SHAPING A HERO

BOB AUSTIN

Copyright © 2019 Bob Austin
All rights reserved.

Book layout by ebooklaunch.com

We live in a world filled with magic, a form of energy that exists within plants, animals, and of course, people. It all started with a catalyst, something that sparked the eruption of energy that flooded the planet. It became so commonplace that no one knows the source; it simply exists as part of the world now. Nature became more abundant, animals grew and evolved with it, and humans learned, through practice, to control and manipulate it for a multitude of abilities. Thus creating a world of balance between those who would use this power to fuel their own desires and those who would stop them from causing harm. For if left unchecked, it would wreak havoc upon the world. Even as we enter the modern age and technology advances, magic is a key part of society. That is what we live in today. - From the desk of Oliver Mansen

Chapter 1

Hide and Seek

Not far outside the town of Merrell, four travelers journeyed through the canyon that connected the small town to the rest of the region. The canyon was usually brimming with wildlife and plants due to the natural stream that ran softly through it. But recently, it had felt barren and empty since something had scared the animals away. And so the young mages had been hired to find the cause. They were not simply scholars looking to study magic. They were prepared for battle, holding an array of weapons at their side, and they had come to flush out a dangerous beast that stalked the canyon and preyed on traveling caravans.

The leader, Claire, walked in front, followed swiftly by Ewan, Lilla, and Arden, who all hoped that Claire had more of a plan than to simply chase the beast. All except Arden, who would have happily run in swords blazing. Luckily for them, Claire was more levelheaded than that. After seeing the system of caves that were dug out by the creature, Claire came up with a plan.

Having split up, Claire and Ewan made their way through the caves. With nothing but darkness in the tunnel ahead of them, Claire, leading the way, focused magic through her arm and manifested a ball of light which fully illuminated her, hovering inches above her hand.

She held it out for Ewan, who had to jog to catch up, and he was greeted with the sight of her short, golden hair shining. He squinted, her light temporarily blinding him, and Claire, blissfully unaware of this, walked closely next to him to light the way ahead.

As they walked side by side, Claire looked at her teammate and couldn't help but notice how he did not look suited for combat. His well-kept hair coupled with his smooth features looked more suited to the classroom than the dark cave they found themselves in. From experience, she knew he could handle himself, but it was amusing to see him out in the field.

"Is there a problem?" he asked, noticing her staring.

Claire smiled wryly and looked ahead.

"No problem. How far in do you think we should go?"

"We shouldn't go too far," Ewan replied calmly. "I'm hoping the tunnel opens up soon since we're going to be running back out."

Claire's smile faded at the idea of it, and Ewan took the opportunity to promptly remind her that it was her plan.

"Yeah I know it was my idea, but I don't like that you're assuming *we* will be running away and not the monster."

Claire was starting to regret her choice of action. But someone had to make the decisions, and since no one else wanted that part of the job, it fell to her. A firm believer in leading by example, Claire was willing to use herself as bait while her teammates readied an ambush outside, but she couldn't help but feel a little relieved that Ewan was with her. Pushing the negativity from her mind, Claire carried on into the cave and crossed her fingers that Arden and Lilla would be ready outside.

****

Lying in wait above the cave entrance, Lilla slowed her breathing and felt the gentle breeze pass by. Like most people who had a strong Elestran heritage, she had a golden tan that complemented her dark brown eyes. Ever prepared, she had a short hunting bow in her hand and a quiver of arrows at her side, ready to use. She readied herself for the first sound of trouble, which came promptly as her partner yelled over to her.

"The rocks are all set, Lilla! Are you done feeling your surroundings?"

Lilla did her best not to react as Arden broke her concentration and waited until he walked over to glance at him casually to answer, "I'm ready."

Arden had no trouble moving the rocks due to his muscular physique; with that done he was left with nothing to do until Claire came back. He had never been any good at sitting still, and he couldn't seem to get anything out of Lilla in the meantime. She was so talkative on the journey to the canyon, but ever since they arrived, she only spoke the bare minimum. Even stranger, she painted markings down her face as soon as they came up to the cliffs. Arden thought it suited her, but he knew that whatever the reason for this strange fashion choice, it probably wasn't done for appearance.

Standing next to her for a moment, he tried to coax her into a conversation.

"So you're Elestran, right?" he asked, looking for anything, *anything*, to break the silence. "Don't see many people from that far west. Did you move here when you were younger?"

"Yes," she answered plainly.

"My family comes from a little down south," he continued, "but you'll find us all over the place now."

Lilla didn't respond; it seemed she wasn't listening to him. With nothing but the sound of the wind going past, Arden gave in and waited with her in silence.

****

After a few minutes of walking carefully, Claire and Ewan emerged into an open cavern with light pouring in from a crack above. Looking around, there was no creature to be seen, but it looked like a den of sorts. Claire turned to Ewan, who nodded for her to proceed.

After a couple of breaths, Claire shouted into the darkness, "Helloooo!" which echoed down the surrounding tunnels.

"Marco!" she called, and Ewan gave her a look that seemed to emote, *"Marco? Really?"*

Claire smiled at him.

"Well, if we hear something reply with polo—"

Almost on cue, a combination between a roar and a grunt echoed back from one of the tunnels. Something large started to move, and Claire and Ewan stood, fully prepared to bravely run back the way they had come.

The two unconsciously took a step back when the beast emerged across from them. The light from above was reflected off its rough, white skin. Looking to find those that had stumbled into its lair, the creature pulled itself forward on eight bulky legs with its tail being dragged on the ground behind. The merchant who hired them did say it was the size of a truck but seeing it in person was far more intimidating. It barred its chunky teeth at the intruders, daring them to come close.

Claire instinctively put her hand over her sword, but she held her ground. They couldn't run yet as they had to make sure it would follow them. Ewan raised both palms at the monster, and with a glow running down his arms, he fired two yellow projectiles which quickly arced toward it. His magic resembled a flock of birds as they flew through the air and slammed straight into the creature. They bounced off without doing any real damage, and the beast knew it was time to take its prey. As soon as it readied itself to charge, Claire and Ewan turned and ran for the tunnel behind.

Claire ran just ahead of Ewan, back toward the entrance. She could hear her friend was right behind her, which was good as there was no time to be looking back. The thunderous crash of footsteps behind them had a rhythm now as if to inform them of the impending death that followed. Up ahead, an exit appeared that signaled their freedom. But before Ewan came out, he touched both sides of the tunnel with each palm and marked them with a yellow circle. It took him mere seconds to leave his mark, but it felt like he was cutting it close as they proceeded to gain distance from the tunnel.

The creature, to which they affectionately referred to as Marco afterward, stormed out of the tunnel and planted its feet when it emerged outside. Ewan clenched both fists together, and the markings he had left exploded into each other, closing the dark mouth of the cave they came out of. Claire wondered if they should have used that trick to blast the monster, but they were already in the thick of it. Drawing her sword and standing firm, she was ready to engage the creature. Although, the sword was more a last resort. Getting close was something she definitely wanted to avoid.

Arden and Lilla watched Marco advance on its small opponents and swiftly moved to spring their ambush. Arden moved to his line of rocks. Each of them was the size of a grown man and far too heavy for even someone of Arden's strength to throw effectively. He had no need to use his arms though. Instead, he stood next to the first, and after channeling his magic through the ground, the rock launched itself upward. It was catapulted into the air to slam back down as planned. The beast was struck and immediately turned to see where the attack had come from. As soon as it faced them, two arrows stuck its forehead with little penetration.

With new targets, the monster began to charge back toward them and simultaneously swung its tail around. Claire and Ewan instinctively ducked under the massive tail as the impact would have guaranteed some broken bones.

Lilla continued to fire arrows. With the wind arcing around them and propelling them forward, she seemed to be pulling in gusts around her as it aided in her arrows' flight. Another rock flew and smashed down on the beast's leg, but Marco continued his rampage. It raised itself upon its hind legs and brought his face up to their level. Its gaping mouth snapped at Lilla who narrowly jumped back out of the way. Instead of retreating, Arden took two pouches from his belt and lit the attached fuses as he held them. Once thrown in front of the beast's face, they let off a fiery blast which forced Marco back down.

More streams of fire came forth as Claire caught up; she summoned them from each hand one after another. Between this, the arrows striking its head, and soaring yellow projectiles all focusing around it, Marco was starting to slow down.

Drawing his battleax, Arden prepared to jump down, thinking one final push was what they needed. He charged his magic into the weapon and attacked head-on. With a mighty swing, the ax cracked down on the creature's head. The ax failed to cut through, but the sheer force of the strike was enough to drive the creature down. Jerking its head up, it tried to shake off the unwelcome pest. Arden had to hold on tight to avoid being eaten.

Keeping a reasonable distance from the fight, Ewan directed his hand toward Claire, and a yellow platform appeared beneath her. Knowing what he was planning, Claire willed her sword to sharpen to try to finish the creature off. She nodded for him to proceed, and the platform beneath boosted her into the air. Marco was still trying to shake off one nuisance when the point of Claire's sword came down on his temple and pierced through. The creature stood motionless for a moment while Claire planted her feet. Without warning, the large body slumped to the side and let its passengers fall.

All four of them looked at each other for a minute, and once it was clear everyone was okay, they let out a relieved breath. All aside from Arden who proceeded to shout in celebration and laugh at the sheer joy of what they had accomplished.

Claire hadn't noticed how fast her heart was beating until the excitement was over. Despite her doubts about leading them, the plan worked, and the beast was slain.

****

Walking back out of the canyon, Claire caught Arden's contagious joy now that she was able to enjoy the victory. Lilla, after removing her face paint, was back to the lighthearted way she had been known for before starting the job. And Ewan, even if he kept quiet, felt proud they had finished their first job together. Without much chatter, they emerged back into the open where a tall, plump merchant waited by his truck.

"Ah, my friends. I take it the job is done," he greeted them as they approached.

Claire was happy to inform him. "The monster's taken care of, Mr. Partell. It's safe to travel again."

"Ha-ha! That is excellent news. Here's a well-earned pay for your efforts."

He handed Claire a card with 300 credits, fair pay for their efforts. Along with it was a business card that was signed Rumen Partell, with his big smiling face drawn on it.

"Now that business is taken care of, let me drive you kids back home eh! I look forward to getting back to work tomorrow."

Happy to return home, the group climbed into the back of his truck. It was a rickety old thing, and from the ride, it didn't seem as though it was designed for being off-road. But nobody complained at being given travel for their first job. In the future, they would have to make arrangements themselves.

The town was only an hour away, but they enjoyed the short rest. Claire noticed Arden frowning and asked what he was thinking.

"You don't think it'll be a problem leaving that big body on the road, do you?" he asked.

Ewan immediately took the chance to lecture him. "With the beast's magic gone, it will decompose rather quickly. Some animals become too dependent on it, and the magic is all that's holding its body together."

Arden accepted this. None of them even asked how Ewan knew these things anymore, better to assume he was right.

Looking at the others anxiously, Lilla had to ask, "I know you guys wanted to test me out there, how did I do?" She looked toward Claire who scoffed.

"That's pretty extreme for a test. Ewan told us you were skilled, or we wouldn't have brought you along, right?" she directed at Ewan.

"Well, it was a test of sorts. It was important to see how we worked as a team. It only makes sense if we're going to be working together in the future."

"I think you did great," Claire added, to stop Lilla fretting. "We watched each other's backs and got the job done. I think we're more than ready to head out on our own. If we're all committed to this, we can head for Verras in a few days. Are you all up for it?"

With no hesitation, Lilla answered, "Yes! There is nowhere I'd rather go."

Arden leaned back and grinned. "You already know I'm in. There's no way I'm going through training with the council for the next five years."

Ewan looked less enthused. "I'll follow your lead."

Trying to keep her excitement in check, for now, Claire asked each of them if they were ready to move. Everyone claimed they were ready. Even Lilla, the new addition to their team said she was fully packed.

"What about you, got any last-minute sorting?" Arden asked, hoping he wasn't the only one that still had to organize himself.

"Nope. I'll call my brother tonight to make sure everything is waiting for us. Then I'll give my parents a last visit before we go."

"Oh, right," Lilla replied softly. She wasn't sure what to say after that, but luckily Arden chimed in.

"You know, her brother's the one who got us a place to live in the city. He's a hotshot in the Council of Magi which gets him all kinds of perks."

Claire wished he would stop telling people that. "He's not very high up in the council. He helps organize the mages working for them. He doesn't spend his money on much, so he's been able to pay for my lodgings and got us an apartment in Verras to start us off."

Lilla had been told this by Ewan, but she was happy for something to change the subject as they rode back into town.

A short while later, the truck returned to Merrell and carried its passengers to the middle of town where the merchant dropped them off. Before splitting up, Claire gave them a reminder not to tell anyone where they went today as students were not permitted to go on jobs of any kind before graduating, never mind one as dangerous as this one. The merchant, Partell, didn't seem to mind ones so young taking up the job if it meant getting it done faster. He either had complete confidence in their abilities or was in a hurry to clear the road for his business. Claire was certain it was the latter.

It was a brief walk home for Claire after she left everyone. Opening the door to her family home, she wondered if she would miss having her own space. She changed out of her leather armor and turned on the television to have in the background. It was tuned into the city of Verras so she could catch the news; it was a good source of information about how things were run there. Claire was half listening to some stories about the economy until it moved on to something she was interested in. It was an update on developments within AMTech, a technologies firm that specialized in Anti-Magic technology. They were recently working on arming a special division to combat any magically enhanced threat.

It made sense for governments to look for a way to combat magic users themselves rather than relying on the council to set things right. The two largest regions, Dottinheim and Elestra, were not permitted to have mages in their military, as per the armistice between the two powers. The Council of Magi did its best to maintain good relations between them, but both were intent on handling these issues themselves. Verras seemed to be against magic users in general.

As Claire and Ewan had discussed, it seemed the perfect place to get set up as there was no competition. People would always choose mages working under the council due to their experience and reputation, but if they were the only magic users in town, then there would be some demand for them. After all, Mr. Partell had a business in the city, and he had taken them on. They would have to keep their distance from AMTech, but it should be easy enough to keep a low profile.

After catching up on AMTech's recent projects, the report moved on to a short interview with the CEO, Corrin Walker. Corrin wore an expensive-looking suit and sat ready in a small meeting room with a female reporter. He was in his late thirties with sleek brown hair and a calm, content expression. Claire had studied up on this man. On camera, he was suave and relaxed on the magic issue, but from what her brother had told her, it was like AMTech was preparing for war.

"So, Mr. Walker, I understand you have plans to expand your technology in other cities even beyond Dottinheim. Is this your way of pushing for more stringent security in areas were Magic is commonplace?"

Corrin replied in a deep, graveled voice, "Not at all, Miss Joyce. We don't have a say on how the governments look after their citizens. We simply want to make our advances readily available to them should they have a need for it. The Council of Magi have done a fine job protecting those of us who don't have those kinds of abilities, but it's time we had another option. I want to make it so the local police can deal with any threat to the public's safety. And with the new Tech Soldiers we're developing, we believe magic users will be obsolete."

He was cut off by a video call coming up. The name Isaac came up on the screen, and Claire answered her brother's call. The video that came up was dark, but Claire could see her brother in what looked like a dorm room. It didn't help the video any that he was always dressed in black.

"Hey, Isaac. I was catching up on the news. Have you seen the latest interview with AMTech?"

"It doesn't matter. They always say the same thing on camera—protect the public, the council won't be needed anymore, etcetera. They really know how to talk in circles."

Despite being involved in politics, Isaac wasn't a fan of how the game was played. It was obvious to them that Walker had a hidden agenda, but they couldn't investigate, not without drawing the council in a bad light.

Moving swiftly on, he enquired about the move tomorrow. He had given them directions to their new apartment, but they would have to get around on their own. Even though he was helping, Isaac looked a bit concerned about the whole thing.

"I wish I could come and visit to see how you get on, but I won't have time for that kind of trip."

"We'll be fine. We'll keep our heads down and help people in the area. Give it some time, and we might be able to change how they see us," Claire said, trying to sound hopeful.

"That's optimistic."

"One of us has to be," she joked, but Isaac did not look amused. "Seriously. You don't have to worry about us."

"Claire, do you know what my job is?" he asked in all seriousness.

Claire regarded him before she answered. "You're an operator. You assign the mages to different jobs and keep track of their progress." It was simple to answer. There was no way she wouldn't know.

"In short, yes. I have to decide if I think the people available are ready for the job. It looks like I'll be your unofficial operator while you're working in Verras."

"Ooh, a possible glimpse of my future then. It's nice to know you're looking out for me."

"As long as you keep out of AMTech's way. If you see those Special Forces moving around you, keep your head down." Isaac looked more concerned the more he went into it. "It would have been easier if you followed the council option. You could have worked your way up with us."

Having had this conversation before, Claire wished she had a better answer for why they were doing this. Her brother had already been supporting them and arranged their lodgings, so surely he wouldn't pull out now. After a moment of silence, she came out with what she could. "You chose your path, and I'm choosing mine. The others agree with me on this. We can do more good in Dottinheim, and maybe someday the council will recognize that."

Isaac sighed as there was no talking her out of it. "All right. You've been set on this for a while, so I'll trust you. I have to go, but I'll check up on you soon."

"I'll let Mom and Dad know you're doing well, okay?"

"Thanks."

****

With the sun about to set over the horizon, Claire left her home. Walking through the town, she realized this would be one of the last times she would be in Merrell. She had lived here her whole life, and she felt a wave of sadness for all the places that she would miss; the people passing by looked so content. Claire knew Verras wouldn't be this peaceful. Merrell was a small town with not much happening. A great place to live if you're looking for a calm and quiet life. She often wondered how her life could have been different, but this wasn't the place for her anymore.

Walking up through a park, the sun shined down on her as she passed rows of red and yellow flowers. Claire was determined to make a difference and protect people. When she thought about Arden, Ewan, and Lilla, she was sure she would look after them.

The path led her on until she cut across the grass and arrived at her destination. Claire stopped and knelt in front of two graves.

She took a slow breath and spoke quietly. "Hi, Mom. Hi, Dad." She paused. "So I'm going to be away for a while."

Chapter 2

Obstacles

The mage academy in Merrell was built a hundred years ago and was named after a man who defended the town during the war. Arkon Academy had been the starting point for many mages over the years, and even with Dottinheim looking for alternatives to magic, Merrell would continue to fund the academy for each new generation to learn magic.

As well as the main building itself, several plots of land were owned by the school for training purposes. Their proudest location was the field on the outskirts of town. Half an acre of open land for complete creative freedom, allowing the students to tap into their power without fear of causing damage.

Two years after the land was bought, an ambitious old headmaster had the idea of hosting an end of year obstacle course to test the students' abilities and put on a show for the town. The Council of Magi and other interested parties were invited to watch and scout the local talent. Other academies were known for different courses or tests to show what the past year had brought, but Headmaster Boyle preferred the idea of throwing his students right into the action. Many refinements were made over the years to make the most challenging but non-life-threatening hurdle.

Preparing to run the course herself, Claire took a moment to watch the townspeople gather to the stands. The reserved seats were all filled, and although representatives from the council were here, she already knew Isaac wasn't among them. When he told her he couldn't make it, she played it off like it was nothing, but in truth, she felt disappointed he wouldn't get to see this. Maybe he wouldn't worry so much if he saw firsthand how strong she had become.

Claire let out a tired sigh; she knew Isaac wasn't happy with her choice to go to Verras. It would have certainly been easier to follow in his footsteps. After graduating from a mage academy, you could move on to further training and education under the council. After a few more years of studying, you could qualify as a regulator. These specialized mages worked to maintain peace under the council's ruling.

Since learning who the regulators were, Claire aspired to be just like them, but she couldn't wait four more years to go out into the world. Claire was ready to make a difference now, and if she had to do it as a freelance mage without the council's backing, then so be it.

A loud air horn shot her back to the present, and she saw the instructors signaling they were ready to begin. Large screens appeared on either side of the course that showed brief glimpses of what was in store for the students. To introduce the course, a local news anchor was brought in to commentate on the action.

"Hello, everybody, and welcome to the twenty-third annual Arkon Academy Obstacle Course! It looks like the stands are packed for today's show. I hope you're all ready to witness an array of talent from Merrell's best and brightest. I'd like to welcome you all, and I want to hear you cheer for our young mages!"

Everyone waiting on the field heard spectators as they cheered for the future mages and regulators among them. It was a bit intimidating, but it was a reminder to do their best for everyone to see. Claire stood ready next to twenty or so of her graduating classmates, who were preparing either mentally or physically. Whether or not they made it through the course, they all knew where they were going next; the course was simply to test their skills and prove themselves capable before moving on. Since Claire was ready to go, she looked around for her teammates and how they were doing. The first she spotted was Ewan, who was walking around the outside of the course while examining it.

"He made a bet with me." Lilla appeared as Claire was watching him. "I said with all his preplanning that I would get a better time out there."

Claire was surprised Lilla got Ewan to compete. It was nice to see him showing an interest.

"As much as he tries to play it cool, he can't resist being challenged I guess. Do you think you can beat him?"

"I hope so. I want to show him that when it comes to a fight, you need to be ready to improvise. I'm going to teach him something today," Lilla announced proudly.

Arden came over by this point; he couldn't help but overhear the bet. "That would be fun to watch, but you won't be the only competition out there."

Before she could reply, Lilla noticed something change in the air. It was nothing but instinct, and she didn't know what it meant until a girl appeared out of thin air at Claire's side.

"The course looks so cool, don'tcha think?" she said, trying to startle them.

Only Arden jumped back at her reveal.

"Aagh! Shell, where did you come from?"

Lilla was more surprised this girl had managed to sneak up on them. Without any reaction, Claire answered her. "That was pretty good. You keep practicing, and you might actually scare me."

The young Shell stood pouting now that she failed to catch Claire off guard. Claire laughed at how easy it was to tease her.

"I'm sorry. I saw you hovering around and knew you would try something. Why are you down here anyway? You're not running this course."

"I wanted to test my abilities too, and this was my last chance to get you."

"Well, you have another year to practice. Maybe after you graduate, you could come looking for us," Claire told her with a big grin. She liked trying to be a mentor figure to Shell even though they were only one year apart.

Lilla still observed this odd encounter for a moment before introducing herself. "You two seem close. My name's Lilla. I'm going to be joining Claire's team bound for Verras."

Shell shyly replied with a simple, "Hi."

Claire noticed this and spoke for her. "This is Shell. She's like a little sister that kind of pops up every now and again."

"Oh, speaking of going to Verras," Arden said, interrupting them. "I think I finally came up with a name for us!"

Claire wanted to cut him off since she had already told him they didn't need a name, but Lilla encouraged him.

"We can be Team Arkon, so everyone knows where we come from!"

"I like it," Shell said quietly, but Claire dismissed the idea.

"Do you even know who Arkon was? You know they call him the deserter, right?"

"Yeah, but he's still regarded as a war hero. He defied orders and saved the town. They wouldn't have named the academy after him if he wasn't a hero," Arden said defensively since he had spared a minute to find out where the name had come from.

With Claire busy trying to stop Arden from making that name a thing, Shell remembered the reactions she got and asked Lilla, "You…knew I was there before I revealed myself. Could you sense my magic that easily?"

"Not exactly. It was like an instinct. Something in the air changed, but I wasn't sure what it was. I guess I'll know how to keep an eye out for you in the future." Lilla winked.

Shell was sure to take a note of that for later, but now the fun was about to begin.

The screens facing the audience lit up to first show the entrance to the course. One of the instructors, Hendrick, stood dramatically on top of the gate at the entrance while the announcer introduced the course. The second instructor, Shultz, directed the spectral cameras with his hand as the course was shown in detail.

"The students will make their way through the first gate where the timer will start. Keeping to the path, they must run across the two-hundred-meter-long bridge while dodging the cannons on either side."

As Hendrick pointed toward the cannons, they each fired a shot on their own. Fast cannonballs from some and short bursts of flame from others made it look like they would be running through a war zone.

The view on the screens moved around to the second area where six mannequins stood in a small, arena-like setting with the next gate behind them.

"Next, we show our students' combat abilities with the dummy soldiers we've set up. They are armed with electric batons and imbued with the instruction to attack anyone who comes within twenty feet of them. They're not the most intelligent adversaries, but their attacks do more than sting you. In order to move past the next gate, you will need to disable all of the soldiers."

The dummies stood completely motionless as you would expect of them but with a glowing sigil on their forehead. Past the final gate was an open area with shifting sand below and rows of pillars leading to the end of the course.

"As you can see, in the final stretch, the students will have to navigate over the pillars and avoid the shifting sandpit below. That sand will be controlled by instructor Shultz and will pull you in if you're not quick on your feet. And to make it trickier, Hendrick will be moving rocks over the pillars to throw you off balance and into the sand. You'll have to keep your attention both above and below in order to make it through. At the end of that stretch is the last obstacle, a fifteen-meter-high wall to climb. Once they've landed on the other side of the wall and pass through the last gate, the course is complete, and they will have proven themselves ready for whatever lies ahead."

He finished with as much showmanship as he could muster. The students were all aware of what was waiting for them, so this was all for the crowd's benefit. "Now, if our first mage is ready, we can begin."

The mage in question was Arden, who was too impatient to watch the others go before him. He was sporting two steel gauntlets with small spikes on the outside and a twin-sided battle ax on his back, fit for his muscular physique. He certainly had the best-looking weapons of the students there. He stood at his mark waiting for the green light, focusing on the path ahead. As soon as the archway above him lit up, he bolted forward and ran like he was ready to tackle something. Before even reaching them, the cannons ahead started firing along the path from either side. As promised, stray cannonballs and streams of fire shot across.

A few stray cannonballs hit off his armored hands, but he shifted his weight to knock them away, with no sign of him slowing down. The fire came out in sequence, and when the flames blocked his path, he covered his face and ran straight through, maintaining his speed to come out with only minor singes.

Approaching the next stage where dummy soldiers waited for him, Arden drew his ax while passing through the archway. As the dummies took a step toward him, he jumped into the fray and slammed down his ax with a mighty roar. The force that followed the ax exploded off the ground and knocked the faceless soldiers down all at once, clearing the stage with one attack. His satisfaction was short-lived, however, as the ax he held cracked, and pieces broke off. Keeping on the task at hand, Arden lifted the remains of it over his back, and it clipped on to his leather jerkin, the crowd cheering at the spectacle.

Back at the sidelines, Arden's classmates were equally impressed, as to most of them, he had never shown this level of power before. Claire felt a sense of pride watching her friend go. Having grown up together, she knew he wasn't all talk. But seeing him here, it was clear to everyone that he had the strength to back up his boisterous attitude.

Next to her, Shell stood in amazement. "How did he do that?" she asked no one in particular.

Claire felt like answering as Arden had shown her his gear beforehand.

"He has a Force sigil inscribed on the blade of his weapon, which is his uncle's handiwork."

Before Shell could ask, Ewan approached and was all ready to explain. "The mark known as a sigil helps guide magical energy. The magic reacts differently to each sigil, allowing you to unleash a variety of techniques simply by charging up the object. I hear these kinds of weapons are his family's specialty in the blacksmith trade. Arden has been practicing, but it appears he may have overdone it."

He may still need to learn to hold back a bit, but Claire was happy with his progress. She could remember Arden excitedly telling her about sigils and how they worked when they were kids. Now she could watch his demonstration.

Back on the course, Arden was making his way to cross the boulder field. He tried to take the most direct path while jumping from pillar to pillar. But soon enough, he was blindsided as a floating boulder caught him and pushed him toward the edge. Refusing to be knocked over, Arden dug his feet in and came to a stop with the rock pushing at him. Through shear strength, he forced the rock back and slipped away. He couldn't enjoy the minor victory because of the time it had cost him; instead, he pushed on to clear the rest of the field to reach the wall.

Wasting no time, he began to climb up by digging his hands into the rock. Although it looked as if he was simply punching his hands into the rock, he was using his own magic through his hands to break handholds as he climbed.

Reaching the top, he went for a quick finish by jumping straight off the wall. It was a harder landing than he expected, which caused him to limp over the finish line.

****

It was a great opening run to set the scene for the rest of the afternoon. A good time, and flashy for the crowd to enjoy. Claire and the others waited for Arden, who looked a little less cocky than before, to return.

"I think I did pretty good."

"A little clumsy perhaps," Ewan muttered loud enough for Arden to hear.

"Hey, I got the job done. I'd like to see how everyone else does." He folded his arms defensively.

Claire raised her hands to stop them arguing further. "Well, you'll get your wish. We'll all be up there soon enough."

Taking them away from their squabbles, they could watch the other students try to follow up on Arden's time with varying results—until it was Ewan's turn. While he left to take his mark, Shell started nudging at Claire's arm.

"Can he really fight?" she asked, which made Arden chuckle.

Claire swiftly elbowed Arden before answering. "Yes, he can fight. His magic is more...creative than most," she said quite ominously. Before Shell could inquire further, they heard the klaxon for Ewan to begin, and all eyes were back on the course.

As soon as the signal went, he sprinted across the bridge without difficulty. Any cannonballs that came his way were blocked with the palm of his hands as a flash of yellow deflected anything that hit them. He made it through without incident but may have lost time ensuring he safely blocked any hits.

Reaching the target dummies in good time, he tagged the first in the chest and circled around. He dodged any blows and threw one of them over his shoulder and into the others. At which point he detonated the first dummy to wipe them out. Without missing a beat, he aimed at the remaining three and shot out his projectiles, only taking down one, with glancing blows on the others. Ewan took a blow to the head when a dummy got too close; he regained his balance while retreating to set off another explosive glyph, which finished them off.

Moving on to the boulder field, he started taking what appeared to be a roundabout path. But this was the most efficient way he came up with to navigate it. Ewan had seen that this path would completely avoid the boulders and made it to the wall without incident.

He took a moment to focus at its base and threw out yellow shards, which dug into the wall heading up it. Creating a pad on the ground, it boosted him to grab onto the shards he left sticking out of the wall. It was a bit of a slower climb than he wanted, but he made it to the top only slightly out of breath. He then was able to jump down and materialize another pad that softened his landing and crossed him over the finish.

After witnessing the fastest time yet, Claire and the others waited for Ewan to return. Ewan seemed confident he pulled it off.

"Was that blow to the head part of your plan too?" Arden said mockingly.

"That was…improvised. In any case, at least I didn't freefall onto the ground."

"It was the fastest way down. It didn't even hurt."

Claire ignored them this time, knowing it was her turn next. After hearing her name called, she gave a quick look to her team before walking up to the starting line. She too was eager to impress. A good time wasn't important to her, but she couldn't allow her teammates to show her up, so she went in determined to win.

Claire ran, ducked, and weaved her way across the bridge; it felt more natural to evade the incoming attacks than try to block them. She was most cautious around the fire, wanting to avoid getting burned on the way. When it came to the target dummies, she even used a nonlethal approach of hitting them with magic from a distance, and when they got close, she used the blunt end of her sword to knock them down. Even against target dummies, she wanted to get used to attacking human targets without fatal injury. They were easy for her to dispatch as Claire had often sparred against Arden in close combat.

Moving above the sandpit, Claire also chose a more roundabout path to get across easier. The sand rose but was blasted away with pushes of air from her palms. She continued using the blast of air to jump farther and maneuver around the obstacles. Before reaching the wall, Claire again picked up the wind beneath her to help boost her further up and grab on. Unfortunately, she was all out of tricks and had to climb up without any aid.

Following her teammates' lead, she jumped down and used more gusts of air below her to soften the landing, managing somewhere in between Ewan's soft landing and Arden's crash landing. She felt some pain in her legs but easily walked off. After passing through the gate, Claire looked up in anticipation to see she was only seconds behind Ewan's time.

Rejoining the others, she noticed Ewan avoiding looking at her in case he appeared smug. She felt a quiet frustration as it would have been nice to come up and beat all of them. She ignored Ewan and checked on Lilla who had applied her war paint and looked ready to go.

Once again focused on the task ahead, Lilla approached the starting line. As soon as the horn sounded, she darted forward. Light on her feet, she ran across the bridge, dodging everything that came her way. She matched Claire as one of the few students who skillfully weaved her way to the other side without a scratch.

Reaching the small arena, Lilla placed her hands on the archway, and several head-sized rocks broke off and flew toward the mannequins, immediately taking a few out. When the remaining charged her, she drew a combat knife and ran in to rip them apart.

Arden laughed nervously while watching her. "She is definitely going for the lethal option."

She was a bit more ferocious than necessary, but Claire was nothing but impressed with her flawless run and wondered if Lilla was still trying to prove herself.

Continuing at full speed, Lilla made her way across the boulder path. Nimbly she jumped from platform to platform taking the most direct route. It was already clear she was making her way across faster than anyone else until her perfect run was ruined as one of the boulders caught her from the side and threw her off balance. Lilla attempted to jump away, but without any platform behind her, she was heading straight for the sand.

Claire and Arden felt sympathy as her impressive run was about to come to a sudden end. Ewan, on the other hand, looked almost relieved.

The sand formed into a hand and reached up for her. Everything happened so fast, but to Lilla, time slowed down. She felt a burning refusal to give up in front of everyone, even though it seemed too late. Without any plan, she summoned up all the power she could and aimed it toward the sand. Her own power overwrote Shultz's control, and the form in the sand broke away and scattered. Lilla landed on the sand, but it hadn't captured her. Carrying on the momentum, Lilla gathered the wind beneath her and propelled herself upward and back onto the pillars.

Somehow with power still left, Lilla ran at full speed and launched herself toward the wall, acting solely on instinct. She hurtled toward it and readied herself to catch onto it. But the second her hands came into contact with the rock, it crumbled at her push. Instead of finding a way over the wall, Lilla crashed straight through to the other side and even landed across the finish.

Lilla kneeled on the ground, breathless from her efforts. The crowd remained speechless until Arden cheered out in front of everyone else. The people soon followed suit, and the area erupted at the spectacle.

Bringing herself back to reality, Lilla turned to look at the broken wall with amazement. She had barely gotten back on her feet when Ewan ran up to check that she was all right.

Feeling a bit faint, Lilla leaned on him a little. "I think I…overdid it. I don't have any power left after that."

Seeing she was fine, Ewan sighed. "That was definitely the clumsiest endings we've had, and I thought Arden was bad."

Oblivious to the impact of his words, Lilla felt disappointed before he continued. "But…it was very effective, and you did win our bet."

Although Lilla was delighted at the praise, she contained herself because she knew he wasn't wrong. "I wanted to win, but I lost control a bit. I won't be as clumsy when we work together, okay?"

"We can work on that," he replied and offered her a hand.

She took it happily and stood to see everyone cheering for her. With time to breathe, Lilla quickly wiped off her face paint. But before she could finish, Arden came out of nowhere and hugged around them both.

"That was awesome! Man, here I'm was supposed to be the strong one here, but I didn't even think of smashing through the wall."

Claire joined in but gave her a bit of personal space. "That was really impressive. Well done."

Arden pulled Claire in so any personal space was gone. "Yeah Team Arkon is ready to roll out," he announced.

Claire let him have that one so as to not dampen the celebration. But all the officials watching would remember the four of them standing together as the team from Arkon Academy.

Chapter 3

A Mage's Best Friend

The newly formed Team Arkon was to meet up at the train station in the morning. The train in question was an armored vehicle designed to ensure safe travel throughout the continent. With monster attacks showing no sign of slowing down, local governments needed to show they could provide a safe way to move and trade between neighboring towns. Although more ambitious traders would pack a truck full of wares and head out, this ran the risk of being attacked and at the very least losing their wares. Any average person looking to travel had to rely on the railways.

Ewan arrived with a sizable backpack and suitcase to find several travelers that came for the graduation now waiting to leave. He saw that Lilla had arrived before him. She looked a little anxious to go, but her face lit up when she saw him approach.

"I thought I'd be the first one here," he remarked instead of a greeting.

"Well, I'm usually awake pretty early, so I came here to wait for you guys. Do you think Arden and Claire will be down soon?"

"Claire will be here in about ten minutes, and I guarantee Arden will arrive five minutes before the train is due to leave. In saying that, I was wrong about your arrival."

"I guess you can't predict everyone. Maybe when you know me a bit better." Lilla smiled. Ewan returned the smile only a little as he noticed Lilla only had one worn backpack on her.

"You're traveling quite light. Are you planning to buy more in Verras?"

Lilla was slightly taken aback by his question. "Uh, I didn't really have much I wanted to bring. I can always get more stuff when we start working." From her reaction, Ewan chose not to pry. It wasn't his business what she brought with her anyway.

Following Ewan's prediction, Claire and Arden arrived in time to head out to their new home. But first, they planned to stop at a blacksmith owned by Arden's uncle, Tohren. From there, they could get the lay of the land and see about some new equipment.

The train took them the long way around the cliffs that separated Merrell from the rest of Dottinheim, the eastern region of the continent. They passed through another small town before circling around to the city of Verras.

As soon as the team stepped off the train, they could see the huge cityscape before them. Right outside the station was a wide path with a tramline going through the center. There were roads for local traffic, but the main mode of transport in the city was its tram system. To encourage this public transport, they ran in every corner of Verras and were kept under constant management for the utmost efficiency.

The group wasn't too far from their destination, so they decided to walk and take in the sights along the way. Above them was another rail system that also seemed to run all over Verras. Except this one had nothing running along it at the moment.

"What do you think those are for?" Arden enquired.

Ewan, having done his research, enlightened them as they walked. "That is the Emergency Rail System. It's how police, paramedics, and firefighters make it to their destination. It's only been implemented in the last decade or so but their response time for anywhere in the city is incredibly quick."

Claire felt like a tourist taking in this knowledge, but it was useful to know how Verras worked.

Arden nudged at Ewan. "So hey, if we work hard enough do you think they'll deploy us from those emergency rails?" His question only received a tired sigh in return.

****

After turning off into a market square, they soon found the shop displayed as Lindhelm Armaments. Arden pointed to it proudly as his family name was displayed for all to see. After giving him a moment to show off, Claire shoved him forward to head inside.

Arden's eyes lit up at the displays of all manner of weaponry. According to the sign, they were all forged in-house. After telling the shopkeeper who they were there to see, the young man happily went back to fetch Tohren. As they were examining a display of the most common sigils, a large man with a great black beard walked in from the back to greet them.

"Arden, it's good to see you. Are you here to get armed?"

"Armed to the teeth, Uncle. What can you show us?" Arden replied, immediately forgetting what else they were here for.

"Straight to business then. Come round the back. I'll take a look at what you've got."

He walked with a slight limp as he led them into a back room with a hand-carved table and more weapons with a faint glow hanging on the wall behind. Tohren stood on the opposite side of the table and nodded toward Claire, who walked in. "You there what's your name and choice of weapon?"

Claire smiled at his manner; Arden's family were always to the point. "It's Claire, and I've been using a short sword."

On hearing the name, Tohren gave her a closer look. "Ah! You must be Claire Butler. I've met your brother a few times. There's a definite resemblance now that I look at you."

"Oh. that's strange he didn't mention you. After Arden's parents took us in, I've met quite a lot of your family."

"It's not so surprising. You'll find us Lindhelms on every corner of the continent. I fixed Isaac up a few weapons in the past. It sounds like it's your turn. Lay down your sword so I can have a look at it," he said while knocking on the table.

Claire took her weapon out of its scabbard and laid it on the table. Tohren examined it closely and ran his finger along the blade. "Mmm not bad, a fine start…and no wear from its use. Yes, this will serve you a while longer. The blades still sharp and precise. Why I could shave with this. Bahaha!"

He placed the blade back on the table for her. "You let me know if the metal starts wearing down. Continual magic use will wear down the blade even if you've mastered the amount of charge it can take."

"Thanks, I'll keep an eye on it. I might look into upgrading once I've gotten used to it."

"Aye, that's how it's done. Once you've gotten used to charging the weapon without damaging it, then you can move up to finer material. All right, next up."

He looked over to Ewan. "What about you, sir. Name and armament?"

"My name is Ewan Solace, but I don't carry a weapon I'm afraid."

"Oh? You're going to rely on magic alone. I know a few who do that, but it's not an easy path to take."

"That's why it's worth taking. I want to learn and advance my magic as soon as I can. With nothing but magic to rely on, I'll have to develop faster or risk being a burden to my team, and I do not plan on being a burden I can promise you that."

"Well-spoken, lad. I'll respect your wishes. How about the young lady? Let's see what you've got."

"Yes of course." Lilla hurriedly laid her bow on the table with the few arrows she had left.

"I carved the bow myself, so it won't be the best quality," she told him, thinking he would judge it harshly.

Tohren delicately picked up the bow in his massive hands as Claire picked up on what Lilla said.

"You carved it yourself. Who taught you that?"

"My grandfather was a hunter. I loved spending time with him and hearing about his hunting trips. He took me out sometimes to train me." She paused softly. "When I realized I was going to be leaving Merrell soon, it took a few tries, but I carved a bow and bought some arrowheads to make them too."

Tohren gave his opinion of it without taking his eyes off the bow. "It's impressive carving it yourself. The wood is decent, and the bow is well shaped for a person your size. You could use a better string though. This one won't hold any magic in it. It'll snap instantly."

Lilla looked surprised at his suggestion. "I've only been charging the arrowheads. I didn't know I could enhance the bow too."

"Of course! Putting energy in the string allows for a better draw distance or more power at close range. Hold on, I'm sure we keep string in here somewhere." He turned toward the doorway, but without moving closer, he instead yelled, "Caleb! Fetch me a bowstring, would you?" The man at the counter hurried back to hand Tohren the string. Tohren thanked him and began fixing it to the bow. Once in, he gave it a simple tap, and the string and bow flashed a deep orange hue before fading. He held it up and extended the string a couple of times to measure it.

"There you go, lass. Now you'll get better use out of it."

"Thank you. Umm, how much do I owe for that?"

"It's only string. I can replace that for nothing. Come back to me once you feel you've mastered it and I'll find you a bigger bow. If you need to replenish your arrows, go talk to Caleb. I doubt you'll be able to carve your own while living in the city."

"Thank you. I do have something else. It was my grandfather's, so I don't want to change it, but I was hoping you could tell me about it." Lilla pulled out a silver hunting knife from her belt and showed it to Tohren. He leaned in close to examine it in her hand. "That's some good silver you've got in your hands. It can take over twice the amount of magic common steel can. Three times if it's purified, which looking at the branding on the hilt, I'd say it is. That will be harder for you to charge at first, but you'll find it far sharper than other weapons once you've mastered it. It's an impressive blade your grandfather passed on."

It was clear that Lilla was brimming with pride. She bowed while thanking him and excitedly ran around to the counter to speak to Caleb.

"All right, Arden, you're last up. Show me your ax, boy. I'll see how it's looking."

Claire and Ewan started looking elsewhere in the room as Arden awkwardly took the remains of his ax that was fastened to the back of his rucksack. He unwrapped the blade to show the shattered remains on the table.

Tohren stood at a loss for words. After stuttering for a while, he looked directly at Arden and began shouting. "How in the deep south did ya manage that!"

"I had to let out a lot of force and the ax kinda…broke."

"You overcharged it is what you did. Titan's beard, I only sent you that a week ago."

"Okay I overdid it a bit, but I thought the ax could handle it."

"The ax ain't the problem, boy. You need to get a feel for the weapon. You rushed into it too fast. Well, don't think I'll be giving you another one of those. You're getting something smaller until you learn to manage your energy." He reached back and pulled a mace off the wall. "I'm only giving you this 'cause I won't have you running around unarmed out there, but anything else you want you're payin' for. Now show me the shield, assuming you've not busted that too?"

With a nervous laugh, Arden put his buckler on the table, which luckily for him was intact. Tohren sighed and murmured to himself while examining it. "Mmm….basic material….decent enough and no previous sigils."

"Don't suppose you'd also offer to brand a sigil on it for me?" he asked, pressing his luck.

Standing in the corner, Ewan remarked quietly to Claire, "That was brave of him to ask." Claire had to look away at this point out of embarrassment.

Tohren wasn't at all surprised he asked. "Oh no, if you want your sigils done you're gonna learn them yourself. I'll be in Verras for a while longer, so if you stop by at the end of each day, I can teach you how to make your mark."

Arden seemed to forget his ax and was again happy at his uncle's offer. "That would be awesome. I could create them in the field if I learned from you."

Lilla came back in looking satisfied with a full quiver. With the weapon fitting done and the shouting over, they were ready to move on to more important matters.

Claire began. "So can you tell us about Verras? Our apartment should be a few blocks away, but it would be good to know where we can get started."

"Aye, I hear ya. I bought a map the other day when I arrived. The streets have changed somewhat since I was last here."

He rolled out a map of the city on the table, which had a red circle drawn around his shop. From the map, they could see the city was divided up into five sections. They were on the south side with their new apartment building a few blocks further in.

"You should be able to find work at the Contractor's Office here," he said while covering the building with his large finger. "See, the way it works everywhere else is people post up jobs, and any regulators or freelance mages would sign up for it and meet the client. Since there aren't many magic users around in Verras, the jobs go mostly unfulfilled. You'd think with AMTech promising to replace regulators, they would help people in their place. Dottinheim tries to resolve issues without our help, but Verras practically drove us out and left their own people to fend for themselves."

"Isaac told me Verras, in particular, refuses the council's help for anything," Claire added.

"Speaking of which, do you work for the council?" Ewan inquired.

"Oh yes, I was a regulator myself until an injury crippled my leg. I could still crush some skulls, but I wasn't going to catch anything with this limp. Now I forge weaponry so others can take up the fight in my stead. I even work special requests if they've earned the right to a real weapon."

It wasn't hard to imagine given Tohren's size and his expertise with weaponry. It seemed that Arden had inherited a few family traits from Tohren's side. There was some definite similarity between the two.

After a moment of basking in the glory days, Ewan brought the topic back to Verras. "The news has hinted at replacing mages, but I never knew they were near driving them out."

Claire saw this as a lucky break for them. "It's exactly what we wanted. People are looking for work, and we're the only game in town. Once the word gets out, we can build a name for ourselves."

"Like Team Arkon?" Arden quickly threw in.

"Oh, I like that. Named after the hero of Merrell who left the front lines to defend the town," Tohren added, causing Claire to sink her head in her hands.

"As long as we avoid the attention of AMTech," Ewan said, again trying to keep them on track. "I feel they won't appreciate us working in their territory."

Lilla disagreed. "But if we aren't doing anything wrong then they can't stop us. We'll be helping people."

Tohren nodded in approval. "I like the idea, but I would watch your backs, all the same. They may not have made a direct move against mages, but it sounds like they're leading up to it."

****

After absorbing all they had learned, the newly armed team left the shop to head to their new home together. Tohren even let them keep the map so they could make their way through Verras. The south quarter didn't seem too busy as it approached the late afternoon. The tallest buildings in this section stood at several stories with mostly apartment buildings and small businesses, but you could see toward the center of the city there were more industrial skyscrapers and what must be business and industry. As they all could guess, AMTech central offices and research facilities were located there.

Their new home was several floors up and spacious, with a central living area, kitchen, and four bedrooms ready for them. Arden started by lobbing his luggage into his room and sitting on the couch while the others got unpacked properly. Once this was done, Claire laid out the map to start planning for tomorrow.

Chapter 4

Birds of a Feather

At the crack of dawn, the party left to check the Contractor's Office in the south quarter, with Arden and Ewan heading to one back near the station, and Claire and Lilla passing through a marketplace on their way to the second. They found an array of stalls with everything from clothing to freshly cooked meat. Most appeared to be brought from other lands to display. The two were curious to look around, but they had to find their first job and couldn't be distracted. In any case, they had no money so looking for work was the best idea.

Claire eyed a stall showing off pottery from further north than she had heard of.

"We should check the next market once we're making a living here," she told Lilla while trying not to get sidetracked.

"I wonder how long until we're settled in. I don't even know what kind of jobs we'll be doing."

"I'm hoping for some hunting to keep ourselves active, but we might be doing odd jobs like construction to keep the money coming in."

"Is that what you had in mind, doing odd jobs around the city?" Lilla asked.

"I'm trying to be realistic while we start up, but we won't be doing the easy stuff forever."

"So what do want you to move up to?"

"Maybe work for the council, become a full-fledged regulator, that kind of thing." Claire smiled to herself at the thought. "Maybe my brother will be sending us out. He's doing his part for the world. I want to do my best too."

Lilla could tell she'd thought about it before. "That's very sweet. I'm sure you'll do great."

"Oh here I'm saying us, but I didn't ask what you want to move on to. What's your idea of the future?"

Lilla blushed at the question. "Awww, it'll sound selfish after what you said. I like that we'll be helping people, but I didn't have any big plans behind it."

Claire wasn't going to let her shy away from her answer. "Come on I want to hear it. Do you see yourself as a badass hunter like your grandad?"

"Something like that. I'd like to be more independent. I want to be able to survive on my own and go wherever I want. I love nature, and I want to travel to the most remote locations and see everything there is to see."

"Ah, so you want to be an explorer. I'll be telling people I know the most legendary explorer out there, traveling the deepest reaches with nothing but a bow and her trusty hunting knife."

Claire received a light shove for her jest, but she was excited about the prospect. "If you stick with us and build up your magic, we'll find a bright future ahead of us."

"That's a nice way to think about it. We all have different goals, and we can use magic to reach them."

The two continued in high spirits as they came up to the office and Claire calmed down. "All right, all right. We need to look professional. Deep breaths."

Opening the door, they found an older man by the counter writing out envelopes. At the side, there was a noticeboard with old requests hung up. The man gave them a quick look as they came in and then a second look when he saw their attire and weapons. "Are you two some sort of adventurers?"

"Yes. We're here for work. Do you mind if we look at your notices?" Claire enquired.

The old man waved toward them. "By all means, but you might find they're a few weeks old at best. We haven't had people like you in here in a long time."

On the wall, there was a display of notices—older ones at the top as old as three months and newer ones ranging after a few weeks. Lilla took the newest one for a look, even then it was dated ten days ago.

"Someone's looking for people to build the foundation for an extension to their house. It was over a week ago, but we should be able to help if they're still looking. It says they don't want weeks of construction and figure magic users can do it in a day or two. The money's good, and it won't take us long."

"Eh, hold on to it if we don't find anything else," Claire said without much enthusiasm. After scanning the notices, she picked one out and read it aloud.

"My family wants to expand the farm out further west, but anytime we move in, a swarm of flying monsters attack. We need someone to destroy their nest and chase them off. After that, we can graze the land and make sure nothing comes back. Amy MacFarlane."

In large letters below that, it read a reward of 400 credits and gave directions to their farmland.

Lilla looked doubtful after reading it herself. "It's been up for over three weeks. Are you sure they've not already done it?"

"Well, if nobody helped them, then they might not have been able to chase these creatures off, and they'll need our help. Four hundred credits can cover the rest of our month's rent and give us some extra for ourselves." Claire thought about how few options they had with the other jobs, even if Ewan and Arden had better luck. "I think we should take the extension job as a backup. We'll go down to the farm and see if they're interested. If not, we'll head back and see about your notice, or maybe Ewan will bring something else." Claire looked at Lilla, hoping she would follow her lead. To her joy, Lilla agreed, and they took both notices.

The man at the reception took them and scanned the two notices they picked.

"I'll take a copy of these for you so you can keep them with you. Normally, if anyone else asks about the request, I let them know the two of you signed up for them, but I doubt we'll see anyone else come in. We'll contact the client in a couple of days to see if you were successful. All that's left is to wish you luck out there."

****

Claire and Lilla arrived at the meeting point at a tram stop closest to the train station. The trains ran underground to each section of Verras, but for more specific travel, they had to rely on the tram system. It was busy with people commuting to work, so they waited in the most obvious place they could so Ewan could spot them.

It didn't take long for the others to finish their business and find Claire waiting. Arden looked somewhat anxious when he saw them.

"Please tell me you found something good."

Claire could guess why he was asking. "Did you guys not have any luck?"

Ewan seemed unfazed about it. "I wouldn't say that. We took with us two odd jobs to start us off. A librarian wants to collect information on monsters and will pay for knowledge of any we've encountered, and there was a rather odd request for samples of frogs from a nearby lake. Both are about a month old, but I assume the librarian would still be eager for anything we could offer."

"Well those sound tempting, but Lilla and I found something a bit more exciting."

Arden's spirits picked up as Claire detailed the job.

"Yes, we have to go for it. We can't spend our first day catching frogs and talking in a library." He shot a look to Ewan, expecting a counter-argument. Ewan rolled his eyes at the challenge and agreed to follow Claire's lead. Based on directions given on the notice, they could see a tram would take them close to the edge of the city, and a short walk would lead to the farmland.

The public transport was easy to use, and before long they were on their way to the west gate. The gate itself was open to travelers, and the guards standing watch gave them no trouble. From there, it took over an hour down a dirt road leading away from the city and into the farms.

Approaching the farmhouse, they were spotted by a man in his midforties, and he came to greet them. "Hi there. What brings you to the farm?"

Claire stood at the front to represent them. "We're here about a job posted a few weeks ago. It says you were looking to expand the farm further west. It was posted by an Amy MacFarlane."

The farmer looked surprised but grinned widely. "What do you know. I didn't think anyone would answer that. My name's Drew MacFarlane. My wife sent in that request after we argued about expanding. I mean I'm willing to spread the farmland out, but I didn't think the request would do anything, and I'd be crazy to try and chase them off with pitchforks, so I figured it was no good."

It sounded hopeful for them, so the others traded looks and Claire asked the question. "So can we take the job?"

Drew laughed and gestured them outward with him. "Let's go find the wife and go over the details."

Up ahead past the fields, they met up with the wife in question and a few farmhands. They laid out a map for the team and showed the area they wanted to extend onto and where the ravenous birds attacked.

While looking at the area, Arden threw out the question, "How did these things get this close to the city. Aren't there border patrols or something to stop this?"

Amy MacFarlane scowled in response. "I went to those tech freaks around the border, the ones who're supposed to be protecting us. Cowardly lot said it had nothing to do with them, that they were to stay and protect our border. Now, what's the point in standing over there with their watchtowers if a pack of flying beasts have already snuck past?"

"Man, these guys are useless," Arden commented, and nobody seemed to disagree.

Ewan cleared his throat through the silence. "Getting back to the job at hand, do we know where the nest is?"

Drew shook his head. "They attack from the hills, so we know a rough area but those stretch on for miles going north toward the mountains. I couldn't tell you exactly where."

After listening to their direction, Claire made the decision to find some of the creatures and see if they could drive them back toward the nest.

****

Claire and her team walked beyond the farm to see the new grazing land, hoping the four of them appeared defenseless enough to draw attention. Lilla had her war paint on, and they scanned the skies for any sign of attack. Once they were out in the open, it didn't take long before a high-pitched squawk sounded from nowhere.

Turning their attention to the sky, they could see high above them was a flock of giant birds descending and circling. The group stood back to back and readied their weapons for the creatures to come within range. It was difficult to tell their size from so far up, but they were definitely not normal.

"How many?" Claire questioned to the group, unsure if any of them could determine that. Lilla was the first to get a head count. "There's seven of them. They're coming down for a closer look."

As predicted, the creatures hovered short of a hundred meters above them. The team stood their ground, but Arden was getting impatient at them staying out of his range.

"Dammit. How long are they going to stay up there?"

Lilla kneeled and notched an arrow to her bow. Claire took that as a sign that she could get a shot toward them.

"Lilla, we need to scare them back to their nest. This might be asking a lot, but do you think you could kill one from here?"

Lilla considered it for a moment. If Tohren was right about charging the bowstring, she should be able to get a further distance with it. "I can aim for a kill shot."

"Good. If we kill one instantly, that might be enough to scare the rest of them off. Get ready to defend yourselves if they decide to dive-bomb us. Lilla, take your shot."

Lilla gripped her bow tightly while charging magic into it. She drew the arrow back and focused on the slowest moving target. She could imagine her grandfather's voice guiding her. Though he never said these words, it helped to hear any instruction as if he were giving them.

Feel the direction of the wind, and let it guide your arrow.

After another second, she let loose her arrow which shot upward at high speed. The arrow hit right on target into the bird's neck, and it instantly fell. With a hard thump on the ground, it landed only a few meters away from the group, and they could see it was the size of an average human. The other birds squawked wildly and flew around faster. After seeing the first one downed, they swooped to a retreat toward the hills.

Claire turned to the others instantly. "They're retreating. We need to get after them."

Running north toward the hills, the group had to cross over the train tracks to chase after the birds. There was no barrier around the tracks as no one was expected to be wandering around the countryside, and the trains were designed to plow through anything in their way.

They could see the birds flying off into the crags up ahead. Claire and the others were close enough now to see them landing on the cliff. They couldn't see a nest, but there was a landing up there, and they could still hear the birds screeching. After taking a moment to catch their breath, Ewan spotted a rough path leading up.

"I think we can approach from there and catch them off guard."

Claire felt an odd rush from the pursuit and immediately started issuing orders for Lilla and Arden.

"You two are our best bet. We spot the nest and Arden can toss a bomb or two in there, then Lilla can pick off any who try to fly. Ewan and I will support you two and wipe them out, got it?" The two nodded in response; it was a simple strategy to follow.

Advancing upward, they quickly made it to an open landing around the corner from the loud, screeching creatures. Preparing to make their move, Lilla readied her bow and faced away from the cliff for any that tried to escape. Arden lit two bombs for good measure, and the three of them rounded the corner, swords and bombs blazing. Arden threw his bombs before his brain even registered what he saw. They landed in the group of eight or so smaller birds, smaller being a relative term as they were approximately six feet tall; this was relative to the mother bird who stood at twenty feet tall right next to the nest. The bombs did a good job of scattering them as they detonated and sent several sprawling off the cliff. Ewan and Claire shot off some projectiles and lightning, respectively, to clear a couple of birds left standing, but none of them had yet touched the mother, who stood ready to retaliate.

She let out a deafening screech at the attackers and received a few strikes of lightning in return for it. She whipped her wing at them, which knocked Claire back near the edge. Arden stood his ground with his shield raised, and Ewan kept to the inside of the large landing. Lilla ran around at this point, and without even hesitating at what stood before them, she took aim and fired an arrow that scratched across the side of its face. The beast pushed forward and pecked at Arden, but he braced himself and refused to budge. The impact of each peck echoed along the cliff.

Claire circled to their other side away from the cliff and saw Ewan moving in close under its wing. Not knowing what Ewan was up to, it seemed like the best course was to keep the giant bird distracted. Claire shot a stream of fire with her left hand, and in return, the creature tried to throw her back with its wing. Claire was pushed back, but she slashed with her sword from her right and drew blood.

Arden moved up in front of Claire to catch the next attack as it again thrust its beak toward her. This time, he blocked with his shield and bashed with his mace. The beast shook off the impact, but as it reared its head back, it received an arrow into its eye from the right.

From the injuries, it took a couple of steps back and was against the edge. Ewan found the chance he was waiting for, and the ground beneath the beast lit up as Ewan had placed glyphs all over. They detonated and crumbled the ground beneath her feet, causing her to fall off the cliff. Claire waited for it to fly back up but instead, they all heard a thunderous crash below.

Surprised, the group stood for a moment, still ready for more while Ewan carefully moved to look over the edge. "It's all right. The creature's dead." With a sigh of relief, they all lowered their weapons.

Claire turned to Ewan. "How did you know it couldn't fly?"

Ewan smirked. "The sheer size of it and the fact it sends its offspring out for food. When I circled the creature, I could see a pile of animal carcasses and other such food sources over there." He gestured to a disgusting-looking pile in the corner.

Claire wasn't sure if it was necessary anymore, but she quickly burned the nest all the same so nothing would come back. With their first job done, they were happy to report their success to the local farmers.

The team finished up their first job with high spirits. As they made their way back to the farm, they had to wait for a train to pass. Unbeknownst to them, they soon wouldn't be the only magic users in town, as a powerful mage sat aboard this train on his way to the city.

****

Ignoring the passing farmland, a man in a private carriage sat reading the paper. He was wearing crimson armor and had black streaked hair. The paper's title was on AMTech's industrial revolution. He sat it down next to a now-cold cup of tea and started writing in his old weathered journal.

It seems they seek to replace magic with their technology; I wouldn't mind so much if not for the arrogant one leading the charge. Make mages obsolete? They have no idea what we're capable of. But they'll soon burn for underestimating us. It may not help with my primary mission, but everyone needs a hobby. He smiled softly as he tucked the journal back into his inside pocket. He pointed his finger at his tea, and a small fire started to heat it.

Chapter 5

Adventures in Verras

With the reward of 400 credits as promised, the newly formed Team Arkon had set themselves up in the city and were free to split up as needed and cover any jobs they were suitable for. Arden kept up his training with Tohren as promised and came home each day looking drained. Ewan wound down each day with his reading material. Lilla and Claire explored Verras when they could to learn more about their new home. Lilla wanted to find any parks or open space around, and Claire wanted to find if there was a nearby spot they could train privately, with no such luck. As the weeks went by, they each made themselves at home and worked their own missions.

The Scholar

From as early as the second day, Ewan chose to go to the central library to explore and find out if the head librarian was interested in his information. He arrived in the central area of Verras via the trams and was dropped off near a university with the grand old library standing apart from the rest of the square. It was a majestic sight and had clearly been there for a long time. He saw many students passing through and did not look out of place among them.

Arriving at the reception desk, he decided it was best to seek out the professor who posted the job before getting lost among the texts that were collected here; he was curious to see the collection and would easily lose himself in the number of texts that were gathered. There was a polite young woman ready to greet him as he walked up and, after seeing the job request, was happy to escort him upstairs.

"Are you sure the professor will still be interested in this? It has been a month since it was posted," he asked on the way.

The young woman giggled. "He definitely will. He's got a deal with the Contractor's Office. They refresh that post for him every few months to catch attention."

Every few months must mean he's organizing a lot of data, Ewan thought. *What could it be for?*

They reached the top at the third staircase and found his office. The young woman went in ahead, and after a moment, she told Ewan to go on in. He entered the office and found more bookcases inside. A short, elderly gentleman under a dapper hat with a thick mustache waited for him. His desk had scattered papers and weathered books that he was looking through. He looked up to greet his guest. "Ah, it seems we have an adventurer before us. How do you do, young man? I am Professor Oliver Mansen. It's a pleasure to make your acquaintance." He extended his hand, to which Ewan firmly shook.

"Good to meet you, Professor. My name is Ewan Solace. I'm here about a request you posted looking for information on any monsters in the area. I take it you study them?"

The old professor looked pleased. "Well, I study monsters, history, archaeology, anything of cultural significance. But yes, in this case, I am compiling a database of monster species. You see, I was reading over the *Bestiarum Vocabulum* from the history section, and I realized it had been far too long since one documented such things. With recent monster populations increasing and them becoming more territorial as of late, I feel it essential we update our records." The professor seemed happy to go into detail on this.

"A noble idea. I'd be happy to help. We don't have much experience yet, but we have encountered several creatures thus far."

After the professor took a notebook from his desk, Ewan began to describe the creatures he personally encountered, starting with the most recent job that was fresh in his mind while Professor Mansen scribbled down all the details. He confirmed the birds they encountered were known as Reavers and were native to the mountain region to the north.

He was fascinated to hear about the mother being unable to fly while watching her offspring.

Next, Ewan described the reptiles near Merrell that were local to the forest east of town which the locals had named Drakens. They weren't much of a problem, but the professor took note of all the information nonetheless. Lastly, Ewan described Marco, without using that name, and the professor fell silent. As soon as Ewan's description was finished, Mansen stood and moved over to a bookcase to find something.

"Is something wrong?" Ewan asked.

After taking another few seconds to grab down a journal, he answered, his voice taking on a serious tone. "I have seen a creature very similar to the one you described in the Deep Wastes. My team and I were investigating ruins close to that area. As we camped for the night, it attacked in the darkness. The creature we encountered, however, was black skinned and had armored scales covering itself, making it almost impervious to harm. It destroyed our camp and forced us out of the area. Even the regulators we had guarding us were only able to hold it back. We haven't attempted a return trip since then."

"The one we fought definitely was not armored, and its skin was white as chalk. Are you sure they're related?"

"Yes, the rest of the description is spot on I'm certain. I didn't expect to find something like it this far north, but it begs investigating. The Deep Wastes contain many mysteries and hidden relics lost to this world. If not for that monster, we would certainly have found something of value. I have always wanted to return, but I have lacked the manpower to attempt it. Many lives were lost down there, and I would not attempt it again without proper precautions."

Ewan didn't even entertain the idea of his team's help; if the one they fought had been armored, then the battle would not have ended as smoothly as it did. The Deep Wastes were not a land to take lightly, even the most experienced of mages would need to be well prepared to attempt it.

"I've talked your ear off now. I thank you for the information. I'm sure it will prove invaluable," Professor Mansen said as he gathered up his notes.

"I hope it helps, Professor. I would gladly come back once I've had more experience. In fact, I could see myself coming here quite regularly to browse your collection."

"Ah, we have a fellow scholar I see. What is your field of interest?"

"I want to study magic itself. I want to understand how it works and where it comes from."

"That is definitely worth pursuing. There is still much we don't understand about our own abilities. Theoretically, anyone can learn any magic, and yet everyone finds a particular style they excel in. I would recommend the theoretical section or perhaps start with historical on the second floor. There should be several books with varying theories on magic. In fact…" Mansen trailed off and looked through several disorganized shelves until he pulled out a large book.

Ewan noted it was a first edition while examining the cover. "*Mordecai: The First Mage?*"

"The title is a bit of an exaggeration. It's not a proven fact that he was the first, but Mordecai is the earliest record we have found of a magic user. It's a lot of speculation, but I think you'll agree it's a fascinating read."

"Thank you for the suggestion," Ewan replied, happy for the new book. "I hope to see you again."

Before leaving, Professor Mansen scribbled a note for Ewan to take with him. "Take this to reception downstairs for your contribution today."

With that in hand, Ewan browsed the library and collected his pay along with several books to take home. He made sure to separate his new pay to split among his team before making his own purchases. Now he could end each night learning what he could from previous research.

The Explorer

Lilla woke up on the floor of her room with the window opened wide like she did every morning. She couldn't seem to get used to sleeping on a bed anymore, but the cool city air was close enough to what she was used to. She opened her bag to see she was on her last set of clothes before having to wash everything. It had only been a few days living here, and she wasn't comfortable with the others knowing this was all she had. Luckily for her, they agree it was a day off today. They could look for work if they wanted to, but the work was steady enough that at the end of the week, they could relax. Which gave her a chance to go shopping and get enough supplies to last her.

In the living room, she found Ewan and Claire already up and studying the map laid out on the table. She could hear the end of Ewan informing Claire, "It seems to be our only option."

Claire looked unsure. "Do you think they'll be up for it? I don't want to make this like a chore they have to do."

Lilla approached at this point, sure they were talking about her. "What are you guys talking about?"

A little off guard at her approach, Claire tried to explain. "Oh, we…uh, I was hoping that if we have the time, then we could find a day to train together. But the only suitable place is outside the city limits, so it would be a full-day thing."

"You're not thinking of using our day off for that, are you?" Lilla asked fretfully.

"No, no, no. I was thinking of the day before. We take the day to go out and train with each other."

Lilla breathed a sigh of relief. "If you think we should then I'm happy to do it."

This made Claire relax a little. "I knew you'd be on board," she lied. "We've worked well together so far, but I think we should practice with each other more. I feel we don't even know what each other is fully capable of yet, and I have a few ideas on how our magic can work off of one another," Claire continued, working out the plan in her head.

Lilla liked that Claire and Ewan were looking out for the team. It was nice to have someone who cared for your wellbeing. After getting herself ready, she let the others know she was going out and went into her room. She opted to use the window as it was the size of a door and easy to shimmy down to the bottom. This left the others confused and believing she was still in the apartment for some time.

Though the foreign markets had cleared up, there was a busy shopping district to explore in the east quarter. Lilla was half tempted to walk the whole way, but she would see more of the city from the trams as most major landmarks could be seen from the track around the outside of the city. Maybe on her next day off she could go sightseeing and climb up some of the landmarks. It would only be illegal if she was caught, after all.

Browsing through the crowded shopping district, she made sure to stick to her essentials or risk getting lost in the range of products available. She found an outdoor clothing store which suited her needs and chose a variety of clothing. Even though she had her boiled leather armor for missions and only needed casual wear, she only chose clothing that wouldn't be too loose or constrict her in a fight just in case. She even found a proper traveler's backpack like Arden had for when she was ready to move on. While looking at the pack, Lilla wondered how long they'd be working together in Verras. The idea of staying together as a team sounded good, but it wouldn't work out that way forever.

A couple of hours later, she was on her way back with everything she needed. On the tram, she couldn't help but think of her idea for the future as Claire has asked her. Yes, she wanted to travel the world like her grandfather, but she wasn't sure if she could do that kind of thing alone. While she was lost in thought, she spotted what always made her feel at ease. Nature.

Lilla jumped off early to find a naturally preserved park. Even though it was open to the public, it was well taken care of with some wildlife running around. Her face lit up at the sight — she had already found a peaceful place within the bustling city.

Soon after walking in, she strayed off the path and through the trees. The wind picked up around her and blew the leaves up to move along with her. Even as a child, she was able to gather the wind around her and make the leaves dance through the forest. She hadn't had a chance to do this since leaving Merrell. Even when they left to hunt the Reavers down, she had to stay focused on the task at hand.

Emerging from the bushes, she came across a collection of large rocks arranged in a circle like a small monument. It was a peaceful spot, and surprisingly, nobody was around. Lilla placed her hand on one and recalled her performance in the obstacle course. Breaking through that wall was a feat she had never pulled off before, and she didn't know if she could repeat it.

Lilla took a stance to face the rock. She breathed deeply and thrust her palm into it like she did before. There was a bit of a shake, but the rock remained intact. Disappointed, Lilla turned away but then took a minute to realize it was probably a bad idea to go around destroying things in a park and would have felt rather guilty if she had succeeded.

Moving on, Lilla made her way through the trees and found a lake which seemed the perfect spot to sit for a while. On her command, the leaves blew over the lake and swirled around. She was so relaxed she didn't even notice two children watching her in awe. There was a silence as Lilla didn't know how they would react, but with the amazed expressions, she decided to keep going and made the wind circle her gently while she smiled at them. The kids couldn't have been more than eight years old, and without knowing any better, one boy shouted, "Wow! Are you a witch?"

Lilla giggled at the idea and answered. "No, I'm a mage."

The two boys looked at each other confused. "What's the difference?"

Lilla stood and pretended to think about it. "Well"—she frowned at them to start—"witches are mean old women who lure in children to eat them. You don't want to meet one of them." She then smiled innocently and continued. "And a mage is kindhearted and uses magic to help people." A bit theatrical, but with any luck, it would stick in their minds so they wouldn't go around calling people witches.

It seemed to work as the kids warmed up to her. She was able to show them a couple more tricks over the water. They wanted to see more, but she had to head back to see what everyone else was up to. It felt like a productive day in her mind; her shopping was done, and she even found her new favorite spot to relax in. Maybe the children would find her there again sometime.

The Apprentice

A few weeks into working with his uncle, Arden was ready to show what he had learned. He rushed into the living room, excited to test something out. To his dismay, however, the place appeared to be empty. Hoping Claire was around, he knocked on her door and, hearing no response, let himself in. But no luck. She wasn't there either. He immediately noticed the difference between her room and his. Her bed was unmade, but other than that, it was spotless. Whereas in the few weeks he had been here, he reduced his room to the same condition he was used to back home.

He was about to leave when he noticed a familiar picture next to the bedside and took a moment to examine it. It was a photo of Arden's family with a young Claire and Isaac with them. Arden remembered they took this to help them feel welcome after Arden's parents took them in. It was years later that his father told him the full story of why they needed a new home. Although Isaac didn't want to be involved, Claire was front and center with a beaming smile.

Arden knew he should go and find Claire, but his eyes were drawn to the next picture on her bedside. It was the only picture of Claire's real parents. Arden used to sneak in to look at it as a kid. He would look at the once happy family and wonder why there was no one to save them. From all his family's stories of heroism, it seemed unfair that none of them were there to help. Maybe it was strange to think of them this way, having no idea what kind of people they were. All he could see from looking at it was the dad was huge with a great big beard, and the mom was a beautiful woman in a flowing blue dress. There was one other thing he could pick up from it. Claire got her big ridiculous smile from her dad.

"What are you doing?" Claire asked from behind him.

Arden jumped suddenly as he didn't hear her come in. "Have you been taking lessons from Shell on how to scare me?"

"It really doesn't take much." She smirked. "I'm lucky you weren't holding that, or you would have dropped it."

Arden took a glance back and stood defensively. "I'm not allowed to hold it. I remember that."

"Oh yeah. Isaac made sure of that. I don't blame him. I wouldn't trust you with it now, never mind a six-year-old Arden wanting to look at it."

"Hey, I only break my own things, okay? I'm careful with other people's stuff. I actually wanted your help with something if you have time."

After getting kicked out of her room, Arden told her about his progress with sigil work, and Claire agreed to let him demonstrate with her sword. They both sat cross-legged on the floor of the living area with the blade between them. Arden placed his hands on the sword, visualized the sigil, and focused his magic through his hands. When he raised them, there was a spiral marking that was now branded on the blade. Arden handed the sword to Claire, barely containing his glee. "All right, give it a try."

Claire took the sword from him and held it up between them. The sigil then started to glow, and fire surrounded the blade. The fire burned softly between them. Claire was pleased with the results as she held a flaming sword in the middle of the living area.

They both looked at it until Claire's smile faded, and she had to ask, "How do I get rid of the flames?"

She saw Arden's expression turn from pride to confusion, and it was clear he didn't plan this far ahead. "Can't you just turn them off?"

"No. The magic's already in the sword. I'm not doing anything at this point."

Arden looked at the sword for a minute and thought hard, then embarrassingly got up and walked over to the sink and started filling the basin. Claire groaned; this was most likely the stupidest position she had ever found herself in. Arden soon came back to douse the fire. The fire went out, and Claire was left with a puddle on the floor. They both took a sigh of relief, and Arden made his way outside to get back to the drawing board.

The Law

In the dead of night, Claire sat on a rooftop carefully watching the building opposite. She was getting tired of waiting, but it would be worth giving it a couple more hours in case her target appeared. She was starting to worry that she was wasting her time here. After spending the last week tracking an elusive thief, she was confident this would be his target, but it was tough to know when he would appear.

Eight days ago, Claire took a job to hunt down a thief in the shopping district. The victims were shop owners who came together to request this job and catch the culprit. The last one caught the thief on camera, but the authorities hadn't managed to track him down yet. He was seen on camera levitating down from the roof and stealing everything, using magic so as to not leave a trace. He was young, slender, and wore a mask that covered everything but his eyes. Since the thief was revealed to be using magic, the local PD was cracking down on young suspects, but so far none of them fit the bill.

Collecting details from each of the victims and going over the intel with her team, the only pattern they came up with was that each establishment was in proximity to each other and had higher and higher levels of security. It didn't even seem to matter how much he was stealing; it was more like he was building up to something.

Thus leading Claire a building over from two local jewelers. If the pattern held and they stuck to their schedule of the end of the month, then they should attempt another robbery in this area in the next couple of days. It seemed like a long shot, or maybe it wasn't. It wasn't like Claire had ever attempted this before, but she was stubborn enough to try.

Finally, on the second day, after a few hours of patience, she saw a figure make its way to the jewelers. Only his outline was visible, but it was clear he was messing with the ventilation, and after a minute, he slipped inside. The second he went in, Claire shot up and, using her preplanned route, made her way across to where the duct had been ripped off. It was better not to rush in after him, or they could end up trashing the place. So instead she drew her sword, took her stance, and waited.

After only a few minutes, he crawled back out with a bag tied around his waist. But before he had a chance to stand, she called over to him. "Stop right there!" Claire shouted with practiced authority.

He froze in place on his knees but slowly looked up to face her. He looked more aggressive than surprised, meeting her unflinching stare.

"Drop the bag. Now."

He looked defiant but did what he was told. He held the bag away from him but, without moving a finger, the vent cover lifted and flew toward her. Using both arms, she deflected the cover with her sword, but he was already fleeing across the rooftop.

Claire chased after him while he made his way to the next building. Unfortunately for her, there were loose bricks and scattered debris that flew toward her while she pursued. She felt like she was on the obstacle course again, ducking and dodging.

They crossed several more rooftops with her keeping pace. The thief clearly knew where he was going; there were no wasted movements as he charged ahead, insistent on losing his pursuer. Tired of deflecting loose bricks, Claire kept looking for an opening. Her chance came after following him up onto an apartment complex. The rooftops where now a straight run with no corners to duck around and no buildings to jump to. With the open target in front of her, Claire took the offensive. Sword still in hand, she charged it up, and it lit ablaze—Arden having since reapplied the sigil since the last attempt. She stopped running, held the flaming sword behind her back and swung it toward the thief. As the sword came down, the fire gathered to the tip and launched forward at a high speed. The resulting fireball hit him dead-on and knocked him down before the next jump.

He struggled on the ground with his back on fire and was left with no choice but to throw off his jacket and mask. Claire caught up and got a clear view of the man in question. She was right in thinking he was young, about the same age as her in fact, with short spiked hair and the same defiant look in his eyes as before.

"Are you ready to give it up?" she asked, ready for another fight. He was out of breath but did not look ready to give up. From the left, a chimney ripped itself from the ground and came at her. She expected as such, so she held out her left hand, ready to break it to pieces, but the moment she raised her hand he did the same. Claire was suddenly frozen as his invisible grip held her in place long enough to get battered by the flying chimney.

Claire quickly pushed the remains off and hauled herself up to see him again fleeing. She stumbled forward for a moment but knew immediately she was in no condition to run after him. Nothing was broken, but the heavy impact had left her battered. It was frustrating watching him flee, but there was no chance to catch him now.

After pulling herself free of the remaining bricks, Claire sat back and looked up at the sky, though she couldn't appreciate the starry night. It was disappointing to experience her first failure, but there was nothing to do but learn from it. Watch out for flying chimneys seemed to be the only lesson she could glean.

In the dead of night, she made a promise that she would meet the thief again. Leaving a job unfinished didn't sit right with her. Hearing thunder in the distance, she decided it was best to head back before the rain started.

Claire didn't know at the time, but it wasn't thunder that echoed in the night. In the middle of the industrial district, a factory exploded outward into a bright flame.

Chapter 6

Where there's a Will

Claire was used to sleeping undisturbed. For the past month, they'd had no major issues, save from the odd fire or the very odd Lilla napping in the middle of the kitchen floor. Of course the one morning she could do with the extra rest after running across rooftops all night, Arden burst in to wake her up.

"Oh are you awake?" he asked as Claire shot up at his sudden entrance.

"Sorry, but you have to see this news report it's huge," he said excitedly and promptly left Claire dazed and confused. Resisting the urge to roll back to sleep, she hoisted herself out of bed to follow.

Everyone was gathered, with the TV in the middle of a report. Ewan paused it when Claire approached.

"All right, what's so important?" she asked while stretching her muscles which still ached from the night before.

Ewan turned over to Arden. "I told you we didn't need to wake her up yet."

"But we need to figure out what we're gonna do about this," he argued. Lilla kept silent but looked apologetically toward Claire.

"We may not have to do anything. The authorities will be pooling their resources to find the culprit." Ewan continued to lecture him.

Before the argument could get any more heated, Claire interrupted. "Would one of you please show me what's going on." Ewan now seemed to remember she was standing there and rewound to near the beginning of the report.

A male reporter stood in front of a fence with the smoking remains of a building behind him. The text at the bottom of the screen labeled it as an AMTech munitions factory.

"Disaster struck the industry today as a munitions factory downtown erupted in flames late last night. Authorities were quick to contain the destruction left and prevent any further damage. Fortunately, no one was working in the area, so there are no injuries to speak of. The damage in question appears to be a deliberate attack on AMTech or possibly Verras as a whole as a man was caught on camera entering the facility and destroying it."

As he spoke of this, the footage changed to the night before. The view was security footage facing the outside of the building. Clear as day, a man in his midthirties with dark streaked hair strolled up into clear view and stopped in front of the camera. Facing the building, he stretched out both arms and pointed his index and middle fingers toward the closed metal shutter to the building. From the angle, you could see he wore heavy metal gauntlets despite the rest of his armor being much lighter. From his fingertips, there was a brief flash, and suddenly the shutter was blasted open, giving him entry. There was no sound from the recording, but when he entered the building, you could see the ground shaking violently in stages. After a moment it looked still, and the man emerged from the hole he created. He could have walked away, and the scene would have been over. Instead, he stopped in his tracks, faced the camera directly with a smile and took an exaggerated bow as the building collapsed behind.

The group watched in silence and took it all in. Claire having seen it for the first time was shocked at the man's abilities but more shocking was his approach.

He wanted everyone to see him doing it. It's a message. That cocky smile, the look in his eyes. He wants someone to come after him. She felt anxious; it was clear to her that he was trying to bait someone.

After the report ended, the room fell silent as Claire absorbed what she saw. "He's dangerous," she said simply.

Ewan nodded. "The question is, who was he targeting? AMTechnologies is the most obvious answer."

"Whoever it is, he's going to put innocent people in danger. He can't start blowing things up in the middle of a city without catching people in the crossfire." She looked at the others before continuing. Ewan and Arden looked tensely for her final say. Lilla, on the other hand, looked unsure.

"We'll do what we can, and if we catch any sign of this guy, we'll focus our attention on him."

Arden was the first to speak up. "Shouldn't we be looking for him, like any place he would hide?"

Ewan shook his head. "It wouldn't do us much good. We don't know Verras well enough to track where he would go. For that matter, we don't know anything about him, not even a name. There are too many unknowns for us to do anything right now."

Claire appreciated him backing up her opinion.

"That's why we'll keep working. We can meet people, build up trust, see more of this city and wait for any clues that come up."

With an agreed consensus within the group, they split up to continue as normal, each of them determined to do as much as they could. Claire went to get cleaned up, feeling glad everyone was behind her on this. There was no use in blindly searching for the most wanted man in Verras. Claire felt sure this was the best course of action. To be safe, she decided to send out a message to Isaac, to see if he could offer some advice for dealing with something like this.

****

With a sense of purpose, Ewan and Lilla were on their way to the Contractor's Office together to check on what else today had to offer. On the way, Lilla was unusually quiet to the point that even Ewan felt the silence wasn't normal.

"Is something bothering you? You seem pensive."

Lilla was gripping her hand, clearly uncomfortable with answering. "I don't know if we should be going after this guy. He might be too much for us."

Ewan was surprised she felt that way. She had been gung-ho about their jobs so far. "We didn't say anything about facing him alone. If we find clues to his whereabouts, we could follow up and call in the authorities to deal with him. Verras has specialized SWAT teams for this situation."

"That doesn't sound like what we agreed on. Claire sounds like she wants us to take him out."

"Claire's only concerned about people getting hurt. If there's any way we can help prevent that, then we should do what we can."

Lilla sighed. "I know, and I want to help…I'm just worried we're not ready."

Ewan had nothing to say to that. It was always a possibility, but all of this was purely hypothetical. They may find no trace of this man.

****

Back at the apartment, Arden and Claire were going over their weapons and corresponding sigils. In the event they got pulled into a fight, Claire did not want to be caught unprepared. They talked through this and went over the battle strategies they had been working on, which ones were practical and what they still needed to improve. The time passed faster than they realized, and when they were near finished, Ewan and Lilla had returned to offer up any jobs to get started for the day. Lilla was feeling better thanks to a new job she found for them.

"I think we should look into this." She held out the request to Claire. The job in question was a mother's plea to find her son. He had apparently run away and hadn't been seen in weeks. After getting worked up over this latest incident, the idea of finding a missing person seemed ideal.

"We could help find this kid," Claire agreed. It seemed like a good objective for now. Arden and Ewan also seemed on board. Ewan was glad to see Lilla perk up since they found this job. With a clear goal for today, the group headed out to meet with the client and find out what clues they could.

****

Claire and Ewan met with the client while Arden and Lilla waited outside. From there they learned the boy's name was Will, he was twelve years old, Elestran, and had been missing for a couple of months. Will had been getting in trouble using magic in school which caused several arguments at home as he wasn't giving it up. While it sounded like a runaway, after two months, anything could have happened. They decided to follow up where the mother had tried with his friends and see if they had any idea where to find him. There were a couple of addresses and areas to check so they split up to find out what they could and meet back home once they were done.

****

With the sun showing the midafternoon, Claire and Ewan found a decent lead after talking to a few of the local kids. They were told Will's friends would be hanging out by a bridge nearby. Spotting them from a distance, they found three boys messing around near some graffiti under the foot of the bridge. Although none of them had any spray cans with them, they weren't doing themselves any favors hanging out right underneath it.

The youths stopped and watched when the pair approached. Who knows what they were thinking, seeing a young couple in light armor and one with a sword at her side. The skinny boy at the front of them boldly asked what they wanted.

Claire smiled at the trio, noting one looked nervous behind the other two. "We're looking for Will Rainey. He's been missing for a long time, and we're trying to help find him. Are you friends of his?"

The three boys looked immediately shifty. Again, their skinny leader answered for them. "Yeah, Will's our friend. I heard he ran away."

Ewan opened with his line of questioning and watched their reaction. "Have any of you seen him? Is he still in Verras, hiding at a friend's place maybe?"

"We don't know where he is, so just leave us alone." The other two stuck with that answer, and the one with a shaven head continued to stare at them while the other kid looked nervously at his feet. Claire stayed composed, but she was desperate for a straight answer.

Be patient with them, she thought. *I'll get nowhere if I push too hard.* She made sure to address all three of them, hoping one of them would respond. "Look, his mom's worried about him. He's been missing over a month and could have gotten into trouble. We need to make sure he's not hurt." This did get a response as each of them looked at each other.

"He's fine," answered the one who was staring at them.

Keeping up the gentle approach, Claire pushed for more. "Are you sure he's all right? You guys looked kind of worried when I mentioned him getting into trouble."

This time the nervous boy cracked and murmured to the others. "What if he's part of that gang?" he said to the others quietly.

Claire's eyes lit up. "Gang?" she asked innocently.

The leader scolded him for blurting that out. "They're not a gang. They're a stupid club." They started bickering among themselves, and Claire tried to listen in. Before she could think of her next move, Ewan interrupted them with something unexpected. "Do they have something to do with a revolution?"

Claire turned to him. *Where did he get that from?*

Ewan gestured above at the graffiti. She hadn't paid it any mind until now, but the most prominent part claimed REVOLUTION with a glowing hand painted beside it.

"It's a stupid brand. A bunch of kids got together to play with magic in secret."

"Do you think Will could be in trouble by joining them?" Claire asked, again sounding as innocent in her questioning as possible.

The boy had his arms folded and was grumbling. The quiet one answered with his own question. "You're only checking he's okay, right? If he doesn't want to come back, it's his choice."

Claire hadn't thought of it that way. She did want to help this kid, not drag him back.

"Yes, we want to give his family some peace of mind."

"He joined a gang called the Revolution. They got together to practice magic, and Will ran off to join them. They say it's a safe haven for mages to hide. We don't know where they are though."

"That's a great start. Thank you."

Before she was about to leave, Ewan posed one last question. "Out of curiosity what kind of magic does Will use?"

The kids looked at each other, and the leader answered, "He plays around with computers, makes them do stuff."

The nervous one started giggling. "Remember when he made the teacher's computer say stuff, and he couldn't figure out how to turn it off?" They all started laughing as they talked about their friend, leaving Claire smiling as they left.

Ewan asked Claire if she had heard of young mages learning outside of a school, but she had never heard of it happening. "How can they develop it without the proper training?" she asked him.

"It's quite rare for one to develop magic on their own without someone to show them how to tap into it. Once they get a feel for it, they could be self-taught."

Ewan started thinking aloud based on the research he had been doing. "Magic responds to the will of the user. This is a common theory I've found, and it confirms what we've seen so far. The stronger the will of the user, the stronger the magic they can wield. You are its guide. The magic responds to what you want to happen."

That's a cool way to see it, Claire thought. She remembered first unlocking her magic; Isaac had shown her before she could start school. She first learned to focus inward and find that tiny spark. Once unlocked it would start to grow stronger. When she concentrated, she could still feel how much magic was waiting to be called forth.

Thinking about how she started, Claire emphasized with Will. "You know it's sad. If Will had been doing that out our school, he would have been commended."

"Yes, it's an interesting trick. I've not seen that kind of magic before. It's possible this Will has a rare talent."

"All the more reason for us to check up on him."

Having only unearthed a few clues, however, it was time for them to regroup and plan where to look tomorrow.

****

They both arrived back home to find Arden and Lilla waiting. Also waiting for them was the video screen with Isaac, who sat ready. Once she saw this, Claire noticed all three of them looked tense.

"What's going on?"

Lilla walked up to inform her. "He's been waiting for all of us to be here. It's about what happened this morning."

This was the first time Lilla had seen Claire's brother. He was tidy with short, flattened hair, and there was only a vague resemblance to Claire in his face. His stern expression drew attention to the pale blue eyes they both shared.

Now that they were all here, Isaac could tell them the reason he was calling. "I got your message about the mage who attacked in central Verras. I need to tell you to stay away from him."

There was a silence after this. Arden most of all wanted to argue, but he held back since Isaac had been the one helping them set up.

Claire broke the silence in a demanding tone. "Why?"

"His name is Daniel Serco. He's a former regulator for the council, and now he's one of the most wanted criminals on the continent. He's far too dangerous for you to get involved."

Ewan was the one to question this. He was as enthusiastic as the others to go after this guy, but there must be a reason Isaac seemed concerned. "What makes this man so dangerous?"

"He leaves us a trail of fire and death everywhere he goes. He makes it theatrical like he's putting on a twisted show. The only reason I think he's there is to strike at AMTech for challenging mages." He paused before continuing; this clearly wasn't enough to sway them from this path. "There is something else, a specific reason I don't want you anywhere near him. It's not about how many people he's killed before but the way he does it."

They could all see Isaac's hesitation at telling them. Claire had never seen her brother worry like this but unless he told them the truth, she would not give it up.

"We've known from his record that he uses fire and explosive magic, but there have been several reports of him…causing people to explode. Worst of all, the latest report states he did this to a former partner, somehow bypassing her own magic and killing her instantly." Isaac gave them a minute for that to sink in. He knew how disturbing this news was. The idea that a mage could kill you without any way to defend yourself. Isaac had heard of Serco long before there was any sighting. Because of this terrifying ability, only their top-ranked specialists were permitted to go after him.

After a minute of hard silence, Arden broke it out of frustration. "So we're supposed to do nothing and let him go?"

"That's exactly what you should do. If you go after him, you will die. It doesn't matter how strong you are."

Isaac took a breath after his harsh reply. "We're going to work with Mayor Hargrove on this and provide him with everything they need to stop Serco. It pains me, but we don't have any of our best to send in."

Lilla was the only one who looked almost relieved at this news; they couldn't possibly go after him now that they'd learned this. It would be suicide for them.

Claire remained quiet, but her hands were shaking. If she were alone in this, then she would gladly take the risk for the chance of stopping this guy. But how could she put her friends in such danger when she knew they weren't ready for it.

"Fine."

The others turned to Claire, but she kept her head low. She couldn't bring herself to look at them. Isaac wanted to push for more, but he could see she wasn't saying it lightly.

"All right, I'm sorry it came to this, but we will handle Serco. I'll leave you guys to it today, but if you want to talk about this, you can call me tonight, okay." Claire didn't speak, but she nodded that she understood, and just like that he was gone.

"What are we supposed to do?" Arden asked softly.

Finally, Claire looked up at the three of them. "We're going to go find that missing kid."

Chapter 7

Keeping Up Appearances

Despite the recent revelation, the team had a clear objective. Claire and Ewan shared their lead to Will's whereabouts with the Revolution. Arden and Lilla hadn't found much else, but when the graffiti was mentioned, it sparked Lilla's memory.

"I've seen that marking a few times around town. They were all around the same area." Lilla went to get the map and spread it on the table, willing herself to remember. She pointed at three different locations where the marking had been seen. It was clear from her directions that they were all on the west quarter. This was a big lead especially considering that's where Will lived and where they found his friends by the bridge.

"Are you sure it's only here? Nobody's seen this in any other part of the city?" Claire asked.

They all shook their heads.

Ewan offered another idea. "Do you see how the first sign we came across was near the bridge, in clear view of anyone crossing it?" They saw where he pointed. Claire didn't realize at the time, but this bridge crossed the invisible border from west to north.

"I see where you're going with this. You think it's a welcome. The Revolution is here for members to find."

He nodded in approval. "It seems likely."

Satisfied, Claire traced her hand around the western border. "We can already narrow down our search here. We'll all split up and look for any sign of the Revolution or this mark. Keep in contact and call in if you've found something." They each seemed a lot more motivated than they had been only moments ago. For Claire, this was a crutch to move on from the more serious matter, but they had a real chance to help someone, and no matter what else was going on, that counted for something.

****

The four of them split up to comb the western district of Verras. They went unarmed and dressed casually to appear less threatening, but the search would take time as there was a lot of ground to cover. Claire and Ewan were stopping to talk to any teens they encountered who might know something. Claire stuck to her method of being curious but not too pushy with them. Lilla took a less sociable approach and checked out alleyways and rooftops for any sign of the mark, while Arden moved in the less populated areas for anything that stands out.

After searching nonstop for two days, things were getting uncomfortably quiet at home, the main cause being with Claire. It was one thing to be determined to find Will, but any attempts to talk to her was met with brief answers if any at all. Lilla most of all tried to see if she was okay, asking if what her brother said was bothering her, but Claire dismissed it. "It would be crazy to go after Serco the way we are now. We've been over this." But Lilla was still concerned. What if they couldn't find this kid. If she was using this to keep herself busy, could she accept if they failed?

Another day of pounding the pavement, Ewan had organized a grid search pattern to save them going in circles. After getting nowhere with the search, Claire decided to take a breather as things were weighing on her mind. She leaned over a barrier overlooking the river.

Lilla's worried about me. They all are. If I don't reassure them soon, I'm going to lose their confidence. So why can't I? Even in her own head, she refused to answer.

I can't give up on this job. I refuse to give up. It's one thing to get knocked down by a damn thief but to abandon people who need our help!

She threw her head up and started taking deep breaths; the cold air was always good for calming her down. After pushing out the dark thoughts, she turned to get back to it. Thankfully for her, she was saved by a simple message not an hour later.

"I found them!"

****

Arden sat smugly at a table outside a cafe with his find. He had told the others to meet here to see the Revolution's club; he couldn't wait to see the look on Claire's face. They were all feeling the pressure to find this place, and in the end, it was all about knowing the right people. Arden had spotted them a few hours ago, a small group of boys a few years younger than him ducking into an alleyway together. He followed them carefully and caught a peek of them showing off some magic in what looked to be an old skating rink. Truth be told, he was hoping this was going to be where they all gathered but it wasn't going to be that easy. The place was too easy for people to walk into. He gathered his nerves to approach them.

They were aggressive toward him at first, but he put up a front of looking for somewhere quiet to test his magic. This was met with suspicion until he came out with a whole spiel of AMTech kicking in his door and forcing him to run. "I tell ya, if I build up my power, I'll show those tech freaks what magic can do." This seemed to win him favor, and after ranting about AMTech for a while, one of the boys finally mentioned a revolution.

Once the team grouped up again, they followed Arden's directions. The four of them walked casually by a nightclub. It was still early afternoon, so no one was around, but they didn't want to stand around staring at it. The neon sign was dark, but the title was clear. "Haven."

Claire felt her excitement but managed to contain herself. "You sure this is the place?"

Arden radiated confidence. "It sure is. The guys I spoke to told me to come here for a revolution. I'm supposed to go in when the club opens, and I'll find someone who can initiate me.

Claire did indeed smile and patted his back a bit harder than necessary. He felt it was a mix of relief and excitement as they could move on to the next stage—infiltrating the club to find Will.

****

After checking out what they could without going in, they prepared to enter the club that night. Lilla and Ewan were left on standby outside as they decided Claire and Arden should enter on their own. Claire could lead the way with Arden as her muscle. After all, without weapons they looked fairly ordinary. They acted casual to gain entry to the club with no issue. It seemed there were no special conditions for entering through the front door. Arden did say they needed to be initiated so maybe this was a meeting place.

They saw, as expected from a nightclub, a bar for over eighteens, several booths, and a dance floor in the center with blaring music all around. The place was packed, and the colored lights were changing so much it was hard to focus. They walked across the dance floor with Arden casually greeting strangers as they passed. Claire wasn't entirely sure what to look for, but nothing stood out to her.

At the far end of the club, they saw another bouncer standing by the door marked Employees Only. As they aimed toward it to get a closer look, a younger man with spiked hair and a dark outfit started talking to him. Upon seeing him, Claire ducked behind Arden to block any view.

"What's wrong? We should go see what's back there," Arden said while Claire held him still.

Claire refused to move from behind him. "The guy talking to the bouncer. That's the thief I chased down the other day. He'll know my face."

The thief in question turned toward them. Claire hadn't even considered he could be a part of this. Claire grabbed Arden's hand and retreated into the crowd. "We have to move before he spots me."

They made their way onto the dance floor and tried to blend in. Arden kept his back to the far end and started shuffling casually while Claire kept an eye out. She saw them move in her direction, and convinced they would be spotted, she pulled Arden with her straight into a booth to hide. As they sat though, she realized there were two guys already there sitting opposite. They stared at the two who had suddenly thrown themselves down in the booth.

The two regarded the newcomers suspiciously. After staring at each other awkwardly for a minute, Arden attempted to break the ice.

"Sorry for jumping in but my friend's ex just walked in, and we're trying to avoid him," he said and signaled toward where the thief was. Claire went a shade redder as he said this but whether this was out of annoyance or embarrassment was anyone's guess.

The ploy seemed to work well with the two boys as the smaller one with jet-black hair replied, "I get that. If his ex walked in right now, he would be under the table."

To which the taller boy with his hair in a ponytail giggled. "Like you would do any better. You would be hiding in the corner!"

Claire eyed the crowd to see that he wasn't following. The two boys also looked at the crowd, curious to see who was there. Luckily they had lost sight of him.

Claire sat back again. "This is going to be a problem."

The boy with long hair leaned over to her. "Hey, you can't let him get in the way of a good time, right?" Claire smiled at the fact this guy was trying to comfort her without knowing what was going on. Arden did a good job of getting the boys talking as they may be able to provide information.

"Are you guys new here?" asked the chatty one with the ponytail.

"Yeah. I'm Claire, and this is Arden. It's our first time coming here."

"I'm Jamie, and my happy little companion here is Wren." Wren gave him a look of derision for this but nodded at the two. They were an odd pair with Jamie being outgoing where Wren was keeping quiet but listening closely. Jamie was clearly curious and continued to question the two. "So what brought you two to the club?"

Arden took the lead and seemed happy to make up a story. "We met a guy who recommended this place, said we might meet people we can relate to." Claire listened intently for their response. This was a perfect chance to learn about the club and if these two knew anything about the revolution.

"It sounds like you're looking to meet some like-minded people here in Haven. You came to the right place. We accept all kinds here." Jamie leaned in close to ask them quietly, "Are you looking for a revolution?" And there was the magic word.

"Definitely," they both answered.

The other two looked at each other, Jamie smiled at them and stood up. "Follow me."

They made their way back toward their original goal. Claire was cautious about who would see her. They reached the back, and Jamie spoke to the bouncer for a moment to let them in. They entered a stairwell that split into two paths, one leading led down and outside or the other that continued straight across. They went straight into the opposite hallway of what Claire would presume was the next building attached to the club. They went straight across the next hallway, ignoring the open doorways that looked from a glance like locker rooms and a row of stairs leading to some ornate double doors.

"Holy crap this place is huge." Arden stared in amazement.

Before them was a large hall that looked like it was a sports arena before. It was split down the middle with half a thin wall, and there were dozens of people around talking and wielding magic. Several smaller areas were split off like a range with targets and an unfinished pool, even the music leaked in from the club for a nice ambiance. Even grander though, was behind the wall was a giant cage that took up a quarter of the hall.

Claire wasn't sure what she was expecting, but it wasn't this. "How do you guys afford this place?"

"The drinks are overpriced," Wren replied with a straight face.

Claire was sure he was joking, but with the bland tone he had, it was hard to tell.

"Now that you're here, we can show you a quick tour of this place before you meet our friends in charge and you can decide how involved you want to be. Wren, why don't you go see if Sam's free to meet these two after we look around."

"All right. I'm not much for touring anyway."

Wren left to go find the people in charge as Jamie had suggested. Claire wasn't sure she wanted to stay long enough to meet them, but she had to play it cool. She looked to Jamie who was preparing to show them around. "I'm getting the feeling you've done this for people before?"

"Oh yeah. It's funny you bumped into us. We're actually recruiters for Haven. We normally come to you, but you fell right into us instead," he answered cheerfully.

They were getting into the thick of it, and Claire remembered to look for Will. Would they have to commit to being full members to find him?

As they made their way around, they had the chance to ask some more questions. "So you call this a revolution. I take it that means more than showing off your magic?" *Like stealing from people*, she thought.

In his so-far friendly manner, Jamie was happy to elaborate. "That is a big part of it, and if that's what you want to contribute, we're happy to have you here. We are also trying to push the government into allowing magic practice as a regular education again, but you don't have to get involved with that if you choose not to."

Claire eyed him suspiciously. *That was way too good an answer. It must be part of his sales pitch.*

They came up to the cage. Nobody was in at the moment, but it was surrounded by spectator seats. "Now I know this might look distasteful at first glance, but if you want to train to become a fighter, where else can we allow you practice. You both look pretty tough, so I'm guessing you're no stranger to this." They both agreed. There was no point in denying that with both clearly showing some muscle behind their casual clothes. So far everything seemed normal, for an underground group of teenage mages in a city that was looking to outlaw them that is. Still, they had only seen the friendly face of this club and Claire was sure there was more to see behind the scenes. She scanned the crowd for Will, but before she could get a good look, Wren came back for them. "They're ready to see you."

"Oh good, I was worried we'd have to wait until tomorrow. So are you guys ready to meet our boss?"

Claire nodded, but internally she was worried they were going in too deep. *We need a lucky break here. Just sign us up for membership and let us leave. We can come back later to find Will.* Still, as much as much as Claire was nervous about keeping up this charade, she was curious about the club's intentions. It seemed like an honest attempt to support mages, but the idea of rising up against the government could be dangerous.

They were led back and up the stairs into a standard-looking office that overlooked the hall with two people waiting inside. It seemed everybody here was in their late teens at most, as even the boss in front of them was young. In front of the desk stood a tanned woman with her hair tied back. She stood politely with a welcoming presence, which was in direct contradiction to the enraged, spikey-haired individual next to her.

"You!"

The doors behind them slammed on their own, and Claire was pushed up against the wall. Arden held back while everyone else turned to the angry youth.

"Hunter, what are you doing?"

He directed his response to the unknown woman in the room. "This is the one who chased me through the rooftops!" With that accusation, all their attention was on Claire.

Wren made it worse with his comment. "She's not your ex?"

The boy now known as Hunter didn't so much speak as growl in response.

Jamie looked offended. "Did you lie to us to get in here?"

Arden articulated his response of, "Uhhh?"

Hunter was still shouting over them. "Did you track me here? Come to finish the job?"

"Enough!" The woman silenced all of them. Her voice seemed to shake the room, and Jamie and Wren took a step back. Even Hunter gave her the floor, but he never released his invisible grip, keeping Claire to the wall. "Sam," he started, but she raised a hand to him and stepped between them to face Claire.

"Is what he says true?"

She knew there was no point in denying it. "Yes."

With no visible reaction, Sam continued. "Why did you attack him?"

"He was stealing from people. I wanted to stop him."

"Is that why you came here, to turn him in?"

"No, we didn't even know he was here," Claire answered calmly despite her predicament.

Arden glanced between the people in the room and the window, most likely wondering if they could fight their way out. Claire wondered the same, but it might not come to it yet.

Sam scrutinized her for a quick minute and then walked back to face both of her guests. She gave Hunter a nod, and he lowered his arm, letting Claire land on the ground.

She cautiously stood back up and looked to Sam. "Thank you."

"You can thank me by telling me why you are here," she asked in a calm tone.

Arden and Claire exchanged a look. What they said next would determine everything— be honest or lie thier way out. Claire sighed and took a chance on it. "We're looking for a boy called William. He ran away from home, and his family's worried about him. We heard he joined this club and thought he might be involved in something dangerous. Were we right?"

Sam seemed to appreciate her honesty. "So you chase down thieves and help find runaways. I can assure you that we help guide people here and unlock their potential. We also protect them from anyone who would threaten us. If William's a member of this club, then he's safe."

Jamie stepped forward on this. "I met Will. I introduced him when he first came in here. I knew he had run away from home, but that's his business. No one was keeping him here."

Now that they had opened a sort of awkward dialogue, Arden pushed for their goal. "Can we talk to him? Finish what we came for?"

With a moment to think about it, Sam replied. "You may."

Claire and Arden finally exhaled, although Hunter was still staring them down. It may have been some shaky negotiating, but they could finish their job. But even with that, Claire still wanted to understand their purpose, if it was as good-hearted as they advertised.

"Before we go can I ask you something?"

"Go ahead."

"Why are you stealing from good people?"

This question, of course, angered Hunter again, but he said nothing this time, letting Sam reply. "We're not proud of that. We did what we had to do to get this place off the ground. We wanted to get our funding from AMTech. Steal from them as they've stolen from us. But we couldn't risk confronting such high security early on." The three beside her all broke eye contact, but Sam held her steeled expression.

They really do feel guilty, and even faced with this, she didn't shy away from the truth.

"Why don't you guys take up job offers to fund this place?" Arden chimed in, but Sam chuckled at the idea.

"We're hardly regulators."

But Claire agreed this was a better idea than stealing. "Neither are we. You don't need a badge or official ID to take these jobs. If you feel you're qualified, you take the job and meet with the client."

Sam considered this for a moment and turned to the others. "Jamie, Wren, I want you two to look into this tomorrow and let me know if this is possible. If what they say is true, we can encourage our members to take these jobs, work together and commit some of the earnings to the club."

Hunter didn't seem as on board. "You think you can trust them?"

"I think we can find this out ourselves. If we can find a better way to support this place, I want to know." With her orders given, she again looked to Claire. "If this pans out then you've done us a great service. Go with Wren and find the boy you're looking for. We need to convene on what's happened here. I appreciate you've been honest with your intentions here. If you choose to come back, we could consider working together in the future."

Claire was shocked at how smoothly this went. She thanked Sam again and made her way out of the office with Wren leading them. Claire still had questions about their intent, but she at least left with a respect for the courtesy Sam showed them.

****

They didn't get a good look at people on the way through as Wren found Will near the target range for them. He told them to go ahead as he waited nearby, clearly not interested in what they had to say. Several kids were using the targets and fired a variety of spells at them, but Will sat to the side on a laptop, occasionally stopping to watch. They knew his face from a picture shown to them earlier. Even without that, he was easy to discern from the crowd as one of the few Elestrans in Verras.

"Will?" The sound of his name caused him to jump at the two.

"Wha...what is it?" he asked timidly.

"Your mom sent us to find you. She's been worried since you ran away."

He looked back down to his computer. "Oh. I didn't want her to worry."

Claire smiled gently at him. "She really worried. She has no idea where you went. Maybe you could talk to her and let her know you're doing well?" It would be a good start if Claire could help open a dialogue.

Will clammed up at this. "You could always tell her. Tell her I'm fine, and she doesn't need to worry about me.

Claire looked at Arden who shook his head. "If he doesn't want to go back, we can't force him. Are you sure you're okay here by yourself?"

Will looked up at the two of them now. "Yes, they accept me here. I can use magic however I want, and I get to see other people's magic too. People understand me here, not like at home."

Claire did feel sorry for him. It was tough for her to relate to the kind of life he grew up with, but she could at least try to understand. "I know you've had problems at home, but maybe you could give your mom a chance. Give her a call or something and talk it over. She'll be so relieved to hear from you."

She could see he was holding back a few tears. He composed himself for a second before answering. "Okay. I'll phone her soon and let her know I'm fine."

Not wanting to upset him further, she risked putting a hand on his shoulder. "It's all right. She'll be really happy to hear from you." After hearing this, he closed his eyes and didn't reply. They took this as their cue to leave and met with Wren to guide them out.

On the way, Arden asked, "Do you think he'll call?"

"I hope so. We'll go see his mom tomorrow and find out."

Although he seemed uninterested, Wren did remind them. "The boss did give you an invitation to come back, so if you want to follow up, you can."

"Thank you." Claire was surprised at how welcoming they had been. Maybe this place was made as a safe haven for mages after all. If so, they could consider working together to help them. One step at a time though.

****

Sam watched from the window as they left. They were already discussing their new guests and the impact this could have. Hunter clearly has misgivings about this, but Sam assured him.

"There's no point in making more enemies for ourselves. We'll have plenty soon enough."

Chapter 8

The Best of Intentions

"Job done!" Claire burst through the door with her announcement. The others were ready and waiting for her.

Arden especially was surprised by this. "She paid us already? I thought we'd have to get him home for that."

"He may not be going home, but we tracked him down, got him to phone his mom, and I may have promised we'll look out for him anytime we're in the club. Honestly, I think she was grateful enough to hear from him," Clare told them with a hint of pride.

Lilla was glad to see her in good spirits again. "I'll be happy to talk to Will when we're there and check in on him. It sounds like he could use someone to talk to."

"That's a good idea. I might see how he's doing as well. If we get to know him, maybe he can be convinced to go home sometime."

After being briefed on yesterday's events, Lilla and Ewan were eager to see Haven for themselves.

"We'll need to see if their boss approves of us. What were your impressions of her?" Ewan inquired.

Arden answered first. "She didn't waste any time in questioning us. I couldn't read her at all, though I was sure she was gonna kick us out."

"She was pretty straight with us and commanded a lot of respect from the others. I think as long as we don't do anything stupid, we'll be able to go back and even help them if their intentions are good," Claire added.

"Are you still mistrusting of them?"

Claire reflected on their meeting. "We didn't start on the best of terms. They were fair to us once we started talking. The only part I'm worried about is spreading the word 'revolution.' I don't want them to start picking fights with the government." Ewan nodded in agreement, so Claire continued. "If they clear us to come back, I'm happy for us to visit and learn more about them."

****

The next few weeks led to a change in the group dynamic; Sam did indeed allow them membership to come and go as they pleased. In doing so, the team helped where they could. Ewan taught those interested about where magic comes from and how it's channeled. Lilla became social within the club, getting to know the people and what brought them there. It was good to learn not everyone was rallying together to start a fight. Most were only looking for a safe place to be themselves. Arden wanted to check into the cage fights, but Ewan and Claire insisted they didn't want to teach them how to fight, in case they got the wrong idea.

Everything was running smoothly until a news report got everyone riled up. Two mages were arrested in Verras for aggressive use of magic toward the public. To make it worse, these two were potential members for Haven. Luckily they didn't know where the club was yet as they had only recently been contacted by Jamie.

Claire and Lilla went to see how the club was faring, and as expected everyone was up in arms over what happened. Some of the young mages wanted to demand their release while the more rational ones were discussing some kind of protest. Jamie seemed to have his hands full reassuring everyone they would be okay if they didn't display their magic outside these walls. He ran up to Claire when he saw her asking around. "Claire, it's good to see you back. Listen, the boss is hoping to talk to you privately if you have a minute."

"Sure. I take it she's up in her office?" she answered while looking up to the window and could see the silhouette of someone looking over the hall.

"Yeah, she's been up there all day meeting with people. She should be free right now."

Claire wasn't sure what to make of this. If this was about the two who were arrested, what was Sam expecting her to do? Regardless, she walked up to the office with its fancy double doors and entered to find Sam waiting for her.

"You wanted to see me?" Claire asked, hiding her curiosity.

"Yes, come one in." Claire did so, and after looking for a moment longer, Sam pulled away from the window and stood next to face her. "I take it you've heard the news?"

"About the two arrests? Apparently, they were acting aggressively."

"Somehow I doubt they were. Mayor Hargrove has been pushing to outlaw magic for some time. The claims of aggression are being used as a pretense."

"Well, I really hope it doesn't go that far. They need to understand magic is a part of life. They can't stop people from using it."

"No, they can't. But now they're pushing us by making false arrests and holding people for showing their natural abilities," Sam said with a hint of resentment. It sounded like she needed someone to vent to, and Claire was happy to let her. She walked back to the window and Claire followed to look at the gathering of people below.

"Claire, do you want to know why I started this club?"

"Of course."

"It was to give people a safe haven to be themselves. To learn about their own potential and how they could use their abilities to benefit people. So far we have eighty-three people who have come here to discover my haven." She fell silent before turning to face Claire again. "But it's not enough. In a city the size of Verras, they should be teaching one hundred times the number in our club. We can only help a fraction of those who want to use magic, but Hargrove and AMTech won't allow us to do more. Tell me, Claire, what would you do in my place?" She gave Claire her full attention.

It was a daunting question. Claire wasn't sure if there was anything they could do, but she knew her answer. "So far my team and I have been working jobs around the city, helping people where they need it. With your people helping, we can make a bigger difference as we work.

We can slowly gain support that way. They can come to realize we can be a benefit for Verras and the world around us. This isn't a problem that will go away overnight. It's a long road, but we have a chance to change things." It wasn't an easy answer to give; part of it came from her talks with Isaac to convince him coming here could work. But Claire understood that asking someone to be patient under oppression wasn't what they would want to hear.

Sam closed her eyes and breathed slowly, considering Claire's answer. "I see. I appreciate your thoughts on the matter. I'll take some time to consider what you've said."

With her cue to leave, Claire went out the door to think about this exchange. She was glad to see Sam thinking about this carefully. If they continued working together then maybe they could find a peaceful solution to this mess.

Lilla was waiting in the hallway. She looked up at Claire expectantly. "Is everything okay?"

"I don't know yet. We should go. There are a few things I want to check up on."

****

They returned home, and Claire started putting a video call through to her brother. The television was already set up and had her phone attached to make the call. Claire sat down to wait because she would probably have to leave a message and pick this up another time. To her surprise, he was able to answer right away. Isaac was in his room in the council offices; he rarely seemed to pick up from his actual home anymore. "Hi, Claire and Lilla. It's good to hear from you," he said formally. Lilla smiled in reply, figuring this was the friendliest he could manage.

"Hey, brother. I wanted to ask about your progress with Serco."

"It never is just a hello anymore is it?" He smirked at her.

"Sorry. Once things settle, I'm sure I'll bug you all the time for a chat."

"I hope you do, but if it's business you want, I'll get straight to it. I've been trying to contact two of our best and brightest who are working in Knoth. It's a town a few days away from Verras. We haven't heard anything from them in days, but if I can get a message to them, I'm sure they could help. I spoke to Mayor Hargrove and their chief of security about Serco. We told them everything we knew about who he is and what he's capable of."

Claire was surprised they let Isaac deal with this directly, but that was soon forgotten when he continued. "They thanked us for the information, but they didn't want any interference from us. They have no interest in cooperating with the council to find him."

Claire facepalmed. *It's like everything I hear about Hargrove he gets worse.*

"But how do they plan on finding him?" Lilla asked with concern written all over her face.

"Hargrove has been waiting for an opportunity like this. He can test his anti-magic tech and show us all they can keep their people safe from someone like Serco. They'll do everything they can to track him and bring him in."

Once again Claire had to remind herself this was out of her hands and moved on. "What do you think of the recent arrests made. I take it you've heard what happened."

"Yes, I'm in charge of the situation in Verras, so I've been keeping up to date. It sounds like they're really cracking down on this. Hargrove has been pushing out magic users since he came into office. It seems like he wants to outlaw it altogether. If it ever gets that bad, I want you guys to pull out immediately. We can find somewhere better for you to set up."

Claire looked to Lilla who turned away. Claire knew she was worried about the people at Haven, but they chose not to tell Isaac about them for now. "Nothing but bad news today. Thanks for keeping me in the loop on this."

With that, the gloomy update was over. Claire turned to check on Lilla, but she immediately went out the door. Claire sank down on the chair after that.

It's one mess after another. Can we please get some good news soon. Some way we can help.

But not one day later she received a message from Ewan that simply read:

"We have a problem."

****

As they were all spread out, the team met up in a café. Ewan was sure to pick a table where no one would overhear them. Claire felt suddenly tense at the implications of what they were told.

"How did you find out about this?" she asked him quietly.

"I was checking on the club's progress today when I heard a young man ranting about taking up arms against the mayor. When I attempted to explain that isn't what the club was made for, he corrected me. He told me that he saw the man from the news who destroyed an AMTech facility going into Sam's office with Hunter."

Claire felt deep anxiety about this. "They could be working with Serco to start their revolution."

"Can we call in the police, let them know we found the guy?" Arden asked, but Lilla burst out in response.

"We can't let them know about the club. They'll arrest everyone!"

"But if they're joining up with Serco," Ewan started.

"Not all of them are like that. They need a safe place to be themselves. We can't take that away from them!"

"We can't let him go either, so what else can we do?" Arden argued.

"We don't even know that it's him," she threw out desperately.

"She's right," Claire butted in. "We don't have confirmation he was even there. We can't turn these people in based on a rumor."

"It wasn't the most reliable of sources," Ewan admitted. "What do you propose we do?"

"We need to see him for ourselves. I know he's dangerous, but we're members of Haven now so we won't look like a threat to him. If one of us sees him enter the club or talk to Sam, then we can decide where we go from there."

They each considered their options, but from the silence that followed, it seemed they had settled on the course of action.

"Jamie's been talking about Sam having a lot of private meetings lately. I could find out when the next one is and see if he shows up," Arden said with confidence.

"If you can do that without arousing suspicion, that would be perfect." Claire stood ready to end this meeting. "We'll break for now and see what we can find out, but be careful."

Once again Lilla was the first to hurry off. She refused to believe Haven's boss, who they all held such respect, for would betray them like this. Lilla rounded a corner so the others couldn't see how upset she was, although she made that apparent in their discussion.

"Lilla!"

She forced herself to stop and wait for Ewan to catch up.

"Hey, do you need something?" Lilla replied, trying to sound casual.

"It felt pretty heated back there. Is everything all right?"

Lilla almost laughed. "Why are you curious?"

"I'm worried about you."

Any laugh was now stuck in her throat, and she had to take a moment before answering. "It's...hard to take the idea that they would hurt people to get their point across. I thought they were better than that."

"This is becoming personal for you," Ewan said, sounding almost judgmental.

"I just feel bad for these people, that's all," Lilla said briefly and turned away.

"No I think it's more than that. Why are you so upset over this?"

Lilla looked him in the eye. He saw no tears, but she was holding something else back. "You'll have to figure that out yourself," she said and walked away, leaving Ewan behind.

Chapter 9

The Planning Stages

The four members of Team Arkon were positioned in the club following Ewan's strategy. Arden had come through and struck up a casual conversation with Jamie to learn of another meeting tonight with Sam, Hunter, Jamie, and Wren attending. Claire and the others waited in different positions to keep an eye out for their target. As a reward for the intel Arden provided, his job was to cause the distraction so nobody would pay any mind to the others. Once he got a signal, he was to join the cage fighting and put on a good show. Ewan was positioned looking up at the office window; he claimed he could see a face if they looked out. Apparently, Sam wasn't here. For that matter, Ewan saw no sign of Hunter, Jamie, or Wren, which was unusual not to have one of the three around the hall. He sent a message to Claire, hoping this was a good sign something was in the works.

Claire received this message while waiting in the hallway to the office. They would need to pass by her to make it there, and she had her excuse for skulking ready. If she was caught, Lilla would be ready in the changing room up ahead.

Someone did come from outside for Claire to see, but it was only Jamie.

"Hey, what are you doing here?" he said in a friendly enough manner.

"I needed a breather. Everyone's pretty worked up in there. I wanted to think for a minute."

"Oh, I'm sorry. Things will settle down I'm sure. Listen, I'm gonna need you to move. Hunter is on his way in a foul mood, and I wouldn't want you two fighting out here." In another circumstance, this would be believable, but this happening now confirmed her suspicions. Claire went along with Jamie; nobody else would come up if she was hovering here. She had to trust one of their backups would work and go back into the main hall.

After she left, Jamie moved to check the changing rooms. Fortunately, Lilla wasn't there.

****

Back in the main hall, Claire hurried to Ewan. "They brushed me out of the corridor. I'm going to signal Arden and find another way around. You keep your eyes on that window."

"Understood." Ewan stood nonchalantly, looking up. For anyone who knew him, it was odd to see him so casual. Luckily, no one in here knew him like his friends did. Claire made her way over to Arden and gave him a pat on the shoulder to begin. He laughed in excitement and headed in. There were a handful of people scrapping in the cage, but all eyes went on Arden as he shouted to them.

"All right, let me show you how magic works in a fight!" He shook his fists down, and the cage rumbled.

Claire looped her way back around the main hall to get back to the corridor; she wondered if Lilla had been caught as well. It was possible she already had eyes on the target, but they couldn't presume that. With everyone's attention drawn elsewhere, Claire made it around and poked her head back into the hallway. There was no one around, but she distinctly heard the office doors close up ahead. Claire slowly approached, trying to subtly listen at the door. Carefully, she moved up the corridor, waiting for any signs that someone else was there. Surprisingly, there was no one standing guard; the hallway was eerily quiet leading right up to Sam's office. Claire leaned close to it but couldn't hear a sound. She was sure people went in there, but she couldn't hear anything inside. Luckily for her, they already had a girl on the inside.

****

Although Lilla's part was to stay in the changing rooms to listen to them walk by and maybe get a glimpse of the target, she had other plans. She wasn't satisfied with just knowing if Sam was partnering with Serco or not; she had to hear what was going on. So the minute she got the message that nobody was there, she crept out of her post and into Sam's office. She and Ewan had been in here once to introduce themselves, so she was familiar with the layout of the room. The large cabinet in the corner would be perfect. It stuck out from the wall and gave enough space to hide behind. Looking at it she couldn't help but hesitate. After all, she didn't want to think of what would happen if she was caught. But part of her would not let this go, so she applied her war paint and calmed herself.

I can do this.

Lilla carefully climbed to the back of the cabinet. There was ample space to stand, and she could maneuver her way back out once she was alone again.

Listen to what they say but do not react, Lilla thought to herself and willed her body to relax so as to not make a sound.

****

Ewan resisted the urge to look at the commotion nearby; he heard a barrage of shouting and crashing and cheering from the cage. He focused magic in his eyes. With a yellow glow to scan the window, he could see shadows moving to show someone had entered the room now. A figure soon approached the window; he focused in on his face to see Hunter, who looked toward the cage. Then a second figure joined him, taller like the figure of a grown man. He focused on the stranger's features and made them clearer. His eyes widened as he immediately recognized them as the man they were looking for—Daniel Serco.

So they are working with him. They must be planning to fight the government after all. Ewan felt disappointed that it was true. He was suspicious of the revolution, but he hoped that he was wrong in this instance. He watched Serco say something and point toward the cage. Ewan wished he could hear as well as see. He wanted to understand what was going on in there.

****

Lilla heard several people come into the room, the first figure to speak was a voice she didn't recognize, a gleeful man's voice. "Oooh cage fighting. Is it to the death?" he asked.

"Get away from that window," Sam ordered. He cheerfully obeyed and thumped on the couch. "If you're so worried about the window, why not have Blackout Boy over there darken it." He gestured toward Wren who silently stood in the corner.

"Because that would draw attention. I've muted the room so no one outside can hear us. As long as you keep your head down, no one will know you were here."

Serco sighed dramatically. "Very well. Let's get on with this. I'm a busy man you know."

"Have you chosen a target?" Sam asked.

Serco perked up immediately. "Oh yes, I found the perfect spot. A little factory where they're manufacturing armor to combat people like us."

Sam scowled at this. She didn't like being compared to Serco, but this was a line she had to cross. "How's their security?"

"It's pretty tight from the outside, but that's not going to matter to us now, is it?" He winked toward Jamie, who was clearly uncomfortable around him. Serco looked around him to see all, but Sam was avoiding eye contact. "What do you all look so gloomy for, this is your big break. We go in, destroy their equipment and leave a lovely big banner for your revolution and job done."

Their hidden guest took this all in. She was almost in a meditative state to ignore any fear of discovery.

Jamie nervously asked, "And you're sure no one gets hurt?"

"Pfft. That's your job. Keep your hostages under control, and there won't be a problem."

Jamie stood more confidently. "All right."

Serco smiled at him. "But it would be naive to think there won't be a few casualties." He lit a fire in his hand and watched Jamie's expression drop.

"Enough," Sam ordered. "We'll keep them out of your way but don't kill anyone unless it's necessary."

He turned his attention back to Sam but never dropped his smile. "You're the boss. On the topic of crowds, how many men did you get me?"

"I handpicked fifteen people for the operation. They're all on board. Any more and I would risk word getting out."

"What about the techno geek? I've never heard of abilities like his. Maybe I should meet with him to see for myself."

Jamie was against this idea. "Will is clearly nervous about the operation. We'll be looking out for him to make sure he does his job, but you would probably...scare him."

Serco erupted in laughter at this, driving Sam's irritation up another level. She spoke loudly to cut him off. "Well is that enough to pull this off?"

He calmed down and pondered. "Yes, yes. It should do. What about the four newcomers? They sound better trained than the usual rabble."

Sam shook her head. "I talked to their leader about the future of this club. It's obvious they wouldn't be on board with this."

Serco shrugged in response. "Their loss." He jumped from his seat. "So if all your preparations are made, then we strike in two days. When the sun goes down, we will descend upon them."

"When exactly is that?" Wren asked.

"I don't know, like nine o'clock or something."

Sam sighed at his pointless detour. "We move in an hour after the night shift, so we'll be dealing with a skeleton crew. We'll contact you for a meeting point." She turned to the others. "Make sure we're clear outside. I'll escort Mr. Serco out myself."

Lilla heard shuffling as a few left. Although she couldn't see it, Daniel Serco was putting on a trench coat and fedora hat as his "disguise" and held his arm out for Sam, which she ignored.

Serco looked to the door. "Do you think they'll be comfortable with how this will go down? Your man James looked a bit squeamish."

She cut him off before he continued. "They'll be fine. They need to see that the path we're taking isn't going to be a clean one. Let's go before you get spotted."

****

Claire and Ewan waited for Arden to finish. Now they had confirmed that Serco was here, their minds raced about what to do next. Claire messaged Lilla already to let her know they had spotted the target, no need for her to take any risks. They weren't sure yet what to do next, but that could wait until they were together and home safe. Claire didn't like the idea of being in the same building as that madman. After some time, she saw Hunter come into the hall, but he stayed by the door. She took that as a sign the meeting was over.

After a few more minutes, she got a reply from Lilla. "I'm outside. I have something you need to hear."

****

"What were you thinking!" Claire shouted clear at Lilla. They were all taken aback by what Lilla did, but Claire was the first to vocalize it. "They would have killed you, do you understand that!"

"I had to find out what they were doing."

"That was a foolish way to do it," Ewan chimed in as Claire paced around, trying to stop from shouting further.

"We had a plan, and it worked. We saw Serco in the office," Arden reminded her.

"It wasn't enough just to see him," she grumbled miserably. "I found out what they're planning so we can do something about it."

"It wasn't worth it!" Claire threw back. "If anyone of them found you, you'd be dead right now."

"I'm sorry. I had to know why they would do it. Why they'd betray the people they brought together."

Ewan kept a calm but stern tone. "There's a reason we discuss these plans first, to limit the risk and find the best option. You threw yourself in danger and hid what you were doing from the rest of us." Lilla shrunk down under the weight of her actions. She apologized again quietly while they all took a breath. After a moment to calm down, Claire came over to sit in front of Lilla. She reached out and took hold of Lilla's hand.

"I'm going to need you to swear to us that you won't ever do something like that again. If you ever think of something that risky, you'll tell us first."

"Yes. I swear I won't hide things from you."

Claire maintained eye contact to drive the point home. "I'm gonna hold you to that. If this ever happens again, then it'll be clear we can't trust you." Claire did feel guilty for chastising her friend, but it had to be done. After Lilla nodded that she understood, Claire looked to Arden and Ewan.

"Are you both happy with that?"

Arden sighed. "As long as she doesn't pull any more stunts, then I'd rather move past this."

"Agreed. We should take a minute to calm down before continuing." Although Ewan was the last person who would need to calm down, the rest were glad to rest a minute before talking about their next move. After taking some time, the idea of what Sam and Serco were discussing was starting to sink in.

Lilla pulled herself together, but she waited until someone asked before telling them what happened. She went through everything she overheard. They all listened carefully and waited until she finished to take it all in. Claire was rubbing her temple after hearing this. "You're sure they said two days?"

"Yeah, he announced it pretty clearly."

"Of course it's two days." Claire leaned on the wall with her head lowered. Ewan clarified if the others weren't told. "There will be no time for the regulators Isaac was looking for to arrive."

"If we call in the troops they'll arrest everyone in Haven. They won't care who was in on it," Arden remembered from their last discussion. "Could we give them a heads-up on where they're going to attack?"

Ewan shot down that idea. "If we do that, they'll question our involvement, arrest us and go into Haven to arrest them too." Claire quietly listened as the two were running through the ideas she was thinking of.

Arden threw in one last alternative. "Okay this may be a stupid idea, but what if their plan goes off perfectly, no one gets hurt, and they get what they want. If we try to stop them, we might end up making things worse."

"Hmm…there are two flaws with that. One you're assuming they can keep Serco in check throughout the operation," Ewan explained.

Lilla added to this, "I don't think they can. I heard it in his voice he wants to kill people here."

Ewan continued. "The other flaw is once the job is done, Serco will escape to do this all over again."

It was obvious where this was heading. They ran through all the options until they reached the only course of action.

"We have to stop them ourselves," Claire finally said to the group. "It's exactly what we were trying to avoid, but now we don't have a choice. People will die if someone doesn't do something, and if Serco escapes, then who knows how many more lives will be destroyed by him. I didn't want us to get involved with him, so I'm asking all of you. Are you up for this?"

Arden was the first to jump in. "We can't do nothing when we have the power to stop this. I'm in." Claire nodded to him and looked at Ewan.

"We may not have intended to go this far, but we have a responsibility. We should do anything we can to stop them."

Lastly, she looked to Lilla. "You didn't want any part of this when we first saw what he was capable of. I'd understand if you don't want to do this."

Without wavering, Lilla answered. "I can't walk away from this after seeing what they've done firsthand. I'm in."

They still had a day to prepare and find out where they would strike. They each settled into their respective roles to prepare. Arden was left with to check their equipment while Ewan had an idea of how to track them. He needed access to something they would carry during the operation. Lilla knew they had a storage cupboard for all their supplies, so they left to investigate. Claire remained to work out their plan of attack based on all the information they gathered. She wrote out everything they knew so she could keep it all in mind to figure out what would and wouldn't work. Claire made it a point to avoid Serco at all costs. The perfect scenario would be to disrupt the operation without having to go near Serco himself.

Not realizing how long she was parked on the floor running through ideas, Arden returned with their weapons ready for use. She had the chance to bounce some ideas off him to help narrow down their strategy.

Shortly after, Ewan and Lilla came back with something to add. They threw Arden and Claire some kind of outfit. Claire immediately recognized it as the clothes and matching mask Hunter was wearing the day she tried to stop him. Realizing what they had brought, she couldn't hold back her impish smirk. "They're going to wear these tomorrow, aren't they?"

"I believe so. They had fifteen of these lying separate in a storage room along with other pieces of equipment. They serve as both something we can track them with and something we could use to blend in."

Lilla added, "They had about a dozen spares aside so we figured they wouldn't notice a few missing."

"That's great but how are you going to track them through these?" Arden asked.

Ewan smiled proudly. "I planted part of my magic as a tracker on them. Once we're close enough, I'll be able to sense where they are."

Claire pulled her stiff body off the floor. "These are perfect. If we follow in after them with these on, they won't look twice."

Ewan noticed her good mood. "I take it you have an idea?"

It was Claire's turn to smile confidently. "Gather round. We'll be in and out before they know what hit them."

Chapter 10

The Frying Pan

"I want you both to take your time and think about what I've said. This won't affect your standing in the club. You can continue to work here and recruit for us as before."

Jamie and Wren left Sam's office. This was how the offer was presented to them almost six months ago. When they returned home, Jamie sat quietly, clearly wrestling with the decision.

Wren instinctively put a hand in his shoulder. "You don't have to rush this. Take some time and think about the right thing for you. I'll be right here, whatever you decide."

Jamie let out a breath and moved his hand over Wren's. "Thank you," he said quietly.

Before Wren could leave the room, Jamie called to him. "Hey, why are you willing to stay with me through all this?"

Wren looked at him as though he didn't understand the question.

"I'm the one who wanted to start using magic. You did the same. I joined a nightclub full of mages, so did you. Now I'm considering joining a revolution. Why would you follow me that far?"

"You're surprised? I said I'd follow you anywhere, that's just how we are," Wren answered and left Jamie to think.

He always acts as though he's done nothing for me.

Wren had first met Jamie in their orphanage in Verras. Wren always used to get in fights even though he tried his best to avoid people. One day, when some kids started picking a fight over his gothic appearance, Jamie stood in. Normally where he'd have to punch them out, Jamie got them to leave him alone by talking to them.

That was always how they worked. Jamie was the talker, and when that wouldn't work, Wren would step in to protect them. It had kept them going so far, and he was sure they could work through anything together.

****

Jamie stood impatiently waiting for the others to arrive. Normally, Wren had a calming effect on him, but even with Wren at his side, he couldn't hide his nerves. They waited in a dingy alley deep in central Verras, next to a door they had broken open. This led down into a sewer tunnel that could get them close to their target. There were only a couple more still to arrive as everyone else was waiting below.

"We'll be starting soon," Wren said, staring at the night sky.

Jamie sighed. "I want to get this over with already."

"We'll be okay, as long as we stick together."

Jamie calmed and leaned next to Wren. "That's how we've always done it. But this is so much bigger than us."

"Are you having second thoughts?" Wren asked.

Jamie took a moment to think about that. "No, I trust Sam. I know we're doing the right thing."

"All right, then we keep going. It looks like we're ready." He saw the last three people approaching, which Jamie waved over. "You're the last to arrive, so we'll be starting soon."

They lead the last of their group inside to find an access ladder into the sewers. As they climbed down, the smell became overwhelming. It was one thing to plan on using the sewers as a way in, but actually doing it was horrible. As soon as they reached the bottom, they donned their masks and made their way through the tunnels as the others were a fair distance away. The tunnels were like a maze, without any preplanning one would get completely lost. Sam counted on this as an escape route as anyone following could end up on the other side of Verras.

They walked in silence trying to get used to the rancid air and found the main group waiting in a boiler room. They had an assortment of weapons ready; Sam holding on to a metal bat, Serco with his steel gauntlets. Wren himself had spiked claws, but he promised it was only for self-defense. Sam and Hunter were waiting at the front. They wore a red-and-white ribbon on their arms so you could tell them apart from the others. They had cleared space by the far wall.

"Is this it?" Jamie asked.

Serco emerged from the corner. He was the only one without a disguise as he was happy for his face to be plastered all over this incident. "Yep, about twenty feet of concrete is all that separates us from our goal."

"Why were you hiding over there?" Wren asked.

With all seriousness, Serco turned to him and answered, "Dramatic effect."

I need to stop asking this guy questions, Wren thought.

Jamie found Will looking nervous by a generator. He was also easy to tell apart from the crowd due to his small frame and his fidgety nature. Jamie put a hand on his shoulder to steady him. "Are you ready for this?" he asked kindly.

Will took a few breaths and stopped shaking. "I...I'll help. I can do it."

Jamie smiled reassuringly at him. "Don't worry. We'll get you access to the security and you can do your thing."

Surer of himself now, Will stood up straight. Jamie was determined to look out for him on this operation. He had doubts Will was ready for this, but they needed his unique abilities.

Sam gathered them all before going in. "You all know your jobs. We do this right, and the government will take notice of our action today. This is our revolution. We do this for future mages of Verras. So let's get it done." She signaled for Jamie to proceed. He placed both hands on the wall and felt for the other side. Once he had its measure, he poured his magic in, and the wall softened and melted down, leaving a hole big enough for them to enter.

On the other side, they found an empty storage room as Serco promised. There was no one here so the chaos wouldn't start until they went upstairs.

Wren and Jamie led the way as they kicked open the door ahead of them. Before them was a huge assembly line with dozens of unsuspecting workers and only a handful of security guards. Not wasting any time, Wren and Jamie ran into the room and aimed straight across for the security booth. Wren stopped and fired black smoke at any guard he saw. They were instantly blinded and tried to wave it off before they were beaten down by the rest of the group following behind.

As they dispatched the guards, Jamie had made his way up to the booth overlooking the assembly line. With the door closed, he touched the metal hinges which instantly liquefied. He could then push the door in and knock down one of the two guards there. The other found enough time to fire two bolts from his taser which grazed past Jamie. He retaliated by pulling the liquid metal hinges of the door and launched them into the guard's hand that then solidified. He then threw one more which solidified in the air and knocked him out.

He kicked the tasers away from them. They had no wires attached to the pins, and the pins themselves held a charge that would incapacitate the target if hit.

The silent alarm would have gone off by then, but that didn't matter. Jamie could see everyone charging in now with Sam, Will and a few others heading straight for the lobby. All the workers were at a loss until Serco jumped on the line.

"Attention!" He shot two long streams of fire into the air, and after a few screams, all eyes were on him.

"If you want to make it out alive, you better do what we say! Group yourselves over there and don't move. We'll lead you to the lobby, and you'll stay there and keep out of our way. If any of you move a hair out of place, I'll be happy to set an example for the others. Understand?" A few terrified nods and they slowly shuffled together as ordered. Serco then waved Hunter in to take his place and ran over to follow Sam. Jamie watched the display with disgust.

He's enjoying this way too much.

****

Sam made her way swiftly through a cafeteria as her people split up to threaten and gather everyone together. Those who didn't have flashy abilities were given big weapons to get the point across. Sam went through the back door of the reception, and armed with her metal bat, took out the unsuspecting night guard. There were two others in the lobby, but as they stumbled to draw their tasers, she hit the bat against the counter. The resulting sound was greatly amplified and sounded like an explosion went off around them, which brought them to their knees. Sam hit it again for good measure before moving in to disable them completely.

Seeing it was all clear, Will ran over to the reception desk and from there accessed the security cameras. His hands hovered over the console and streams of deep blue light emanated from him and sank into the controls. The security footage fizzled out but left one screen showing the outside of the building. He continued to send his instructions into the computer system and closed the shutters on the windows but left the two front doors clear.

By the time he was done, Serco was there checking out their handiwork. He eyed the guards on the ground first. "Nicely done. I doubt I could have done better myself. Well, unless I torched them, but you disapprove of that." Sam ignored the comments; she wouldn't allow him to provoke a reaction from her. He turned his attention to Will who was hoping to go by unnoticed. "Good job, kid. You're handy to have around. Keep it up, and you might not get yourself killed."

Before he could bother Will further, Sam gave him his orders. "Tell Wren and Jamie to bring the hostages here. Then get to work on your charges."

Serco grinned with excitement. "Ah, I love this part." With that, he ran off to gleefully rig the place to explode.

****

Everything continued smoothly from there, and it looked as though the job would be done in less than an hour. But neither Sam nor Serco could have predicted interference from four new Revolutionists entering from the storage room. At first glance, they blended in with the others, but anyone paying attention would notice their array of weapons and pick them out of the crowd.

Claire could hear a lot of movement from the other side of the door. She waited until it fell silent and poked her head in. She was looking into the assembly line to find no one was there. Both the workers and intruders had moved elsewhere.

"All right we're clear." She waved the others to come through. "Let's split up and find the hostages. Remember, you see Serco, you go the other way." The others agreed, and they split off in teams of two, each of them hoping to wrap this up as quickly as possible.

The plan seemed simple enough. Since Sam and her people were in charge of crowd control, they could avoid Serco by going straight for the hostages. If they were freed, then the security forces outside could storm the place and wrap things up while they slipped back out. Serco could be dispatched without them having to engage directly.

Claire and Arden moved up to the far end of the assembly line. With a choice of doors up ahead, they didn't waste time and picked the far right as the closest. They entered another wide open room that connected to the assembly line through the conveyor belts. Upon entering, they instantly ducked behind some large machinery as nobody had noticed them yet. They appeared to be in a smelting and molding room where Hunter and a half dozen of his people were scattered around threatening the remaining workers, but worse than that they could see Serco at the far end messing with something. They stayed hidden for now in case they were spotted trying to leave.

Claire got a view of Serco through a gap in whatever crane-like machinery they were hiding behind. He was holding a breastplate and burning it. When he stopped to see it had no effect, he then started a small, concentrated fire on his fingertip and started burning through it like a blowtorch. After a moment, he examined it again to see he had melted through and threw it aside like trash.

On Hunter's order, several of his people guided the workers back toward the assembly line. They went straight past Claire and Arden without taking notice. She checked again to see Serco leave through another exit and took that as a sign to go the other way and follow the hostages. As they promptly moved toward the door, someone called out to them. "Hey, you two! Come with us. We have more to round up." Claire considered ignoring him, but he was already too close.

They turned to face him, and Arden attempted to answer. "No problem. This room looks clear." Hunter almost accepted this, but he paused as he looked at their weapons and Claire trying to avoid eye contact. The silence went on long enough that Claire had to look, and the second he saw her pale blue eyes, he knew. Within a second of each other, they both raised their arms to attack.

****

Ewan and Lilla made their way through the cafeteria. Lilla had applied her war paint, even though the mask covered them, in preparation for battle. They moved carefully with no sign of trouble and approached the lobby. Through the glass pane, Ewan could see a couple dozen workers and several injured guards huddled together on the lobby floor. He even caught Sam at the forefront waiting patiently. With their objective spotted, Ewan pulled his phone and sent a prepared message.

"Hostages found, make your way to us."

Behind him, Lilla was looking around for something. "Is someone coming?" he asked softly.

"No there's something not right here." Standing in this hall, she felt uneasy but couldn't understand why. She was trying to find a source of her discomfort when she spotted a light glow in the corner. Ewan joined her to investigate, and they found a glowing orange shard embedded in the column. Ewan touched it gently and immediately recognized it. "It's a beacon, the same as the one I used to track them here."

Lilla thought of Serco and backed away. "Is it going to explode?"

"No, there's not enough energy in this to trigger an explosion. This must be how he sets his target—he plants these in key locations and then can target them without a line of sight." Realizing this, Lilla moved to the opposite end to find a beacon on the other column as well.

"Ewan. If he's only here to destroy equipment, why is he setting these on support columns?"

Ewan felt a sudden chill as he knew the only possible answer. "He's not just destroying equipment. He means to destroy the whole building."

"We have to get Claire and get the hostages out of here." She moved to the door, but Ewan stopped her.

"No, that's not enough." His brain raced to keep up with the situation. "If we free the hostages, then the swat teams move in, and they'll be killed instead. Not to mention any workers that they haven't yet gathered."

"Can we destroy the beacons?" Lilla asked desperately.

"Yes. That won't stop him, but it'll buy us enough time. They're easy enough to break, and he won't notice until he tries to target them." Ewan moved back, and with a glowing hand, he chopped the shard, which shattered instantly. He checked the lobby to make sure no one was aware of them yet. With them in the clear, they moved to break the one opposite and track down the remaining beacons.

****

Unaware of the situation unfolding, Sam watched out the doors as a team had already arrived and were lining up with riot shields. Sam purposefully left the glass doors clear, so they had a view of all the hostages in the lobby. The doors were locked of course. After only a few minutes a voice echoed from behind the line on a megaphone.

"We have the building surrounded. Release the people inside and come out quietly. There is no other option for you."

Sam responded to the demand without the use of a megaphone; she held out her arms and her voice transmitted outside. "I will kill one hostage for anyone who tries to enter the building. Remain where you are, and no one will die here. This is a message for those in power, the mages of this city will not disappear to be part of history. This is our revolution." Before waiting for a response, she checked a timer on her wrist then signaled to Wren and Jamie. "Get everyone together and tell Hunter we'll be clearing out soon, our job is almost done." Happy to follow that order, they moved out to find everyone.

It didn't take long as they passed by a few of their own people heading for the lobby. In the assembly line, they spotted two more at the edge of the room facing the wall.

"What are you doing over there? We need to be ready to leave soon," Jamie shouted to them.

They turned around suddenly, and the taller one answered, "Understood."

Jamie was happy to let this go, but Wren stayed. "What were you doing over there?"

Before they could answer, the group was distracted by a crash on the other side of the room. Claire came flying through the door and rolled swiftly to her feet to dodge the incoming tools that were thrown at her. Hunter was in hot pursuit, throwing every bit of scrap that was nearby.

Arden was also occupied right now as he was fighting the other three that were with Hunter. The first took advantage of his diverted attention and started laying into him with solid rock surrounding his fists. Arden took a couple of hits before grabbing his arms and deftly headbutting him. This was followed up by throwing him over his shoulder and into the conveyor belts. He realized he fought this same guy in the cage before and confidently faced the other two. He could check on Claire after he was done, thinking she'd probably want to settle her fight with Hunter herself.

Jamie and Wren were about to move to help but were stopped by the two behind them. Ewan caught their attention with a few of his projectiles in quick succession. A few hit their target but weren't enough to stop them. Lilla moved in close to fight Wren, but a smokescreen skewed her vision, and he pushed her back. Wren stood ready for a fight as smoke surrounded him, and Jamie made his way behind him.

Lilla ran around them, drew her bow and fired a quick arrow at Wren. Another wave of smoke blew past her, and he dodged while she was blinded. Jamie followed by softening the ground, which moved to cut her off.

With them engaging each other, Wren moved in to attack the other at close range; he slashed at him with both hands, but they were blocked by a yellow shield that formed. Wren analyzed the moves and what little of his appearance he could see. He looked surprised once he pieced it together. "You're Ewan, aren't you?"

Ewan was impressed he figured it out so easily. "Here I thought Jamie was the people person," he said while pushing Wren back.

****

Claire continued to move around the assembly line as all manner of objects rained down on her. After dodging this long, she attempted to counter with the new sigil on her sword. She charged it and swung at the tools flying toward her. A gust of wind was released and blasted it all to the side. It wasn't strong enough to push them back at Hunter at this distance, but she could deflect anything he threw. Despite his rage, he was still tactical. With a concentrated effort, he caused part of the walkway above her to collapse and followed this up by holding her in place again. She was expecting this though. Ever since their last encounter, she had prepared for this. Focusing inward, Claire pushed back against his hold with her own force that exploded from her. Without wasting time, she darted forward to avoid getting crushed and sprinted toward Hunter. In response, he reined in scraps of armor like a wall to defend him. Claire continued at full speed, jumped at him and, gathering the wind around her, she started spinning around with her sword out for momentum. The gusts of wind were enough to knock away anything he held, and the final strike at him sent him soaring. Claire barely managed to slow down on the ground and watched Hunter slam into the wall.

****

Lilla was struggling with her opponent. She wasn't used to fighting people, and her main method of attack was too lethal to use against either of them. Jamie waited for her to move with a puddle of what used to be the floor in front of him. It was clear if she got too close, he would catch her, but she couldn't attack from a distance either. Her only choice was to force him back to Ewan and fight them together. Lilla launched another arrow, ensuring it wouldn't hit him directly; it came close enough that the liquid ground rose to catch it. She used this chance to circle around, and as the softened earth reached for her, she summoned an air current behind her to launch herself forward and tackle Jamie the floor. Up close he seemed defenseless. He managed to throw her off but received a swift kick to the face after. He rolled away and stumbled to his feet, but she was already on him and again received another kick for his trouble. She stopped and waited as he was clutching his face in pain.

"Lilla!" she heard behind her, and before she could react, smoke engulfed her. Everything went dark, and she braced herself for an attack. From out of nowhere something slashed her torso and rushed past.

She couldn't do anything to defend herself, so she called on the wind to surround her and push away the darkness. With a blast of air, the smoke dissipated, and she could see Wren standing in front of Jamie, ready to fight again.

Ewan ditched his mask by this point as they were clearly exposed. "You need to get your people out of here!"

Wren didn't answer and still looked as though he would attack at any moment. Behind him, Jamie was trying to recover. Lilla ignored her injury and instead readied herself for another fight.

Jamie was the one to reply. "Why are you doing this? We're supposed to be on the same side."

"You've attacked innocent people and worked alongside a killer!" Ewan shouted.

This left Jamie speechless; he couldn't deny the accusation.

Ewan took the silence as his cue to continue. "It was a mistake to come here. Take your people and go before this gets worse for you."

Wren pulled himself back and looked toward Jamie who was on the verge of panic. Without saying a word, Wren gently wrapped his arms over Jamie, and his smoke emerged and engulfed them both. By the time it cleared, Ewan and Lilla were alone again and, after quickly wrapping Lilla's scratch, they could check on their teammates on the other side of the room.

Arden walked out casually, having had no difficulty fighting, and the four gathered together. Claire noticed Ewan and Lilla weren't wearing their masks anymore. Since it was obvious their cover was blown, she did the same. "Are you guys ready to finish this?" she asked.

From Ewan's expression, however, she could tell it wouldn't be that simple. "I'm afraid the plan's off. We can't simply save the hostages anymore."

"What happened?" Claire asked, fearful of the answer.

Lilla explained to them. "Serco's not destroying the equipment here. He's going to blow the building up and kill everyone inside."

"He's planted beacons on the support columns so he can target and destroy them. We're in the process of breaking the beacons now, but that will only delay him."

Claire remained calm and let him explain the situation. "How can he still take down the building if we get rid of the beacons?"

"He would just have to fire blindly. He could still target a rough area. Like the lobby, for example." With the hostages gathered there, they all knew what that would mean.

The team stood in silence, thinking if there were any other options available to them. But after a short time, Arden was the first to say it. "We don't have a choice then."

Claire wasn't as surprised or upset as they expected her to be. "I thought this might happen."

Her casual response caught Arden off guard. "You figured we'd have to do this?"

She nodded slowly and faced the three of them to tell them what they already knew. "We're going to have to fight him."

They each acknowledged this. They had done their best to avoid this fight, but it seemed inevitable. But that didn't mean they would be rushing in without a strategy as Claire had been preparing for the possibility. "That technique we heard of where he can bypass someone's magic and kill them, that's the biggest danger to us. It can't be easy though. It has to take some concentration to pull off. If we keep the pressure on him and protect each other, then I know we can stop him." As Claire finished, she felt determined to protect her teammates and take Serco down.

The four stood together and mentally prepared themselves to fight Serco.

Chapter 11

Trial by Fire

The mage revolution of Verras. Even the sound of it gets my blood pumping. Fighting for the right to learn magic like any other city, such a noble cause. It makes it all the more exciting that they sought me out to help them. Clearly, they're willing to go to any lengths. Their leader very much believes the end justifies the means, but we'll see how far that gets her. History is written by the winners, after all. I'm curious to see if she ends up being the hero or the villain of this story. We all have a part to play.

Serco smiled to himself while he rode the elevator to the roof. This venture was as much fun as he hoped and it was coming up to its dramatic conclusion. The only thing that would make it better would be some elevator music. Why don't elevators have music these days? Well, life isn't perfect, or he never would have wound up here.

The elevator doors opened, and he found a charming night sky up above. He took a moment to appreciate the still night; it was the calm before the storm. It was a shame the explosion wouldn't impact the surrounding buildings much, but it would still paint a bright message. Serco checked his timer and found he could enjoy the night air for a little longer. Or he would have if he was alone.

****

After Sam had made her demands clear, the police forces gathered outside. The chief of security, Eren Ghehara, passed the negotiations on to whoever was closest as he had decided it was a lost cause. It was his call, and in his experience, there would be no peaceful surrender if they just sat outside. His subordinates out front would provide a suitable distraction while he led a team inside. Some would argue it a risky move, but no one would dare question him here. His stern features and shaven head all gave the impression of a man who wouldn't be trifled with.

When he arrived, he found his strike team suited up and awaiting his order. It was frustrating that the experimental tech armor wasn't ready yet. If Serco was indeed behind this, they would need every asset they had.

Chief Ghehara donned what armor they had and inspected the weapons available, riot shields, stun batons and a few taser rifles. The batons were the size of a small sword and had two prongs with electricity running between them. If they could get close, they should be able to take him out. But from what they were told about Serco's abilities, getting in close would be near impossible for them. Even knowing this, he took one of everything. The rifle he took had a lot of stopping power and a good range, so that was his choice of weapon. With the riot team standing guard at the entrance, they had the perfect cover to move around and ascend to the roof.

They couldn't afford to be reckless with the hostages at play, but if Serco was in there, it wouldn't stay quiet for long, and they had to be ready to drop down from above. The chief fired up a grapple onto the roof and clipped it to his belt with the rest of his team following suit. They had to move up carefully to avoid the windows.

Slowly but surely, they made their way to the top, and upon seeing it was clear, they moved toward the access door on the opposite side. As they approached, a figure casually made his way out and took his time strolling across the roof. Chief Ghehara had spent enough time studying that face to recognize him. He approached while the rest of his team spread out to face him.

His men moved carefully around Serco. Two of them had their rifles readied with the others charging their batons.

"Get down on your knees and surrender. We have you surrounded!"

Serco seemed unfazed by the team and cackled in response. "Surrounded by what, those bug zappers?"

Eren ignored the jibe. "You're not walking away from this one, not after the damage you've caused."

Again feeling unthreatened, Serco raised both his arms with a cocky smile. "Then, by all means, come and stop me."

The moment Ghehara gave the order, fire and electricity shot across the rooftop as the fighting commenced.

****

Claire and the others were climbing the stairwell when the explosions went off above them. Claire feared they were too late as a few more shook the building. Regardless, she ran up the stairs and burst through the door into the open air. A distance away from them she saw the remains of a battle. There were scorch marks all over, and only two of the swat team remained on the roof but weren't moving. Serco stood over Chief Ghehara and took no notice of the others who had joined them.

"You know, even though you brought cheap plastic to a firefight, I'm glad you were here," he mocked the downed chief and pointed his palms toward the ground. "You kept me entertained just long enough, and now you get to bear witness to the grand finale!"

Claire and the others crept up slowly since they already knew what was going to happen. Serco's mind reached out for the magic he left in the building. After finding nothing, his smile faded and was replaced by general confusion. "That's odd. What happened to—" He turned quickly as he only just noticed the group advancing on him. They all froze, and Serco looked at them quizzically as his brain was piecing together what happened.

Claire chose to enlighten him first. "Your beacons are gone, Serco. We won't allow you to kill the people here. It's over for you."

They all had their weapons ready for his response. Serco looked the team up and down as he realized what was going on.

"Ha…hahahaha…ahahahahaha. Incredible!" They all looked at him like he was crazy. It was a look he received often.

"You infiltrated our operation, broke my beacons, and fought your way up here to face me. I love it!"

Claire watched with disdain at how much he was enjoying this and tried to stop him. "Do you not understand what's happening? The fun's over. We're going to make sure you pay for your crimes."

Serco continued to laugh in excitement. "Over? The fun's just started! Oh, why would I bother with some rebellious mages with daddy issues when *you* are far more interesting?"

Claire scowled at him, but Serco became more excited in his movements as he rambled. "I thought Sam was determined, but you four...the shear strength of will to make it this far." After giggling to himself a bit longer, he finally exhaled and calmed himself. "But I'm getting ahead of myself, aren't I? You still have one more challenge before you." Serco faced them from the side and pointed with his finger and thumb extended. "Stop me, and you'll be the heroes." A jet of fire erupted from his finger and raced toward them.

Having mentally prepared for this encounter, the team moved in formation with Arden up front to block the incoming fire while the others arranged behind him. The flames struck his shield and continued burning against him. The prepared fire sigil on his shield prevented the heat from coming through so he held his ground. With his free hand, Arden unclipped a bomb from his belt and threw it back to Lilla. She understood and hurriedly tied the bomb to an arrow. Claire lit it between her fingers, and Ewan readied a platform beneath her. She cocked her bow and Ewan propelled her up above the fire. Giving her a clear shot, her arrow landed at Serco's feet and detonated, forcing him back a few steps.

Ewan and Claire took this chance to circle around him. Serco shot an arc of fire their way, but Claire dissipated it with a swing of her sword. The wind still following every slash was enough to blow the fire away from them, with Serco's hands focusing fire on Arden to his left and on Claire to his right, who was looking for a chance to fire back. Ewan's projectiles and Lilla's arrows came at him from both sides, but with minimal effort, he hit them away with his hands and in turn countered with more fire.

This continued until Serco ran forward and turned to let loose a much larger arching flame toward both pairs. Claire stuck down and blasted away the fire from her end and Lilla ducked behind Arden for protection. Claire and Ewan attempted a few more shots but didn't notice Serco now pointed both his index and middle finger toward them. Instead of a jet of flame, a single shot fired toward them. Ewan created his own shield in time to catch the shot which exploded on impact, sending him spiraling through the air. Serco turned his attention to Claire, and after what she saw happen to Ewan, she knew it wasn't worth trying to block. She barely dodged to the side as his missile shot past and blew up the next building over.

On the other side, Arden's shield took a dent from an explosive round. It was tough, but he was strong enough to hold steady. Lilla tried to fire back, but when she moved from behind Arden, another shot went speeding past her. She looked at the destroyed wall behind them, and it was clear that a direct shot would have killed her.

Lilla moved back further and fired arrows into the air to drop down on her target. He may be human, but she couldn't afford to hesitate. There was a chance her arrows could kill him, but with the skill he'd shown so far, it didn't seem likely.

Serco danced and turned and dodged everything with an insane smile plastered on his face. All while firing potshots toward them while receiving lightning from Claire, arrows from above, and an advancing warrior with his mace at the ready from the other side. To pressure him even more, he took a step and the ground below him lit up, but he instinctively jumped away as the ground exploded. Ewan cursed while still on the ground watching the fight.

He's too fast for my mines. I need something else.

As he narrowly avoided an arrow that scraped his face. Serco changed tactics; he pointed his palm toward Arden, and he got a clear view of the force sigil marked on it. This time instead of shooting toward them, a glow appeared between Arden and Lilla. Lilla tried to move, but the glowing bomb detonated and threw her hard into the wall behind. She felt a sharp pain and was laid flat on the ground. She looked for Arden to see he had been knocked away but was staggering to his feet.

With two enemies down, Serco shot a stream toward Claire with one hand and fired a shot from the other. Claire blew the fire away with her sword but moved in the perfect way for the shot to strike it as it was outstretched in her hand. The explosion knocked the sword sailing off the building and possibly broke her wrist.

The tide of the battle was clearly turning in Serco's favor. With only Arden left standing, Serco playfully fired explosives into his shield. Arden barely managed to hold it together with each impact. With Serco's full focus in one place, he received a shooting pain in his back as an electro dart was shot into him. Taking a fair shock, he turned to see Chief Ghehara struggling to stay on his feet, with a heavy taser weapon in his hands. For the first time, Serco looked angry. He pointed his hand at Ghehara this time. "You're not a part of this!" He aimed to remove him from the fight.

Claire was already moving to intercept with no weapon and no plan. Serco fired his shot, and half a second later, Claire moved directly in its path. She held out both hands in an attempt to block it with no time to even think of forming a shield. The shot reached her and detonated, the resulting explosion being instant death for anyone hit by it. But when the smoke cleared, Claire was still standing.

Serco was the only one who saw how it happened as even Claire couldn't tell how she was unharmed. Hardly a second before the missile impacted her hands, it detonated, and the full force of the explosion was directed away from her and the man she protected. For the second time in this fight, Serco was caught off guard. He stared with interest at the ability he witnessed. He was interrupted, however, by Arden charging in with his mace raised. Arden was too far away, though, and left Serco plenty of time. He was about to blow Arden away when something stopped him. With his eyes on Arden, he hadn't noticed the glyph at his feet. From it, yellow light shot up and seemingly grabbed his arms.

Ewan was kneeling across from him, willing his trap to life. All this happened in a few seconds as the light held him still long enough for Arden to charge and swing his mace clear into Serco's chest. The light released him, and Arden's swing threw him off the edge.

They all watched as everything slowed down to see Serco fall off the building and away from them. Arden looked over to watch him drop. On his way down, Serco let loose another explosion underneath him, which sent his body sailing across and smashed through a window to the adjacent building. Arden was hoping that would cripple him, but they were too far away for this to continue.

All of them lay battered and beaten, but for now, the fight was over.

****

Silence set in as everyone relaxed for a moment. Claire looked around at the aftermath and the state her team was in. "Is everyone all right?" she asked between breaths.

Arden and Ewan answered, but Lilla weakly waved her arm in response. Ewan ran over to check on her. Lilla coughed a reply to him, and he translated. "She'll be all right, but we need to find her a doctor soon."

Claire winced from the pain in her wrist but was relieved that none of them were critically hurt. She turned to the man still holding himself up behind her. "How about you, are you okay?"

"I'm fine," he said despite obvious injuries. He pulled out a radio and started giving orders. "Control, this is Ghehara. Primary target escaped to the eastern complex. All available units must pursue immediately."

Arden was still looking over the edge and informed the chief, "I think your boys are already on it," as he could see teams of officers running in and around the next building. Another riot team also came through the door next to them to secure the roof. They moved up swiftly and aimed their weapons at the injured party—those who could raise their hands.

Ghehara called out to stop them before they could attempt to take them away. "Lower your weapons! These people saved our lives. I want a med team sent up for them now."

They followed his order and the lead officer radioed in for medical. Claire was glad for the reprieve. The last thing they needed was to be dragged away in handcuffs. She smiled to show her gratitude to him. "Thanks. I'm pretty sure you saved our lives too."

Chief Ghehara didn't look particularly pleased by this, but he acknowledged it. They left the cleanup to his men and were taken to get seen to and rest after an intense fight.

It was obvious to them that Serco would be difficult to beat. But Claire still felt disturbed at how easily he had fought all four of them.

But she could leave him to Ghehara's men and focus on her friends. Despite their injuries, they had won the battle.

Chapter 12

No Rest For The Wicked

I met an interesting group of people today, some real heroic types. They put everything on the line to stop a heinous criminal, and by working together, they succeeded. The mage's revolution was dealt a serious blow. But I don't care about that anymore. I have a new interest now. I want to know if any of these four mages have what it takes. If I can craft the right scenario, I can mold one of them into the perfect hero.

****

Lilla woke up in unfamiliar surroundings but was glad to see Arden and Ewan were at her side. She was in an infirmary from the looks of it and must have passed out on the way here. There were rows of beds with several others being tended to. There was a calm atmosphere as medics quietly checked up on their patients and it seemed no one was in critical condition.

Ewan noticed her stirring. "Try not to move too much. Are you feeling all right?"

Lilla was already smiling, trust him to give advice before showing concern. "I'm fine." She looked around a little more to see Arden had a thin cast on his arm.

"The doctors here helped fix us up. You have a few cracked ribs, but they put some gel on and wrapped you up good as new."

Lilla did notice that she wasn't able to sit up yet. "Where's Claire?"

"Oh she's off talking to the security chief. He was asking each of us about how we got here, who the Revolutionists are, things like that."

"What did you tell him?" Lilla asked and tried to sit forward but was met with a sharp pain.

Ewan gently put a hand on her shoulder to stop her from moving around. "We told him everything. We met this gang while working a job. They seemed harmless at first but when we discovered their plan we moved to stop them. We always met under the old bridge on the west side, but we don't know if they had any sort of hideout," Ewan explained to her while emphasizing the key points for their story.

Lilla relaxed back into the bed. "So the people in Haven are still safe."

Ewan looked around to make sure no one was listening. "I don't know if that's a good thing. Sam and a handful of others escaped, but we can deal with that problem later."

Lilla started to feel tense, and she felt a dull pain run through her body as a result. "What about Wren and Jamie?"

"If they fled when we told them, then they got away, but that's not something we can ask about without arousing suspicion. They're still identifying the people they captured, and they aren't exactly updating us." He noticed her discomfort. "Don't worry. It was a tough fight, but we made it. We can rest easy."

She nodded and tried to settle back in. Unfortunately, this is when Claire returned with Chief Ghehara escorting her. He had a clear limp when he walked, and you could see the strain on his face, but he gave no complaint. Claire looked to her injured teammate, but she couldn't hide her unease after their discussion.

"What's happened?" Ewan asked.

"We're all right here. We'll be sent home soon," Claire tried to reassure them.

"However?"

Claire sighed knowing she couldn't hide it. "They didn't find Serco." The shocked reaction she received was much the same as her own when Ghehara told her.

"You're kidding me!" Arden yelled in disbelief. "How could he get away after the beating we gave him?"

Although the chief didn't have to tell them anything, he appreciated the cooperation they had given so far and felt they deserved to know the aftermath of the battle. "My men followed his trail, but he left explosive charges for us. Some went off when we moved too close, and some acted as a distraction, so we couldn't tell where he was going. We don't know how he was able to move so quickly after the hits he took."

Ewan posed an answer. "It's possible he's not as hurt from the fight as we would expect."

Arden refused to believe it. "I hit him as hard as I could off the building. How could that not stop him?"

"Well the longer we use magic, the more it becomes a part of us. Your bones, organs, and muscles continually absorb it, making them stronger. So it's hard to say just how durable he is."

"In any case," Ghehara sternly interrupted, "that's not your problem anymore."

"Hey, we're the ones who fought him off, and you expect us to let him go?" Arden questioned.

"That's exactly what you should do. I am in charge of the security of this city. You may have assisted us today, but we can't let you do whatever you want and go chasing a wanted criminal. If Hargrove were here, he would order me to detain you." This gave them all pause as he was considering it.

"Be grateful I'm willing to let you go."

Arden was about to argue further, but Claire took his arm to stop him. "It's okay. We finished what we set out to do. We need to take a step back and rest for now. Right, Arden?" Arden looked defiant, but he held his tongue and begrudgingly agreed. Claire turned back to the chief. "Thank you for this. We'll try and stay out of your hair."

"Good. I won't let you off a second time. I'll send some of my paramedics to help get your friend home. She should rest up for a few days until those ribs heal." Despite his limp, he left abruptly after that. Even though he had shown them some respect for their help, he was clearly not happy with the situation. They all exhaled together when he left. Alone, at last, it was a chance for them to take some time to do nothing. Claire was happy sitting quietly for a while, but she still felt responsible.

"We did a good job today. We stopped Serco and saved a lot of lives. I feel pretty proud of us." She smiled to herself as the words came out.

Arden and Ewan seemed happy with that. Lilla fell asleep smirking, and they each got a well-earned break.

****

As promised, two medics came around to escort them back home. They brought a stretcher for Lilla and took them to the Emergency Rail System attached to the building. They used a terminal to put in their destination, and a smooth, white shuttle moved up for them. Claire assumed that in an actual emergency, they would be running through this process a lot faster. They stepped on, and it slowly pulled out into the city which glided above the streets toward home. After everything that went down today, it was nice to tour the city at night; everything seemed peaceful with only dim lighting in the distance.

Once home, the medics laid Lilla down gently and made their way out. She wasn't used to being treated so delicately, but she didn't exactly have a choice. Claire and Arden retired to the other room, but Ewan stayed for a moment. The first thing she asked was if he could leave the window open for her.

"Is that why it's always freezing in here?" he enquired, to which she held back a guilty smile.

"I'll check on you in the morning. Hopefully, you'll be able to sit up at least." He sounded oddly gentle despite the formal manner.

Before he left, Lilla spoke without looking directly at him. "Did you ever figure it out?"

"Hmm?"

"Why I was so desperate to help the people at Haven, why I still want to help them." She said this like she was figuring it out herself. She wasn't sure what he thought of her, but she wanted to know.

"No, and I'm not going to." She looked at him quizzically. "It sounds like your own business. It's not my place to pry. However, if you ever wish to talk about it, you know where I am." With that said, he sheepishly retreated. Light tears came to Lilla's eyes.

"I think I will," she whispered in her last moments before drifting off to sleep.

Claire and Arden relaxed in the living area for a while longer. It was good to wind down after everything they went through. Arden was especially proud that he landed the finishing blow but freely admitted it was all of them together that gave them a chance to win.

Some ideas of what Sam would do in response and where Serco escaped to started to creep in, but Claire dismissed them as exhaustion was catching up on her. She could worry about them another day.

****

Through the alleyways in the western district, the walk back to Haven was nerve-racking. Every movement they heard on the way gave them pause. Will occasionally mumbled incoherently to himself, but no one paid him any mind. The whole city was out looking for them, and it took nearly twice as long to get back to the club as it should have. Sam was expecting daylight to pierce through any second, but it seemed it was still the dead of night. If anyone did try to catch them, she would have killed them on the spot. She was tired of holding back, especially after this disaster of an operation.

The others following her walked in tense silence until at last the safety of the club was there. Without any instruction to the others with her, Sam stormed straight up to the office, Hunter followed her and left the others to rest elsewhere. She found her doors open and met Jamie and Wren waiting inside.

If she was relieved to see them, it didn't show. Instead, she threw her bat to the side and sat at her desk silently.

"How many others made it back?" Wren asked quietly.

Hunter thumped into the wall, looking like he was going to break something. "Four."

Jamie looked guilt-ridden. "We should have never tried this. It's all fallen apart," he said to the room.

Hunter still stuck to his guns. "We had to send a message to them," he growled, his hands shaking with anger.

Wren met his furious gaze. "It doesn't matter anymore. We failed."

"We were betrayed!" Sam screamed suddenly. The shock of her outburst silenced the room. "We had everything planned out until they ruined it!"

After some short breaths, she stood suddenly and regained a modicum of composure. "We have to be ready to leave. They'll find this place soon, and I want us gone before they get here."

Jamie was shocked at the idea of having to keep going. "But we have nowhere to go. This is our home."

"It doesn't matter!" she spat back. "They have our people now. They'll find this place soon. Get everyone ready to leave tomorrow. If we want to survive then we keep going."

Her order didn't get the usual reaction as they all stared at her. She had reverted to her icy stare that held back her rage.

Wren then helped Jamie up. "Come on, let's get some rest." The idea of collapsing in a bed and forgetting all this for a few hours was appealing. So they left Sam and Hunter to pick up what was left of their operation.

****

They weren't the only ones to forego any sleep tonight. Chief Ghehara went straight from the medical center where his men lay, to the Central Research Lab for AMTech. To anyone else, it would look like an admin building, but with his clearance, he had access to the basement level. Although nobody would call it a basement as it was the most high-tech laboratory and research site they had. Their best weapons were created here and kept under wraps until they were ready for the field. Ghehara knew he would find Doctor Lambert in the Genetics Research even at this hour. He wasn't sure the man ever slept, and it definitely showed in his haggard appearance.

The doctor was hunched over a microscope, waiting for a result while several beakers of different colored liquids were coming to a boil. The chief coughed to announce his presence, and Lambert made a disappointed noise at his experiment and switched his attention to Ghehara.

"Ah, Chief Ghehara. What brings you here?" Straight to the point, Lambert looked at him with big dark circles around his eyes; the chief was familiar enough to know he always looked like that.

"I need the tech armor you've been promising. We need it finished and ready to deploy now."

This was supposed to be the doctor's primary focus, but he seemed confused by the demand. He mumbled the words back for a moment until it clicked. "Ah yes, your anti-magic armor. I'm afraid there are still some bugs to work out. The charge running through it may be too harmful for the wearer, and wielding it in battle may be too much strain for an ordinary man to bear. I have worked out a solution with a genetic enhancer. We can strengthen the body to better handle the strain. However, we have yet to start human trials you see." He continued to trail off from his initial point, causing the chief to interrupt him.

"Doctor Lambert! We don't have time to wait anymore. I can't keep our people safe without your help. If you need a guinea pig, then use me. I'll test out your armor firsthand."

Doctor Lambert was surprised by his willingness to test this out. "You know the director won't approve of this," he warned, but he couldn't hide the excitement in his voice, like a child about to put his hand in the cookie jar.

"Walker respects my authority to protect this city. This is my decision, and I've made it."

The doctor's face lit up with glee. "Oh, this is exciting. You'll become our first enhanced soldier." He giggled and led the chief away to begin the procedure. The professor seemed far too eager for this, but Ghehara's only concern was making himself strong enough for what would come next.

Chapter 13

Hard Truths

Despite the intense battle last night, Arden was restless. It was rare that he was up before everyone else, but he was still feeling buzzed from last night's battle. It felt like their first real victory together, and he wanted to build on their momentum. Everyone else slept in from fatigue, but Arden had already removed his cast and was gingerly stretching his arm out. It still had a numb, throbbing pain but that would heal in another day or so. When Ewan and Claire appeared, Arden gave them space to get themselves sorted while waiting to talk to them.

At last Claire took notice of him fidgeting. "I take it you're ready for a team meeting?"

He leaped out of his chair and followed her into Lilla's room. They had to talk in there since she couldn't do more than sit up in the bed.

"First things first. How are you all feeling after last night," Claire asked as if she was readying for a pep rally. They all replied, and everyone seemed fine. Even Lilla was content with her condition.

"Down to business then. After our talk with the chief yesterday, it seems his team will be leading the hunt for Serco. I think we should do our best to respect their authority here."

Arden immediately looked disappointed. "We can help though. We've beaten him once."

The others didn't share his gusto, however. "Arden, we did well yesterday but let's not sugarcoat this. We barely managed to fight him off."

Ewan agreed with her assessment. "I do believe if he wasn't toying with us, then the outcome would have been far less favorable."

Arden lowered his head and reluctantly agreed. "All right, but what about Sam and her people?"

"Them I would feel more comfortable getting involved with. We've worked alongside and gotten to know them, and not all of them want this fight. If Ghehara finds Haven, then he'll arrest everyone involved."

"Yeah, I feel bad for Jamie. He's a good guy," Arden agreed.

"Wren and a lot of the others are good people too. If we can turn them away from this fight, we should try. Stopping their operation yesterday might have discouraged them. But I want them to understand why we fought against them."

Lilla felt a pang of guilt. In the heat of the fight she had to take Jamie down, but now she felt bad for hurting him.

As if reading her mind, Ewan interjected. "We shouldn't feel guilty for what happened. They made a poor choice, and they paid for it."

"Do you think they knew Serco was going to kill the hostages?" Arden threw in.

Lilla had to take a deep breath before speaking. "No. Jamie was insistent that nobody would get hurt. They wouldn't have done it if they knew."

From spending time with them, Claire agreed. "That might be our chance. If we can convince them about Serco's betrayal, then we might be able to talk them down."

Ewan still felt skeptical, but he agreed it was worth trying. "We should still avoid the club for now. It'll only be a matter of time before Chief Ghehara's men find its location. I believe Sam is smart enough to realize this and will likely relocate."

Claire shook her head. "Without knowing where they'll go, we're back to square one. The only thing we can do is keep our ears to the ground for any information. In the meantime it's back to business as usual, I guess. We still have bills to pay."

Arden was more than happy to get to it. "I wouldn't mind jumping down to the job list today if you want to come with?"

"Yeah. I need to stop by your uncle's and get a new sword." Claire felt it wasn't worth trying to track down her old one as it was thrown off the roof.

Unable to join them, Lilla asked them to pick up a few more arrows to stock up for when she was better. She had written out a list of different kinds of arrows and a few sigils to try.

"I'm going to stay as well if you don't mind the company," Ewan volunteered, leaving Claire to lead Arden out as he was getting more fidgety by the minute.

Ewan sat and joined Lilla. "I could lend you a couple of my books while you're stuck on bedrest. Perhaps you'd enjoy some of the magical theory I've been looking at."

Lilla looked at him, not sure if he was joking. "Do you have any fiction?"

Ewan had to think for a minute. "Hmm. I have some stories of current heroes and their exploits."

"That still counts as studying." Lilla chuckled. Ewan gave up in his suggestions. Personally, if he had to rest for a while, he would take the opportunity to study further. It went quiet for a moment as Lilla hesitated with something.

"Hey, do you remember when we first met?"

Ewan looked at her suspiciously. "You're not still holding a grudge are you?"

"No no, and it's not like I was mad about it. You surprised me is all."

That's not how Ewan remembered it when Lilla held a knife to him. It wasn't an unprovoked reaction as Ewan accidentally caught her in his explosive trap.

He was testing his glyphs in the Esterwood on the outskirts of town. The only thing he didn't factor was the human element. He waited nearby, and the minute he felt movement on the glyph, he detonated his mine and struck whatever poor creature came upon it. To his surprise, the poor creature was one of his classmates. They had never spoken before but seeing her there on the ground, he ran up to check on her. The second he came close, she sprang up and held a knife to his throat.

She had him dead to rights with a burning gaze. The war paint and the fierce look in her eyes compelled Ewan to immediately apologize.

"I didn't mean to hurt you. I left that trap for something else, I swear," he said in a panic.

She eyed him carefully and without saying a word, slowly lowered her dagger. She stood and tried to walk away without saying a word before Ewan caught her. "You train at Arkon, don't you? I've seen you around." Although when he saw her, she was dressed more plainly.

She replied abruptly, "Yes I study there," and continued to walk away, but she stumbled slightly. That gave Ewan cause to stop her.

"Please, if you're hurt, let me help."

She hesitated but turned around for him. "You hurt my leg," she said miserably.

"Let me help you with that, in exchange for my grievous error." He bowed his head, in way of an apology. She exhaled sharply and smudged off some of the markings. "All right."

She suddenly sounded tired and sat down to let him help bandage the wound. "Why were you laying traps for these creatures anyway?" she asked while he tended to her injury.

"I was training. I need to master these spells for use in the field."

"I don't think any of these monsters will fall for a trap like that."

"And you did?" he boldly asked. She looked irritated at his question but answered. "I've been out here for too long. I was sloppy."

"Well, it's a good thing I bumped into you instead of some creature." This was his attempt at humor, which under the circumstances worked poorly. Nonetheless, she talked about her survivalist training and saw they both wanted to be ready for the future. He was surprised when she spoke to him the next day; he was sure she didn't like him after blowing her up. Despite this, Ewan made an effort to befriend her and the two built an odd rapport and even helped each other by training in the woods. When Ewan was preparing to move to Verras to establish a team, the first person he asked to join them was Lilla.

Ewan was surprised she brought this up, but they reminisced about it. Lilla's version of events made her sound far less threatening than he remembered.

"It's funny looking back on it, but what made you bring it up?" Ewan asked her.

"Last night you said you weren't going to pry, but I think you already know all about me."

Ewan shifted awkwardly as he couldn't deny it. He knew about her circumstances from how they met, but he promised he wouldn't ask about it until she was ready to talk.

"The people at Haven are like me. They're just looking for a place to be themselves."

"Is that what you were looking for in the Esterwood?"

Even though she was sure Ewan knew about her, it was still hard to get the words out. She finally pushed herself to say it. "I was living there. I was living in the woods for months before I met you."

"You were alone?" Ewan asked, encouraging her to keep going.

Shakily she nodded. "My grandfather died. Then my dad kicked me out, and I had nowhere else to go."

Ewan had realized she was homeless from spending time with her, but he didn't know what her family life was like. It was something she clearly avoided, and he was getting an idea why. "I'm sorry about that. I didn't know your father did that to you."

Lilla leaned back and sounded more distant as she talked. "I think he only kept me around because of my grandfather. After my mom passed away, he tracked my dad down so he could raise me. He had no idea what my dad was like. If I had told him then he would have taken me away from there. But it was too late, and next thing I knew, I was all alone."

Lilla was struggling to keep it together the more she went into it. "I knew you figured it out already and I wanted to ask. Is that why you spent so much time with me?"

Ewan didn't expect the confession to turn to him. There was some truth to it. He knew she was by herself so he tried to be a friend to her in his own way. "I couldn't leave you in the woods alone. I didn't know if it would help, but I thought I could at least be a friend to you. I'm sorry if it was intrusive." He started to mumble away from the topic. He stopped once he noticed she was tearing up.

"You gave me a home. Somewhere I can belong."

Ewan placed his hand on her head, somehow thinking this would stop her crying. "You've earned your place with us. You don't need to thank me."

Ewan now understood Lilla's desire to help the people at Haven. He suddenly felt compelled to do the same.

****

Tohren was in his element showing his employees one last trick with tempering the steel for their weapons. He was only going to be in Verras for a couple more days and wanted to ensure the shop was in good hands. As he finished hammering the burning metal, he heard Caleb the shopkeeper call on him to find Claire and Arden waiting.

"Ah, Arden, good timing. I have your new weapon ready for you."

Arden's face lit up. "You got it to work?" he said excitedly.

"You doubted me? You have much to learn, my boy. Nothing is beyond my craftsmanship. The question is can you handle it?" He handed Arden a new mace; this one had a large spiked ball at the end of a dark metal grip. Arden and Claire looked at it carefully. It was an impressive weapon but looking closer the sigil marked on the grip was unfamiliar to Claire. It wasn't a basic elemental one at any rate.

"What does the sigil do?" she asked.

Arden held a mischievous grin. "I want you to see it in action first. It will blow your mind."

Claire moved on rather than give Arden the satisfaction of her asking. "I'm going to need a new sword while we're here. The last one kind of got lost."

"You came to snatch up the last sword made by my hands, aye? I knew you were a clever one."

Claire smiled at his confidence. "You got me. I need a new sword, so I had to come to the best."

"Music to my ears. As it happens, we're making a few tempered steel swords to stock up. I'd say you're about ready for an upgrade. We'll pick one out and see what kind of sigil you're looking for, or if you want, young Arden can do that for you on the go. You'll be ready for any situation with him at your side."

Arden stood smugly from the praise.

"Your nephew's good to have around." She smirked at him. "He didn't mention where you were going though."

"Ah yes. I have a special order coming in, so I'm bound for Karlea."

"Karlea? Is it for the Council of Magi?" Claire asked as the city was home to the council.

"My clients expect some discretion you understand. But, yes. It's for the council," he said, not caring about it being discreet.

"Yeah, I forgot you were only supposed to be here for a couple of weeks," Arden pointed out.

Tohren folded his arms and grunted in response. "I ended up staying longer, with all the trouble going on. I promised your father I'd look after you. I'm sure he needed the peace of mind. But you seem to have adjusted to the city. You don't need me watching over your shoulder all the time. Besides, I get to see my blockhead of a son and make sure he hasn't gotten himself in any bother."

Arden was happy to move the subject along to his cousin. "How is Carter getting on?"

"He's doing well. They've started sending him on real jobs lately. He must be following in my footsteps." Tohren then told about his own heroic exploits and how he expected his son to follow a similar path. As much as the stories may be exaggerated, he was clearly proud of his family. After getting an impressive new sword for a good price, they left to go find work.

Claire waited until they were away from the shop to ask Arden, "So you didn't tell him about Serco?"

Arden faced away guiltily but answered her. "You heard him in there. My folks would be really worried if they found out. Tohren would insist on staying longer when he doesn't need to. Everything worked out fine, so there's no point in mentioning it."

Claire didn't have a reply. It was his choice if he was going to keep this to himself after all. After walking a bit further, Arden posed the question back to her. "Are you going to tell your brother?"

Claire instantly felt nervous about it. She tried not to think about it until now, but she made a promise to him that she couldn't keep.

What would he do if he found out? Would he come rushing down here to make sure I'm safe? That would be stupid. He's in charge of the situation here, and he won't be any help wandering the city looking for Serco himself. If I did tell him, he would only worry about me. It wouldn't accomplish anything.

Claire received a light shove that snapped her back into reality. Arden took her shoulders and shook her as they walked. "Don't worry so much. I'm sure he'll understand if you explain it to him. Even if you don't tell him right away."

"I'll apologize in person for breaking my promise. Once all of this is over."

"You'll be fine. After what we've been through, owning up to your brother shouldn't scare you."

Her conscience aside, she settled on her decision and tried to move on. There were new jobs to look for in the meantime.

****

Arriving at the Contractor's Office, Claire and Arden moved to examine the noticeboard as usual. The man working today gave them a friendly nod as he was used to their visits now. They eyed the jobs posted and saw a few were marked that someone had already taken the job. They continued looking and found one recent job to find a lost pendant.

Please help. My pendant was lost in transport from Hermadale. The convoy was attacked, and they had to leave some of the cargo behind. My father says to leave it, but it's the only memento that shows my family when we were all together. The transport was lost on the road heading west outside the border. 1000 credits for the return of my pendant.

No name or address was left; only a contact number.

Claire smiled and handed the post to Arden. "This looks like something you'll enjoy."

Arden grew visibly excited while reading. "We've not been outside the border yet. I wonder what attacked the cargo. Leopards? Reavers? Maybe bandits?"

"You can find that out from the client, and I think maybe Ewan should go with you this time. I'd like to take it easy for a little while. At least until Lilla's recovered."

Both were happy about moving forward, but Claire was planning on taking her time. They signed up for the seemingly simple job to get back into normal work. After talking with Ewan, they decided to take a couple more days to recover before checking it out. This would give them enough time to prepare. Unbeknownst to them, it also gave other people time to make their own preparations. For between Sam, Serco, and Chief Ghehara, it seemed everyone had a plan in the works.

Chapter 14

Family Pressure

Mayor Hargrove stood ready to address the people of Verras. He was an imposing figure. Big, bald and with a fine suit and cane to add prestige to his look.

"I would like to assure our citizens that we are taking every precaution to protect you. The attack on our property was thwarted and the intruders driven off by our security forces. We have captured several key members of the group. Their leader, the villain known as Daniel Serco has been forced into hiding and will be hunted down by our anti-magic soldiers. We will restore peace to this city and crush the rebellious mages that threaten our safety!"

Sam cut off the speech there. She, Hunter, and Wren were in her new office with nothing but a long table, several boxes of supplies, and a cheap TV hooked up to keep track of the news. Since she was finished listening to one of her least favorite people, she nodded at Wren to finish his update.

"We've told everyone about the move and made sure they've been discreet. Will didn't come back to us though. We haven't seen him since we returned to Haven."

"He probably ran. He never had the stomach for this kind of work," Hunter replied with his usual aggressive tone.

Sam felt disappointed. He may have been timid, but his abilities were undeniably useful to them. She wouldn't allow the others to see how she felt; they had to know she was in control.

"Was there anything else?"

Wren had been thinking about their situation all day, and this was as good a time as any to voice his opinion.

"I think we need to lay low again. We took things too far and lost a lot of good people." Wren was apprehensive about their approach to begin with, but after so many had been arrested, he felt they had to stop before anyone else went wrong.

He couldn't tell if Sam was annoyed by this. She moved around the table silently, as if she was considering her reply carefully.

"I understand. We'll look after our own and keep ourselves safe. In order to do that though, we need to know how safe we are." Wren tensed as he could see she wanted to keep going. Cautiously, he allowed her to continue.

"If we want to ensure our safety then we have one more fight ahead of us. We were betrayed, and we need to find out how much they know about us. If they know our identities. If they do know who we are, then you, Jamie, none of us will be safe."

Wren scowled at her. He knew she was using Jamie's name to convince him, but he couldn't deny that she was right. Still, if she was going to make it personal then so would he.

"And if they found out about your connections then they would crack down on us without mercy." This gave Sam pause, and Wren was sure he saw a flash of annoyance before she returned her normal, indifferent look. "All the more reason to go through with it. I have a trap being put into motion as we speak. We do this one more task, and we can be safe."

Wren was having doubts about Sam's orders and not for the first time. But for their safety, he gave in and agreed to one last fight.

****

As promised a few days after picking up the job, Ewan and Arden were on their way to Verras's outer border. There was no standard transport as the border was far outside the city limits. Luckily, the farms also rented out horses to travelers. It was a beautiful day for it, with the sun shining on the open landscape, it almost felt as though it would be a leisurely trip.

The two galloped through the farmlands at a fast pace. After contacting the client for information, they were ready to find the lost caravan. Ewan planned out their route to save time, but it balanced back out with his awkward riding. It was a skill he regretted not spending more time on, but it wasn't something that he needed to do that often. Arden, on the other hand, seemed a natural rider. He reared his horse back to Ewan's pace to check on him.

"Are you all right?" he called over.

"I can adjust to it," Ewan replied shakily.

They weren't able to converse until a couple of miles down when the horses had to slow to a walk. Ewan was glad for the reprieve as he was sure Arden was enjoying his discomfort. "I take it you've been riding a lot?" he asked Arden while he caught his breath.

"Oh yeah. My family took us horse riding all the time. It was one of the only things that we all had fun doing."

"Your siblings as well? You have a few if I remember."

Arden was always happy talking about this since he came from a big but close family. And getting him talking about this would hopefully stop him from commenting on Ewan's horse riding.

"Of course, my little brothers learned a few years ago. They kept trying to race each other. My big sister, though, she goes at her own pace. When it comes to building up speed, she rides a lot like you." He laughed at the image of it. Ewan rolled his eyes and continued riding, but Arden didn't want the conversation to drop before he asked about Ewan. "Did your family not go riding? There were some great trails around the Esterwood."

"No I never took an interest, and I don't have any siblings to speak of." He stopped there, suggesting that was all he would say about the subject. Ewan rarely talked about his family which made Arden more curious.

"Have you thought about when you'll see them next?"

"Once the insanity has died down, we can think about it."

That sounded like all he was getting for now and since it was time for them to ride at speed again, he would leave this conversation for another time.

****

Claire greeted the man working reception on her way to check the jobs posted. She was keeping Lilla company until she was kicked out for hovering too much. Lilla was recovering well; she was able to walk around the apartment, albeit with some discomfort. Claire was still in the mood for some simple work after their recent misadventure. Like before, several jobs had been taken since she last checked it, and she moved on to the next ones. A thought occurred to her. She looked back at the jobs in the past couple of days and saw the best-paid jobs were taken. She felt a tingle of excitement as it clicked in her mind. Before they arrived, the jobs weren't getting done. The only other people that could be taking these jobs were the people from Haven! The fact that a job was taken as early as yesterday means they were still signing up for work even after the attack. Claire wished someone was there to share the excitement as her mind filled with possibilities.

If they're coming in here to check out jobs, then we can follow them and find where they're hiding.

Claire took a moment to compose herself and stored this idea for later. Not wanting to go back empty-handed, she took the one job that caught her eye. It was another appeal for a lost child, this one younger and it didn't pay well, but that didn't matter. The important thing was, this might be another connection to the Revolution like Will was.

She took it to the counter and the man working was grateful to see someone would help. According to him, the woman who handed it in was distraught and looked on the edge of a breakdown. Hearing this, Claire decided to stop by before home. It sounded like this woman should know right away that they were ready to help.

****

Claire found the clients' house and immediately saw why the reward was so little. The house was run-down, and she could only imagine whatever family was making a life here. She came up to the door to find it was partly open. Hoping nothing was wrong, she eased her way in and called out.

"Hello? I'm here about a job notice. You reported a child missing?"

She heard a gruff male voice reply in the other room. "Sorry, love, I'm fixing the fire. Come on in."

Claire walked onward into a dark living room. She couldn't see the man who responded to her and tried to get a better look. Suddenly a fire did light behind her, and she slowly turned to see the source. A fireplace was indeed lit and sitting casually next to it was a man with steel gauntlets pointed right at her. Daniel Serco sat with a smile, and she felt her blood run cold.

"The fire's ready."

****

The border wall proved no obstacle for Ewan and Arden. It stretched across from the dusty canyons, which lead south toward Merrell, and the rocky hills and highlands up north. The wall was originally built because of suspicion and fear of the western countries, but now it was said to be in place to keep monsters away and allow their farmlands to thrive. It held several checkpoints to keep track of people entering or leaving. There was no martial law, so people were free to come and go through the gates with only a fair warning of what would wait on the other side, but the two travelers today seemed well equipped and claimed it was a short journey to find a lost caravan.

They followed the road as their nameless client advised. A few miles outside the border, they spotted where the caravan had been as the remains were scattered near the road. But the caravan itself was missing. The trail of wreckage continued, but it had been picked apart by scavengers. It wasn't hard to follow as there was a clear trail through the dirt, as if something heavy had been dragged through it.

"This might be a stretch, but I have a feeling the caravan is this way," Arden said, grinning.

"Your powers of deduction astound me," he replied and pressed on down the trail. They paused briefly to check any wreckage in case the pendant was lying out in the open.

Up ahead they saw the trail moved up a small hill with a rock formation on top. They climbed up and moved between the rocks to find the remains of the caravan completely abandoned. It had been ripped apart, and anything useful to whatever creature brought it here had been ripped out.

The two dismounted and began searching through the remains. Most everything was destroyed, but when searching close to the outside, Ewan found a jewelry box with its contents spilled on the ground. Arden was still digging around as Ewan inspected it. He found a sparkling pendant that looked accurate.

Ewan hesitated at looking through the belongings, but the only way to be sure was to open it up. In doing so, he found a family portrait inside. The family looked elegant with a mother, a father, and two little girls looking happy in tailor-made dresses and the father in an expensive-looking suit. Ewan's eyes widened as he examined the faces of the family.

"Arden! You should take a look at this."

No luck getting the horses yet, he hurried over and took the pendant that was offered to him. After a moment, he looked up at Ewan to confirm what he was seeing. She was much younger but one of the girls was definitely Sam, and what's more, they recognized the father.

****

Claire did what she could to contain her fear. She was frozen in place while Serco sat there as if greeting an old friend.

"You don't look happy to see me, Claire," he said as his smile dropped. Her discomfort went up a notch at hearing her name.

"How...do you know my name?" Her voice was barely a whisper.

"Our mutual friend told me all about you. Poor little Samantha." He rose from the chair and again pointed his fingers at her, ready to pull the trigger.

"She must be distraught that you ruined her little plan. Why, she'd probably like nothing more than if I killed you now."

Claire tensed, and although she didn't move quite yet, she was considering if she could make it to the window before he could stop her. Serco noticed her reaction and lowered his arm again.

"Oh don't fret. I'm not here to hurt you. I don't care about their rebellion or the wacky anti-magic anymore. No, I'm far more interested in your story."

Strangely enough, Claire didn't feel reassured by this.

"What do you want from me?" she said, trying to speak more firmly.

"I want to see you live up to your potential. You and your team were pretty impressive, and I'd like nothing more than to see you become true heroes." He emphasized the last word like a romantic notion. "I am right in thinking you're the leader?"

Claire said nothing to this, instead trying to think of a way to gain control of the situation. Serco grinned; he clearly knew the answer to his question.

"You took charge of your team and even faced off against a man like me without hesitation. It must be fate that you came here alone so we could have this talk."

"The woman who gave the job post?" Claire asked shakily.

Serco let out a short laugh. "Ah yes, that woman was very helpful. I asked her to hand in the job notice for a missing child, figuring that would get your attention considering how you came to find the club. I was impressed by her though. I told her to hand in the job for the child, but all the tears and shaking in fear she did really added to the performance."

Claire wanted to push for answers but was cautious not to set him off. If she played this carefully, then she may get to leave with her life. "Why do all this to meet with me? Why meet with me at all?"

"Hmm, you don't seem to be getting it. Here this might explain it better." He held up a small tattered journal.

"This is what it's all about. It's my story. From my time as a regulator to my more criminal escapades and my life's search. Even my encounter with you has been recorded. I expect when my story comes to an end you can keep the journal as a keepsake of our time together." Claire was still at a loss. She began to ask why but he ignored her and plowed on.

"Long story short, I wanted to be the hero but as much as I played the part…well, it got stale. There was no great evil, no final quest, and no big villain for me to overcome. If there was no endgame then what was the point. So I came to a realization. Maybe I'm not meant to be the hero… but I can create one."

Claire stared at him blankly as she couldn't follow him at all. She was listening to a madman, but there must be some logic to his actions.

Serco noticed her expression, and his face sank. He summoned up his enthusiasm again to spell it out for her. "I can be the great villain for the hero to overcome. For you to overcome."

Claire continued to stare blankly and felt her fear starting to fade. "You can't be serious."

"I'll never be more serious. I see great potential in you. With the right guidance."

"Why? Why would you go this far for some story you made up?" Claire forgot her fear as the words came out her mouth.

"No, no, no. This isn't some delusion. The hero's story is as old as time. There is a hero every generation, and we all have a part to play to see it through. So to find the next true hero, I cause destruction and mayhem to inspire others to stop me," he finished as though it was the most obvious explanation in the world.

"Stop." Claire breathed.

"I can mold you into that hero."

Claire's fear was gone, and she forgot all caution. "You murder innocent people all for your delusional story! Do you think I would want any part in such a sick game! I would never…" Her rant came to a sudden halt before she boiled over. Claire lost all breath as a sudden pressure was felt in her chest. Serco was holding up his hand to stop her, the pressure she felt started pulsing like it was alive.

Suddenly the fear came rushing back.

"I see how it is. You're doing well, but you don't understand sacrifice." All humor in his voice was gone. He held her life in his hand and let the pressure build.

"You need to understand you can't save everyone. Some people have to be left behind to make way for the greater good."

Claire started to panic, but she was unable to move. The pressure in her chest couldn't get any higher, and she was positive that this was how he killed his victims. She locked eyes with him and saw his cold expression as he would watch her die in terror. He smiled gently at her. "Don't worry, Claire. I will teach you."

Suddenly the pressure dissipated and Claire fell to her knees, gasping for air. She shakily caught her breath as Serco started to walk away. He looked back to her from the doorway.

"The next time we meet, you will learn what it means to be a hero."

Chapter 15

Fight or Flight

They had arranged to meet that night, but with all the secrecy with their client they half expected it to be a back-alley deal. But after confirming that Ewan and Arden had the pendant, they received the address of a vacant home. It was ready for sale, but the door was left unlocked for them. They had ideas about who was going to meet them, and there were a lot of questions that hopefully, the client was willing to answer.

After some time pacing around the empty room, a young woman came to the door. She cautiously entered and confirmed it was them she had been in contact with. It was an odd sight watching her remove a cloak to reveal an expensive-looking dress underneath. Whomever the cloak and secrecy were for, she seemed comfortable revealing herself in front of the two of them, although she looked anxious about the trade.

"Do you have it?" she asked quickly.

Arden nodded and handed her the jewelry box with the pendant sitting on top. It would have been a waste to leave the rest of the jewelry behind so they brought all of it. She checked the pendant and relaxed when she saw the picture. After staring at it for a moment, she snapped out of her daze and reached into her cloak. "Thank you for this. I have your reward right here."

"Before we get to that, we wanted to ask you about the picture," Ewan politely requested, but the girl looked apprehensive.

"I don't think you—" she started nervously until Ewan cut her off.

"One of the girls is named Sam, correct?"

The girl hesitated. "How do you know her?"

"We've met a few times while working," Ewan answered, which wasn't a total lie.

She shuffled nervously before asking. "Is she all right?"

Ewan and Arden looked at each other as they weren't sure how to answer that. "She's...caught up in some trouble, but she's unharmed if that's what you mean."

The girl looked saddened but not surprised. "Yes, I knew she would be."

Arden stepped forward. "I'm sorry for prying here, but we saw you both in the photo. You're her sister, right?"

The girl gave in, knowing her cover was blown. "Yes. My name is Celine." She looked them in the eyes. There was a definite resemblance, but this girl had much kinder features.

Arden filled in the next part. "Celine and Samantha...Hargrove. The mayor's daughters."

She lowered her head as if she was ashamed of the fact. "Yes, that's right."

Even though they had deduced this themselves, it was still a shock to hear it out loud. The leader of the Revolution, Sam, was Mayor Hargrove's daughter. How did she end up like this? There was no point in speculating as the answers lay in front of them. The anxious sister once again avoided eye contact with them.

"Do you know what your sister's been doing?" Arden asked carefully.

"I haven't heard from her since she left us. That was three years ago."

They weren't sure what to do with this information, but Arden felt he had to push the issue. "Look, she's caught up in some trouble, and it's going to get bad for her if she keeps going. Maybe you can help her."

Celine looked at the two of them with sympathy but shook her head and pulled out their payment as promised. "I don't want anything to do with this. Please just take your money."

Shocked at her response, Ewan stood forward but didn't take the money. "You clearly care for her, for your family. You might be the only person who can help her now."

Celine angrily pushed the money into Ewan's hand and backed off. "She made her choice!" She shouted and was breathing heavily. It felt like they were digging up something painful for the girl, so Arden tried to apologize for upsetting her.

Ewan wasn't ready to leave it there, so after she calmed down a bit he gently asked, "What made her leave?"

For a moment they thought she would storm out, but instead she muttered, "That stupid boy."

The two quietly waited for her to elaborate rather than push any harder.

"One of the servants that worked for us got sick, and then he died. His son blamed our family, said we should have paid for his medical care, but we didn't know that would happen. He broke into our house and attacked my father with magic. The guards came and stopped him, but when they went to take him away, Samantha…defended him." The last two words were filled with anger and confusion. Even after three years, there was a clear resentment.

"This boy tried to kill our father, and she rushed to his side. She screamed so loudly that all the windows shattered. It wasn't until later I found out she was using magic as well. He taught her how to use it, and they attacked us. That was the last time I saw her." She petered off after this; it was clear she wanted to get this off her chest as even after three years the emotions were still burning strong . Ewan only managed to ask one last question as Celine was trying to leave.

"What was the boy's name?"

Celine walked to the door, and it seemed as if he wouldn't get an answer. But before leaving, she faced them again. She suddenly looked a lot more like Sam with a hardened expression. "Emil Hunter."

****

Ewan and Arden walked back in silence, even though they left with a good reward for their trouble. The pair mulled over the information they received but weren't sure if it changed anything.

Arden was hoping Celine could talk Sam down, but there was no chance of that happening. They weren't even sure if this explained Sam's drive to have the mages rebel or if this made it even stranger, and why defend Hunter after attacking her family? They wouldn't come up with the answers talking over it, but they had to let Claire and Lilla in on this development. But when they arrived home, they found Claire hadn't returned yet.

****

Claire stood looking over the river in silence. She always felt more relaxed watching the water. Her earliest memory had been falling asleep on her dad's fishing boat. She couldn't picture his face that clearly but could still remember how peaceful the water was. But it wasn't enough to help her this time. She had been standing trying to calm herself, but her emotions kept moving from one extreme to the next. She was stuck in the range of fear, anger, and shame from her meeting with Serco. She felt tired but couldn't bring herself to leave.

She had been standing there thinking it over for several hours, but she still wasn't ready to see the others after what happened. All that training, and she was helpless against Serco.

The wind blew in with the night air as the temperature dropped, but she ignored the chill. Claire remained still and thought about how she was nearly killed, and why? Because of a psychopath wanting to play at being a villain. He toys with people and throws away their lives for his own twisted amusement. She already disliked the man, but now it had morphed into genuine hate.

Claire forced herself to look over the slow river of water and allowed the rage inside her to fade yet again. She could still feel that sense of helplessness when the pressure was building. In the midst of her turmoil, something else occurred to her.

The fear I felt, how many others have experienced that? That would have been the last thing they ever felt before they died.

This realization hit her hard, and all the heavy emotions she felt for her own life was now directed at the others who had encountered Serco. And how many would come after her? Once he was bored and moved on, how many more would he kill and torment for his own ends?

Claire struggled with these questions until only one singular thought was left.

It will keep going until someone stops him, her inner voice told her. Claire felt the magic within her reacting. It felt warm and almost comforting.

I can't wait for someone else to come along. I have to stop him myself. Whatever it takes, I have to stop him from destroying any more lives.

After standing for hours, Claire let go of the pain that gripped her and chose to focus on stopping Serco. For all the people who were killed for his game. Claire felt the cool wind in her face and allowed herself to settle. With a newfound determination, she felt a strange kind of peace wash over her as her mind was made up. No matter the risk to herself, she couldn't let Serco do this to anyone else. But she would need to be stronger the next time she faced him.

****

After a long wait, the others finally received a message from Claire. She asked them to meet her, with no explanation as to where she had been or what she was doing. It wasn't too far, so they made their way down to the river to find out what she was up to. They saw her silhouette in the distance before the night sky could illuminate her. At least it was easy to assume it was her as who else would be throwing magic around in the middle of the city.

Claire stood with her sword drawn, facing the length of the river. She held it firmly and focused her magic into it; the difference was immediately apparent as it was more of a strain to reach its limit. It was like tensing a muscle. With no sigil in place, she had to concentrate harder on the effect she wanted. Claire swung her sword and sent the force of her swing outward to strike the water ahead of her. She felt satisfied with the impacts as it blasted the water. It would take time to master control of her new sword and attack more efficiently. But she would train her skills as much as it took.

Claire stopped once she noticed the three of them approaching. It was a good thing Lilla was well enough to walk out with them. After the physical and mental exhaustion of the last few hours, it was nice to see her team. As much as she wanted to handle things alone, Claire knew she needed their help. It was time to find out if they would follow her lead yet again.

"It's about time we found you. You would not believe the day we've had." Arden was excited to bring her up to speed. Claire smiled awkwardly thinking at this point nothing would surprise her. She allowed them to get her caught up and was instantly proven wrong about not being surprised. Despite her own encounter, she listened to everything Ewan and Arden had found out.

"Samantha Hargrove…that explains a few things," she said, trying to wrap her head around it.

"It makes you wonder if the mayor knows his daughter's involved in this," Ewan commented. It was a fair question and would be difficult for them to find the answer.

Now that Claire was up to speed, Lilla was finally able to ask where she'd been.

"It's a long story. We should probably sit down for this."

As Claire ran them through the whole story, they held back from interrupting. Though she paused at several points, she saw their expressions change from worry to something close to horrified. She was eerily calm while explaining and was left with a stunned silence once it was finished.

"That's—" Ewan started before Lilla shouted over him.

"Are you okay?"

"Well, I—" Claire began before she was also interrupted by Lilla.

"I'm sorry. Of course you're not okay. We can fix this though. You can leave the city or…we could get Isaac to help…or we could call the chief and raid every house until we find him!" Lilla yelled with frightening enthusiasm.

"Whoa, calm down. We're not raiding any houses. Take a breath."

Lilla did as she was told, taking rapid breaths.

"You've had more time to think about this than us. What are you planning to do?" Ewan asked, keeping his composure.

Arden stood in response. "Isn't it obvious? This guy's a menace, and we need to stop him. We can't let him corner one of us again." Claire looked at him for a moment, understanding that they were all worked up. Arden looked back defiantly. "Don't tell me I'm wrong here."

"Actually, I agree with you."

Everyone fell silent, and Claire took this chance to explain and ask for their help.

"I felt firsthand the kind of terror he inflicts on people, and I understand the kind of pain that comes afterward. I will not allow him to destroy any more lives. I'm asking if you'll help me, but I understand if you don't want a part of this. Taking down Serco is going to be extremely dangerous, and I don't want you to go into this if you're not ready."

Her team shared a look and faced Claire, none of them showing any signs of hesitating.

Arden smirked. "Do we really need to say it?"

Claire could easily see they were on board. She expected as such, but still, she was grateful to them. "All right. Then we take own Serco together."

****

So far neither Sam's group nor Claire's had realized the relevance of Will's location. For he had not simply run away. Instead, he was holed up in a university campus in the tech lab. He was accessing the network and was committing to memory a map of the city and all the travel lines.

He nearly leaped out if his chair when the door was suddenly kicked in. He turned, expecting to be hauled away by security, but it was only Serco. In any other circumstance, this would be the cause of a much greater alarm, but in this case, Will was relieved he hadn't been caught. For it was Serco that brought him here.

He regarded Will warmly. "Hey, buddy. How's my little genius doing?"

Will still wasn't sure how to respond to him properly. "Umm yeah, I'm doing well. I think I have the routes all planned out. All I need is the right access. How was your…errand?"

Serco clapped his hands together with a clang from the gauntlets. "Oh, it went perfectly. I got to meet someone very special. They have a bright future ahead of them if they're willing to learn."

Will nodded politely. He had no idea what Serco was talking about, but he learned not to ask. "Are we going ahead with this operation soon? I'm sure the boss is quite anxious to break our friends out of jail. They shouldn't be in there."

"No, they shouldn't. That's why we'll free them soon enough. You focus on your part. I'll get you the access you need, and you guide everyone to the right positions."

Will let out a nervous breath and got back to work, leaving Serco to his own thing. He looked back at Will working away on the network.

He is far too naive for someone so talented. I sure hope nobody takes advantage of him, Serco thought with a grin.

****

"I'm glad we're all together and ready to fight, but how are we going to find him?" Arden asked.

Claire smiled in response. "I think we already had the right idea. Serco may not be working with the Revolution anymore, but if anyone knows where he's hiding, it's them."

"So we're going after Sam first?" Arden asked.

"I think that's our best shot. I'm guessing Celine's not going to help with that?"

Ewan shook his head. "She was determined to have no part in this I'm afraid."

"Hmm..." Claire pondered what they had told her. "Even so we've learned a lot more about her and Hunter. We might be able to use that."

Lilla perked up at what she was suggesting. "You still want to try and talk them down?"

Arden scoffed. "That's not gonna be easy considering our fight. They think we're traitors."

"But we're not though. Serco betrayed them. He was going to kill everyone," Lilla reasoned.

Ewan was doubtful. "As far as they know, the plan was going smoothly until our interference. Then the operation collapsed, and the majority of them were captured."

"It won't be easy. We need to convince them that Serco was going to kill them. We may need to fight first and reason with them after. They spent time with Serco, they must understand what kind of man he is," Claire said, although she struggled to even think of him as human now.

"As for finding them, I have an idea."

Chapter 16

To Regain A Purpose

Although the plan to track the Revolutionists was solid, it took longer than Claire would have liked. First, they checked the Contractor's Offices one by one to find out which had people coming in for jobs. This wasn't confidential so they soon found out which offices Sam's group were using and could begin watching them. They set up shifts of two at a time to better spot and follow anyone they recognized. Meanwhile, the remaining two could keep up their training for the battles to come. Claire was exhausting herself, often having no magic left by the end of the day.

After some time and several changes to their schedule, they finally spotted someone. They had tried several positions, but this day Lilla and Ewan were waiting on the roof across the street, watching people come and go from the office. The man who entered was about the right age, and on the way out, Lilla got a good look at his face.

"That's Jacob! I met him in Haven when I first joined," she said triumphantly. But spotting them was only one part of the plan. Lilla followed from the rooftops while Ewan made his way down to the street. He stalked their target while wearing a not-at-all silly looking cap and sunglasses to hide his face. Lilla could only follow them as far as the tram he jumped on, but Ewan managed to casually get on and keep him in view.

It all seemed too easy as he followed Jacob into the northern district. There was a concern that they would start the job immediately and go meet the client, to which Arden suggested jumping them and getting them to talk. Luckily, Arden wasn't here as Jacob seemed to lead Ewan straight to what they were looking for. He witnessed the young man circle behind a vacant shop and from there enter a seemingly closed warehouse. Ewan figured they must be in luck, that Jacob was taking the suitable jobs then meeting everyone else to hand them out. Now Ewan gave his teammates the message they had been waiting for; tomorrow they could move in.

****

Physically the team was well equipped for this, but they still had a disagreement with how to handle the situation.

"I'm not going to be able to help talk to them," Lilla told them.

Claire was lost in thought until she heard this. "What do you mean? You spent more time with them than any of us."

"I also kicked Jamie in the face…twice," she said guiltily.

"I understand that might sour your friendship a bit, but we all fought them, and we could end up fighting again."

"That's why I need to be ready to fight. I can't focus on that and convince them at the same time. I can't afford to get emotional in the middle of it. I need to tune everything else out."

Ewan knew her well enough to accept this. "If that's how you operate then you can leave the negotiating to us."

Arden wasn't as optimistic. "I feel like this is going to be a mess anyway, so yeah, it's better you're prepared to fight."

Claire was surprised, but they all seemed adamant, so she accepted it. *That's how Lilla operates.* She took a mental note of it. If she was going to lead them against someone like Serco, she had to better understand her team.

****

They worked on the assumption that if Sam's group was still working like before, then the majority of them would be active during the day. So they left their infiltration until the evening, hoping to get straight to Sam. The warehouse wasn't much to look at from the outside, and after watching for a while, they saw no activity. It seemed apparent nothing would happen if they continued watching, so Claire decided it was time to move in, and they made their way across the lot to the entrance.

Arden led the way into a side entrance, and upon entering, found no one standing guard. The building was pitch-dark inside, and there was no sign that anyone was here, the team said nothing, but the silence made them uneasy. Out on the main floor, they could see only a few boxes scattered by the walls. The only sign that this place wasn't completely abandoned was a light in a room at the far end. They silently moved toward it thinking maybe they had come at the perfect time.

This hope was immediately shattered as all the lights came on, leaving them completely exposed.

"You again!" Sam's voice emanated from above like something from a loudspeaker. Looking up, they could see Sam and Hunter on a previously hidden walkway.

"We were waiting for AMTech's soldiers to arrive but instead it's always you people." Sam was speaking normally, but her voice loudly echoed all around them.

"We didn't come here to fight!" Claire tried before things escalated. "We're only looking to talk."

"You've come to talk after what you did? You betrayed us, and eight of our friends are locked up because of you!"

Ewan attempted to argue back. "We did not betray you. Daniel Serco was planning to turn on you from the start. We had to stop him."

"Lies!" This word echoed louder and rang in their ears. "You sold us out to AMTech, and now you've followed us here."

It was obvious to Claire this was not going well. *Where are Jamie and Wren when you need them? We could really do with someone more sensible to negotiate with.*

"You might not be who we were expecting, but we can still get plenty out of you four." Sam held up her metal bat, forcing them to draw their weapons in response.

"This is for the people we lost!" Sam shouted and stuck the metal barrier. The sound from it exploded around them, causing pain ripple through them. Lilla recovered quickly and fired a couple of arrows at Sam before she could do it again, but with a swipe of his hand, Hunter knocked the arrows away. Their voices still amplified as Hunter called out, "Wren!"

On cue, Wren emerged for only a second before darkness erupted from him and engulfed the group.

Claire tried to catch her bearings. To go from unbearable sound to sudden darkness and quiet was made to disorientate them. She heard Arden struggling nearby but couldn't move to help him without getting in the way.

It was all a trap, she realized. *They kept taking jobs to attract attention and lure people here.*

They had no choice but to fight their way out, starting with clearing the smoke.

It circled around her to the point she could only see a foot in front of her, so Claire called for aid to clear it. "Lilla!"

Somewhere behind her she heard the blind response, "I'm on it!"

Knowing what she would do, Claire swung her sword around in an arc and summoned a gust of wind around her blade. They needed to get this done before someone interrupted them. Somewhere in the dark she could still hear the clash of Arden fighting and then a loud collision somewhere else. She could feel it now. The wind was building and spiral around them, and with the smoke starting to clear, she could make out Lilla nearby moving her hands in the same motion. With one last swing of her sword, the smoke blew away in a wave to reveal the fight around her.

Arden took this chance to push Wren back with his shield. Ewan was recovering on the ground as the remains of a wooden crate lay next to him. With a clear line of sight, Lilla again tried to shoot down the two above. Since she was able to prepare this time, her arrows were blunted so that they wouldn't kill so she could aim straight for them. Hunter effortlessly deflected the arrows and continued throwing the large boxes on the ground toward them. With Hunter watching over her, Sam used her crushing sound wave to cripple all of them yet again. As much as it caused pain, it was also a perfect distraction so Wren could knock back Arden and Claire narrowly avoided more flying crates.

Arden quickly got up and moved next to Claire to eye the two above. "Keep Wren off me a minute. I'm gonna knock those two down." Trusting her teammate, Claire made straight for Wren to engage him. On his way, Arden only now noticed Jamie who had melted the ground beneath Lilla, leaving her stuck. She turned her attention to him and fired arrows to keep him pinned.

Arden joined Ewan who was firing potshots at Hunter to keep him on the defensive. It was tempting to attack one of them directly, but Arden had a better idea.

Charging magic into his new mac,e the sigil on the hilt lit up. With a strong swing, he propelled the spiked ball toward the landing and struck a few feet below Sam. A long chain connected the ball to the hilt in Arden's hand. The length of the chain seemed impossible for the size of the weapon as it easily reached and smashed one of the supports.

The walkway Sam stood on buckled and seized, causing her to lose balance. Before they could react, Arden pulled the spiked ball back and reeled it in a bit before pulling it toward another support. It instantly ripped through, and within seconds the whole landing and its two occupants were sent crashing to the ground.

With practiced ease, Arden again whipped his hand back, and the mace returned to its hilt. He was kind of hoping his teammates saw his new weapon in action. The sigil Tohren placed created a chain from the user's magic that could extend out and retreat as needed. It took a lot to use it, but it had an effective range.

Remembering the point of them coming, Claire tried to stop Wren as they fought. "We are not your enemy. We need to stop this."

Unwilling to listen, Wren launched a cloud of smoke over Claire, which she instantly deflected with the air current from her sword. As this happened, she heard a loud crash behind her and worried for a second it was another one of Sam's sound waves. She felt confident pushing Wren back, at least until her feet started to sink into the floor, giving him the chance to strike. She barely stopped his advance with a streak of fire from her left hand. She didn't know when Jamie had circled around to her, but he kept his distance.

Luckily, before Wren could attack again, a blunt arrow came in and hit him in the head, knocking him back. Claire took the chance to push back the softened ground and jump out of it. She ran back and saw Lilla was still stuck in the ground, but she had bent backward to fire her arrow. It was an impressive move as she was carefully balanced in the sinking earth.

Ewan bore witness to Arden's attack as he managed to ground Sam and Hunter instantly. He noted that the impacts and crashes did not amplify the sound as Sam's attack did. With a moment's reprieve, Ewan checked his surroundings for his teammates. Noticing Lilla's struggle, he quickly aimed one hand toward her and made a platform at her feet to jump out. Effortlessly, she boosted up from the ground and spun around to take aim. With Hunter and Sam back up, she held her fire and waited for an opening.

Sam was unharmed and determined to keep going, so she instantly took a solid stance to strike back at Arden and Ewan. Waiting for her next move, they heard a sudden vibration around them. Not wanting to give her a chance to attack again, Arden reared back and launched his flail toward her.

"No don't!" he heard beside him, but not knowing why, he allowed it to continue which Sam took full advantage of. She batted the mace away, which was more than enough to cause a massive blast of sound around her enemies. Brought to their knees by this, Arden somehow managed to keep his eyes open to see Hunter launch some of the debris behind him. Arden managed to move and shield himself and Ewan. With his ears still ringing, he felt a tap on his shoulder as Ewan ran left to flank them, so Arden reeled in his mace and left Ewan to find a way to counter Sam's technique.

If Ewan was going to handle Sam, then Arden would need to get rid of her bodyguard. He was being cautious now and occasionally glanced to the side where Lilla was waiting. Whether he was going to distract or knock Hunter down, this was playing to his strength. Arden swung his ball and chain around in an arc toward Hunter, but it was easily moved off course. Hunter countered with another crate coming from Arden's rear, but with a flick of his wrist, the mace swung back and demolished the crate behind him.

To close the distance between them, Arden put away his new favorite weapon and raised his shield to charge toward Hunter. He made it over halfway before being stopped in his tracks. Arden dug his feet in to stop from being pushed back as Hunter kept him at bay. Arden used all his strength and pushed one foot forward...then another. One step at a time, he moved closer as Hunter was straining to hold him back. Closing in on him, Arden gave one last push with all his might at the invisible force against his shield. Suddenly, he whipped his shield to the side, causing it to fly off. The sudden release made Hunter stumble in time for Arden to punch head-on. The second his fist connected, Lilla fired her arrow.

****

As this was happening, Ewan ran around Sam to draw her away from the others. He could hear and feel a strong vibration every few steps and knew Sam was tracking him with her power. Before he reached the wall, Ewan stopped suddenly and boosted himself into the air toward her. He fired three of his projectiles, which she easily batted away. As each one hit, Ewan heard the sound amplify to his left but not close enough to hurt him.

Moving in close, Sam took a swing at him, but he ducked under and moved around behind her. He quickly grabbed her bat from behind and tried to hold her still. He received a hit from the base of it for his trouble and stumbled back. Ready to beat her foe bloody, Sam turned to take another swing but was stopped in her tracks, her hands now held in place by chains of light coming out of the ground around her. Ewan caught his breath and slowly walked in front to face her.

"You won't be able to break free as long as I'm holding them in place," he announced confidently.

This didn't stop Sam from struggling, with murderous intent in her eyes. "You can't hold me for long."

"It'll hold you long enough. I know you can't use your amplified sound up close or it will damage you as well. That's why you've used the others to keep us at a distance."

Breathing heavily, Sam's face darkened. "Very clever," she spat. "But you underestimate me. This may hurt me, but it'll hurt you a lot more!" The room seemed to shake as a stronger vibration from before surrounded them both. Ewan knew what was coming, but he couldn't react. He had no moves left to play. Any notion he had that she wasn't crazy enough to do this was gone.

Sam took a deep breath and screamed.

The scream blasted him from all sides, and any form of bracing he did for this felt pointless. Pain coursed through his entire body and topped off at his head. He may have been screaming too, but neither he nor Sam could tell as they were both deafened. Sam maintained her scream until, after what felt like her head would explode, the chains binding her shattered. The noise finally stopped, and by some miracle, they were still standing. Fueled by an insane desire, Sam lurched forward and cracked Ewan over the head.

Ewan didn't have a chance to get his bearings when he was suddenly knocked to the ground. He opened his eyes, and when his vision cleared, he saw a crazed-looking Sam standing over him, ready to finish him off. Even if Ewan did have another spell he could use, his mind was a blur. He was defenseless. He didn't flinch and watched as Sam reared back to strike him. Instead of seeing the bat crack down on him, he saw her stop abruptly. Her body seized, and she collapsed to the ground as an electric arrow struck her in the back.

****

Everyone's attention snapped to the two on the ground. Wren and Jamie ran to see to them, and Claire stepped aside to let them. On the other side, however, Arden was thrown out the way as Hunter barreled toward Sam. As the three checked on Sam, Claire cautiously walked up to see how Ewan was.

"What kept you?" He remained conscious enough to be sarcastic at least.

"Hey, I was buying time for you all right. Looks like it worked, kind of."

Ewan groaned as he forced himself to sit up. "Well, it's your turn now. Time to talk things out."

Arden and Lilla reared up beside them so the two groups faced each other again, unsure of what the other would do. Hunter was busy helping a barely conscious Sam to her feet, so Jamie and Wren stood in front to defend them.

Claire jammed her sword in the ground and called out to them. "That's enough. This fight is pointless."

Arden and Lilla kept their weapons raised in case another fight broke out. At the very least they felt confident they could win as the other team was in worse shape.

"If you didn't want to fight then why did you follow us here?" Wren demanded to know.

"I told you we came here to talk. We want to stop you from planning any more attacks before this spirals out of control."

"We had things under control until you messed it up!" Hunter yelled while supporting Sam.

"He's right. Nobody had to get hurt, but you sabotaged us," Jamie agreed.

"That might have been your plan, but that wasn't what Serco was going to do. He was going to destroy the building and kill everyone inside if we didn't stop him," Claire retorted. Her whole argument hinged on them believing this fact.

Sam slowly eased her way forward. "That's...a lie." She paused between breaths.

Hunter stuck with her. "We had Serco under control. He knew his job."

"Oh come on. Do you really trust Serco over us?" Arden threw this out, making Jamie look uncertain.

He turned uneasily to the others. "Could they be right?"

"No, he didn't turn on us! Things would have gone smoothly if they didn't interfere!" Hunter spat back.

Claire felt any patience she had melt away. "You know the kind of man he is! Did you think he'd be satisfied following orders from you? He can't go anywhere without leaving a trail of bodies behind him."

Wren and Jamie looked to be wavering at this, but Sam and Hunter remained defiant. "We had...a deal with him. He was cooperating," Sam managed to say.

"I can't believe this. How can you be so stupid as to completely trust that man! If you're as smart as I think you are, you'd know he's a psychopath. You can't control him! So why have you put your trust in him?" Claire couldn't wrap her head around it. Sam had always been cautious, planning out every move.

"You knew."

This voice came quietly beside them, but everyone heard it and paused. Lilla stood with paint still applied but a gentler look than before. "You knew what we were going to do, and you were going to let it happen."

Sam tensed up at this sudden accusation. Jamie looked at her but couldn't believe it. "No. No, that can't be true."

"They need to see that the path we're taking isn't going to be a clean one. Those were your words when everyone else left your office. I was there for your whole meeting, that's how we knew what you were up to. I didn't know what you meant at the time, but you meant to kill the hostages the whole time. That was the message you wanted to send," Lilla explained calmly.

Claire was as shocked by this as everyone else. But it all made sense. This was why Sam was defending Serco because she was complacent in his plan.

Jamie and Wren were looking to Sam now. Jamie especially looked horrified. "It can't be true. You wouldn't."

Sam caught her breath slowly, and she couldn't find the energy to lie. "Sacrifices had to be made."

All the shock Jamie had been holding back suddenly hit him. He could barely hear Wren beside him. "We trusted you. You've been using us as pawns in your ridiculous vendetta."

"We are in a war here!" she shouted, all composure gone. "We need them to see what we're capable of, that we will not be swept under the rug like a disgrace in their city."

"No, this is your stupid vendetta with your family that you're dragging all of us through."

Sam recovered enough to stand, and with Hunter, took a few steps back from them. "So you're turning against us too? Fine. We'll win this war on our own!" With that statement, Hunter reached up, and all the lights exploded at once, leaving the group in darkness yet again.

"Don't let them get away!" Claire found herself yelling.

"They're running to the door. I can catch them," Wren answered while moving through the dark. Claire heard the rushed footsteps and summoned what remaining magic she had into light. With both hands, she pulled up two small but bright lights and propelled them toward the entrance. But as the lights reached the other side, she only saw Wren, with no sign of Sam.

Wren looked around confused. "I'm sure I heard them?"

On the ground, Ewan coughed. "Sound...manipulation."

Claire heard this and realized immediately. "It was a trick. They went the other way!" She looked to the office and heard a loud crash from within. She quickly grabbed her sword and ran with Arden toward the light. Kicking down the door, however, they found that half the office had collapsed in on itself.

Jamie caught up to see what remained. "It's too late. We had an escape in place. That crash was Hunter sealing the entrance." Claire racked her brain for a way they could follow but it was no use; they had escaped.

****

Claire's team, along with Jamie and Wren, gathered themselves outside. Since the warehouse was left pitch-black, Arden helped carry Ewan out, and they took a moment to get a better look at him. His vision was still a bit blurry but it focused enough to see Lilla checking on his head wound.

"How are you feeling?" she asked while gently inspecting him.

"I'm very eager to pass out, but I'll wait until we get home for that," he answered honestly.

Arden laughed at his response. "You were pretty tough back there. I don't think I could have handled her better."

Seeing he was okay, Claire turned her attention to Jamie and Wren who sat nearby. Wren looked quietly frustrated whereas Jamie looked defeated.

She approached to check on them. "How are you holding up?"

Jamie didn't even look up as he answered. "She was using us, ready to throw us away at any moment."

"I shouldn't have believed her. I knew this was a bad idea, but I went along with it anyway," Wren said, clearly blaming himself.

Claire tried what she could to be comforting, but they didn't seem to be taking it in. "It's all right. You both made it out, and now you can move on."

Jamie shot up when she said this. "What are we supposed to do? That club was our home. It meant everything to us! But it was all built on a lie. Sam only wanted us as soldiers to fight her father."

"It doesn't have to end here," Claire reminded them. "The people you gathered aren't all a part of this. You can rebuild. You two can take ownership of Haven and lead your friends in the right direction. They want somewhere to learn about magic and discover themselves. That's what you told me when we met. You can't tell me that part was a lie."

Jamie's expression softened, but there was still a look of doubt about him. "Do you really think we can do this?"

Wren put a hand on his shoulder and looked him in the eye. "We should try. We owe it to everyone."

Seeing Wren at his side, Jamie pushed away any doubt and looked back to Claire. "We'll gather everyone tomorrow and tell them the news. Will you come with us? We don't know if Sam or Hunter will show up."

Claire smiled. "Of course. We'll help however we can."

Although this was only supposed to be a stepping stone toward finding Serco, Claire felt a sense of hope that they could help the people of Haven.

Chapter 17

Bringing People Together

Ewan woke up from the sunlight reaching his eyes. It must be early hours as the sun was starting to creep above the cityscape. He took a minute to wake up as it wasn't exactly a pleasant rest with his head still throbbing, but he passed out as soon as he returned home. Although he had no experience in the matter, he wondered if this was what a hangover felt like. Not one for lying around, he shuffled and slowly sat up to check how he was. Only now did he notice Lilla asleep on the floor next to him. She was a curious sight, curled up on a hardwood floor. Somehow she looked completely content lying there. He decided to sit back as to not disturb her and pondered if his headache would stop him from reading.

It was over an hour before Lilla stirred. Well, not really stirred; she snored, coughed loudly, and woke up. She saw Ewan looking down at her with an amused smile.

"Huh? You're awake! How are you feeling?" she asked while trying to subtly wipe her mouth.

"I'm fine. Are you all right?" he asked jokingly.

There were a few cracks as Lilla stretched out to wake herself up. "It was a long night."

"I can't imagine it's comfortable down there, especially with your own bed on the other side of the wall."

"I don't like the bed. It's too soft. If they would let me sleep in the park down the road, I would."

"You must have fallen asleep pretty quickly. You didn't even wipe the paint off." It seemed polite to tell her as it was smeared over her face. Lilla was casual about it so far, but now she was starting to get a bit flustered while wiping her face. Realizing she smudged it worse, she tried to collect what dignity she had by standing to leave.

"Before you go."

Lilla turned back to him and willed herself to not be embarrassed.

"You really came through for us back there," he remembered to tell her.

Lilla's attempt to not be embarrassed was out the window. "Oh it was nothing. I mean I was watching you fight for some time before I had a clear shot. If I had fired sooner, you might not have gotten hurt, but I was worried Hunter would stop me, so I waited until he was down." Lilla's breath ran out.

Ewan shook his head. "I don't mean that. You exposed Sam in the end. Even with your guard up for the fight, you spoke up at the right time. Our argument would have fallen apart if not for you. Now Haven has a chance of being something good."

Lilla was left speechless for a moment, and she suppressed her smile from the praise. She made some awkward incomprehensible noises and left to go clean up.

****

It wasn't until the afternoon that the members of Haven gathered together. Claire and Arden were waiting in the new location for the club where Jamie had asked everyone to come. Wren told them it was one of the last properties that Sam had bought out with the stolen funding from her father. Which explained how she had a whole nightclub running and various abandoned properties. This last location was an old hall with a stage for musicians. It wasn't as spacious as the club, but it was a perfect location for Jamie to address everyone.

They waited in the back with Wren periodically reporting to them as he was ensuring Sam or Hunter didn't make an appearance. It would be hard to face them here with so many people, but if they did turn up, Claire was ready to settle their fight and get answers. It seemed as though she wasn't going to appear. Although what should have been good news left Claire feeling somewhat disappointed.

Before everyone gathering was ready, however, they had business to discuss backstage.

"You have no clues as to where Serco would hide out?" Claire asked again, hoping they could come up with something useful.

Jamie shook his head apologetically. "Sam was always the one arranging a meeting with him, and anytime they met outside the club she only took Hunter with her. He was there to protect her in case the deal went south."

Arden let out a quick laugh. "I don't think that would be enough."

Claire nodded in agreement. "I don't think she understood how dangerous he was. He would have done away with her the minute he grew bored," she said with resentment. Claire dismissed the feeling with a sigh and continued. "So they're the only two who might have a lead on Serco. Do you know where they might be hiding, now that they're on their own?"

Jamie mulled it over. "There were a couple more locations that Sam considered for Haven. She could hide there for a short time. But I'm afraid they're not completely alone."

"What do you mean?"

Jamie's face sank at the question. "The four members who came back with us on our operation. They all refused my call when I tried to gather everyone. Wren thinks Sam contacted them first, and they might be with her. I understand the others were pretty loyal. They were handpicked by Sam after all. But Will…?"

"Will was with them?" Claire asked. *So he wasn't captured.*

With everything else going on she had forgotten he was involved. After how anxious he was during the operation, it would be a shock to learn he was still on board with more fighting. Was it possible he ran off?

Claire sat back now that she had an idea where to go next. "All right. Sam might still have allies. We'll keep that in mind. If you could pass us the locations after you're done here, I'd appreciate it."

Jamie looked rather nervous sitting with them as he had to go out there soon.

"Do you know what you're going to say?" Arden asked.

"Oh man, I hope so. We spent all last night writing out what to say and how to say it. And guess who got stuck with addressing them all?"

"Yeah, I didn't think Wren would do it." Arden chuckled.

"He'll be right there with you though, and we'll stand with you too," Claire said, trying to be reassuring.

Jamie took a breath and looked at them. "Thank you for coming out. I know we couldn't help much with Serco, but I appreciate that you're staying while we sort this."

"We can't leave yet," Arden jumped in. "I have to see what happens with you guys. We need a win."

Arden was right. Although Claire was disappointed that they had no leads to Serco, her focus had to be here. "We'll see this through with you. We'll help with anything you need."

It was only when they started to feel relaxed that Wren came back yet again. "Everyone's here, are you ready?"

Jamie closed his eyes and took more deep breaths. "I'm ready." He stood and practically marched out to the stage with Claire, Arden, and Wren in tow.

The three of them stood by Jamie as he prepared to address what remained of Haven. There were a lot of hushed whispers when they came up to the stage as many had heard Claire and her team were banned from the club. Jamie chose to grab their attention and stop any hushed rumors.

"Sam is no longer leading Haven." Everyone immediately stopped and listened; there was some shock in the crowd as they waited for what would follow.

"Both Sam and Hunter are set on going to war with Mayor Hargrove and AMTech. They wanted us as soldiers in that war, and for a while, we went along with it. Until these two brought us back from the brink."

Claire tried to stand confidently while he gestured to them.

"We made a mistake!" Jamie yelled to the crowd of mages in front of him. "As many of you know, the recent attack at the armory in central Verras was done by a team of us, handpicked by Sam. This was a mistake. Sam wanted us to fight against Hargrove's oppression, but this was the wrong way to do it." He paused to let that sink in as many of them weren't made aware of the operation.

"Many of us involved thought we were doing the right thing, but we put people's lives at risk for our own agenda. If Claire and her team didn't stop us, Sam would have allowed the people there to die in order to send a message. I'm here in front of you now to make up for my part in this. I want to put us back on the right path. I believe we came together for the right reasons. We're a family, and we can continue to learn from each other and work with each other as we have done so far. Sam wants to continue her warpath against Mayor Hargrove and AMTech that backs him. So Wren and I are stepping up to look after all of you and bring this club back to its roots. If you'll stay with us, then I promise to show you what Haven can be. A place for anyone looking to study magic and discover their own abilities, a home for them. Will you stay with us?"

Claire waited anxiously for their response. She couldn't even imagine how Jamie felt up here. He put his heart into this speech as he would put his heart into this club. The group of fifty or so youths looked around at each other for a spell until one girl stood from her friends. "We want to stay!"

Jamie smiled warmly at her. It was only a group of five or so, but still, you could see his gratitude.

"We'll stay with you as well!" another young man chimed in with his friends all nodding behind him. One by one, the young mages called out their support, which slowly turned into cheering. Jamie broke out into tears in front of them as the emotion he was holding back flooded out. He looked to Wren who was standing by his side as always. Wren looked back at him proudly, and although he wasn't as beaming as Jamie was, you could tell he was happy.

Arden started nudging Claire in excitement and applauded the two as well. Claire could almost see the history between Wren and Jamie, as they had stuck together through it all. It was as if it led up to this moment where they had found a true purpose in life. There would be plenty more tears (mostly Jamie's) and a lot more work. Claire wanted to see what they would build together.

****

Over the next couple of days, they searched Sam's possible hideouts. Ewan insisted on coming, but Claire only agreed if he swore to keep his distance if they found a fight. He was still suffering headaches, so the last thing he needed was to face Sam again. He had learned a strategy for fighting her so Claire said she'd take the lead if it came to it.

They moved in each location like a strike team, taking every precaution against another trap. It was doubtful she would prepare a second one, but Claire wouldn't take that chance. She refused to allow her team to get caught off guard again. Unfortunately, their search had turned up empty, both locations given to them showed no sign of people. They checked the surrounding areas, but again they found nothing.

Claire was thinking of their next move on the way back. It would suck to go back to regular jobs until they found something. And she was sure Serco wouldn't sit idle for long. They were on their way home after checking everywhere they could. It was late evening, and the sun hadalready set, only the glow of the street lights led them back home. Claire had the night ahead to come up with a new plan.

Arden then broke concentration. "Hey, I wanted to ask you something."

"Yeah, what's up?" Claire asked casually. Her thoughts were going in circles anyway.

"Are you doing all right? You've been kind of all over the place lately."

"Hmm?" She had to think about it. As long as she kept busy she felt fine. But anytime her mind wandered to Serco, her blood started to boil. She did her best to use this feeling as fuel in her search.

"I'll be fine. I look forward to ending this and getting back to whatever it is we'd normally do. It feels like we barely got started and now we're constantly chasing a killer."

"It'll be okay. Who knows, maybe AMTech will take him out before we even get close," Arden said lightheartedly.

Claire laughed at the idea of it being that easy. "I would like nothing more. But we can't hope someone else will get it done."

"I'm sure we'll do all the work and get none of the credit."

"I know you would enjoy the glory," Claire joked.

"I'm a Lindhelm. I have to live up to that. But I don't need to be famous or anything. I just want some good stories to tell."

They walked quietly on a while longer. They had a brief respite to enjoy the peaceful walk in the night, and they took it in.

"Who would have thought we'd get caught up in all this?" Claire said aloud, as much to herself as to Arden.

"Yeah, it's crazy. We came here and got thrown into a revolution instead of a simple life with the council."

Claire giggled at the idea that training with the council was a simple life.

Arden looked up and sincerely asked, "Hey, do you ever regret coming here?"

Claire genuinely had to think about after what they'd gone through. But when she remembered Jamie and Wren back in Haven, she smiled. "No. I'm glad we came here."

At last approaching home, Claire cleared her mind for the walk home. They could get a fresh start tomorrow. At least that was the plan until they heard a thunderous crash nearby. They stopped dead in their tracks and listened.

"Thunder?" Ewan said, but there were no clouds in the sky. Claire had once thought it was thunder, but she knew exactly what that sound was.

"It's him!" She drew her weapon and ran toward the source.

Chapter 18

Blowing Them Apart

"You better keep your head down and follow my lead."

This was the last instruction Will was given before they entered one of Verras Security's admin buildings. He felt his heart beating faster as they were now in the belly of the beast. Of all the buildings owned by Verras Security, this one held the central hub for the Emergency Rail System. As such, security was tight and anyone who didn't belong there shouldn't be able to make it past reception. Beyond that, every door required the correct ID to enter, and as far as Will knew, they didn't have any passes to get through. But Serco was oddly confident, and Will had no choice but to follow.

He nervously followed Serco, who sauntered up to reception like he belonged. He never explained how he was going to get past the front desk, but as long as he was keeping his gauntlets hidden in his pockets and acted natural, nobody would look at them twice as they came in.

Follow his lead. Will repeated this notion to himself. Whatever plan he had in mind he would need to stay calm and let Serco do all the talking.

"Can I help you?" asked the guard at the desk.

"Oh I'm certain you can," Serco started but was cut off as a back section of the room exploded into a bright flame. Will fell over from the sudden impact while everyone else in the room was put on alert. Several of the guards rushed over to anyone who was hurt and tried to assess what happened. Serco looked at the source as though he was surprised, then immediately punched out the guard in front of him and ran to the escalator with Will barely managing to find his feet and follow.

Within five minutes of entering, the whole building was in chaos. An alarm rang, and everyone started evacuating aside from all the security and the two intruders who ran up the escalator to the next floor.

It was on the second floor that the guards took notice of the crazy guy in a trench coat charging through the building. The moment somebody ordered him to stop, he received an explosive shot that knocked him across the room. Serco fired off several shots to keep the scrambled guards away. He didn't seem to care where he was aiming as explosions fired off one after another. The strategy, if one could call it that, worked as no guard got close to them.

Arriving on the fourth floor, Serco came to a stop and started as many fires in the surrounding area as possible. Will felt disturbed seeing the grin on Serco's face as he performed. He had his back to a secure door and pulled Will in to duck behind him. Before Will could catch a breath, Serco was yelling orders at him. "Get the door, kid! Unless you want to make your final stand here."

Will did what he was told and looked at the scanner next to the sealed door. It had a card reader but was flashing red to indicate it was locked down. Concentrating proved difficult with the increasing heat from the fires and the screams happening all around him—some of them coming from Serco, who had abandoned any sense of sanity. After another minute, Will had the door open for them and was promptly shoved inside.

The room was large with no windows, dozens of computer monitors, and a group of employees standing at the far end. Will didn't have time to take this in before he was then thrown next to the door again as there was another scanner inside for him to close it behind them. More fighting ensued as Serco beat down the two guards inside and drew his attention to the huddled employees who were gathered.

"I'd hate to fry your fancy equipment, so I'm going to politely ask you all to get out of here!" he screamed and let loose another stream of fire above them for good measure. The group scrambled over each other to another door which was opened for them. It may well have led to a bathroom, but the occupants weren't going to be picky as they were then locked inside.

"There. Now that the rabble is gone, we can get on with the show." Serco clapped his hands in excitement. Hesitantly, Will ran to the centermost console and worked his magic.

"Are you all set?" Serco asked.

After scanning the data he was being given, he replied. "Yes, I can keep the police and emergency services running in circles from here. I should be able to get you a transport soon."

Serco watched excitedly at the screens which flashed in front of them. The rail system also came with security cameras that linked to key locations. Serco skipped through the feeds until he settled on a street with a few people walking home.

"The nearest emergency station?" Serco asked without taking his eyes off the screen.

"Southmost Caery station," Will told him, and Serco giggled with joy.

"Excellent, my boy. I'll keep in contact and update you as I go. I can keep the young heroes busy as long as you follow the route we discussed."

This was the only part of the plan Will didn't understand, but he was willing to go along with it if it meant freeing his friends. "After you're done you'll head back here for me, right?"

"Yeah, yeah. By then your friends will be free, and I'll come get you. Now get me to that station quickly. I'll need to make one quick stop on the way."

****

Claire and the others found the source of the commotion in the service station near their home. Smoke was billowing out the windows, and nobody was around to help but them. Cautiously, Claire opened the front doors to investigate. The entrance was flashing red to indicate the danger they were walking into, but it was completely silent inside. They made their way slowly as not only Serco could be here, but it wouldn't look good if security showed up and found them at the scene. From their trip through here the last time, they knew a bit of where they were going. They surmised that this place was mainly used as an access point to the area as many other checkpoints would be around Verras.

"Yes!" They heard an excited voice above them. Before they could react, Serco fled from the overlook, and they could hear his laughter moving away. Claire immediately gave chase up the stairs. She arrived at the top as a shuttle embarked and she caught a glimpse of Serco waving goodbye inside. She looked around at all the injured guards and technicians scattered on the floor. The others took a moment to check on the injured, but Claire moved straight to a flashing console for some indication as to where he was going. It showed a map of the rail with several pathways highlighted. She was starting to make sense of it when Ewan joined in.

"There's something going on in the residential district. The call is for firefighters and any paramedics closest to help," she read aloud to him.

Ewan examined the report with her. "No one's been assigned to it. There's a marker for when a team is on its way but its blank here."

"We have to help them," Lilla exclaimed, only catching the tail end of the conversation. Claire saw another shuttle on standby like it was waiting for them but was still trying to process what was happening.

Is he attacking random points around the city? Is it a distraction for us?

"Damn him," she muttered and moved for the shuttle. She hated moving in without all the facts, but one fact she knew was people needed help, and they had to move fast.

At the front of the shuttle, Claire was faced with a console and some complicated-looking controls. Luckily, she didn't have to resort to hitting random buttons as the console was displaying the possible routes to take and had a flashing icon where the fire was. A few taps on the screen to set the course and the brakes released for them to leave.

Feeling a knot of anxiety, Claire hoped none of the other controls were important. The display in front of her kept up in real time and showed them moving to their objective.

"I just knew you couldn't resist joining me."

Claire froze the moment she heard his voice come through the speakers. She slowly looked up to see a second monitor with Serco waving fancily at her.

Seeing him again brought back a race of emotions, but she settled on angry.

"What is this!" she yelled at the monitor.

From his own shuttle, Serco smiled up at her. "Oh I was out for a stroll, and I happened upon this train, and I thought to myself, this could be fun."

Claire turned and eyed the emergency brake, wondering if it was safer to stop things now.

"I wouldn't shy away if I were you. You may not have been prepared for this, but if it's any consolation, the emergency call is real, and those people need your help."

"What are you up to?" she asked again.

"I'm doing exactly what I said I would. I'm showing you what it means to be a hero." Yet again with that word, there was a sly grin that followed. "So here's your first scenario. An apartment complex has mysteriously burst into flames with no one coming to help. You must put out the fire, help the residents escape, and make it back to the train before the next disaster."

Claire's blood ran cold as she caught the meaning of his words. "Next disaster?"

"Of course, there has to be more, or it wouldn't be much of a challenge now would it?"

What have we walked into?

Ewan moved in to question him. "You can't keep us running around the city at your whim. Security will shut your train down."

Serco gasped for a moment at the idea, then immediately shook his head and dismissed it. "Nope, nope, nope. Well maybe given enough time, but my boy William is in full control of the shuttles, and he can guide us wherever we're needed. So the nefarious Daniel Serco will wreak havoc and you the gallant heroes will chase and attempt to stop him. Not only that, but he can keep any security and service teams running in circles until we conclude this exercise."

Claire looked up in confusion. "William? You mean Will, why would he—"

"There's no time!" Arden informed them as the shuttle came to a halt. Claire snapped out of her daze and saw across from her was a burning building as Serco promised. She followed the others out through the stairs that lowered from the back carriage, to rush into a scene that Serco had prepared for them.

✳✳✳✳

Despite the circumstances, they wasted no time in heading into the fire. Arden used his mace to knock down the front doors from a distance, but the entire bottom floor was ablaze. Lilla and Claire proceeded to blast as much wind as they could manage into the entryway, which cleared some of the way to the stairs.

Claire turned to Ewan. "Can you conjure water?"

Ewan briefly hesitated since he hadn't kept up the practice. "I can."

"Do what you can to clear the entrance. The rest of us will lead people out." With her orders given, Claire swung one more gust to clear the stairs and make her way up with Lilla and Arden following behind.

Ewan couldn't control the elements, but he could conjure them when needed. He aimed to create his glyphs to summon the water. It took some concentration as he was only starting to practice making glyphs from a distance. Despite the intense heat and lack of visibility, he felt his magic take form around the stairs. Instead of his usual traps, he visualized the water erupting from it. After a short delay, water formed as the glyph shrank and then spread across the floor to douse the flames. It was more of a puddle than an eruption, but he couldn't argue with the result. Within the entryway, the residents were making their way down to him. If they had more time, they could have put out the rest of the fire in the building, but they had to get back to the shuttle before Serco caused more damage.

With everyone cleared out, a few only hesitated to watch the curious sight of four mages jumping back on an emergency shuttle and speeding off. Already there was another location on the map flashing for their attention, so Claire set their course.

"Time to spare that was some good hustle out there," Serco complimented them.

"You have to stop this. Why drag innocent people into your obsession just face me and be done with it!" Claire demanded.

Serco laughed at that idea. "And what would that accomplish? You can't jump right into fighting the main villain. It's not the destination that teaches you but the journey."

Agh. Why am I even trying with this lunatic? she thought, frustrated. Giving up on that, she joined Ewan who was eyeing the map.

"Do you see anything useful?"

Ewan shook his head. "I was hoping there would be a point to intercept him, but he's too far ahead and moving to a different track." He pointed to his location. Claire hadn't seen it before, but after expanding the map, they could see the other train ahead of them. There were several others scattered on the rails. She zoomed out more to get a better look, but they were all running in circles, and they wouldn't encounter another for a while.

With some time left, Lilla tried a different approach. "Will?"

Claire stuck to the map but listened intently.

"Will, you need to stop this. You're going to get people killed. I know you don't want to hurt anybody so please stop, and we can help you," she pleaded, but the speakers remained silent.

Serco appeared to be waiting for a reply with them but soon shrugged. "I guess he can't hear you. He must be busy keeping the trains running. Of course I can contact him for you." He put his hand to a speaker on his ear. "Hey, kid, you there?" After a muffled response he continued. "Yeah, I just want to tell you that you're doing a great job. Keep it up."

The mockery of their situation was running their tempers high. Lilla turned away from him and calmed herself. Not so controlled, Claire looked back to the screen and glared at him. *How can he take so much pleasure from this?*

"All right. Now that you're all warmed up, we can jump straight to the best part," Serco announced.

None of them were dignifying him with a response anymore.

"Come on, guys, where's your energy gone? You were so chatty before. You're gonna need to pull it together because you have a very important choice to make."

Arden was the only one bold enough to ask as Claire was still trying to get her head together. "What choice?"

"The choice will be on young Claire's shoulders, but you can always weigh in. You've done well so far. You've rushed into danger to save innocent lives, but of course, you've done this all before. You're still missing one crucial aspect of heroism. Sacrifice."

Now he had all their attention. The dread of being led by Serco was always there, but this was the moment they would learn how disturbed this game would become.

"A true hero needs to make hard choices. To make sure you're ready for the future, I'm going to present you with that choice."

Another flashing icon appeared on the map; this one was yellow and in a different direction to the first. Following his route, Ewan could see Serco's train would intercept the yellow icon while they would head to the red. Ewan's eyes widened as he recognized the yellow location. "What is this?" Ewan questioned.

"This is a split path. At this very moment, I am heading to a certain abandoned music venue where the mages of Haven have set themselves back up. When I arrive, I plan to go in personally and kill everyone I find."

"No!" Lilla screamed first. "They aren't part of this anymore. You can't kill them!"

"Well, that's where your choice comes in!" Serco yelled back, causing a silence on the shuttle. "You'll see a lever on the console in front of you which controls the rail you'll stay on. If you hit it left, you'll head to a hospital which is somewhat on fire, and the main entrance has suddenly collapsed. If you hit the lever to the right, you'll make it to New Haven before I get there, giving you the chance to face me and save your new friends. Now make your choice, who will you save and who will you let die? You can't save them all."

Each of the four had reached a breaking point. Ewan desperately searched the map for somewhere else to go or a way to reach Serco's train. Lilla moved to the window somehow hoping his train would appear and she could shoot him down. Arden started shouting at the monitor as if he could convince Serco to stop.

Claire blocked it all out and looked in horror at Serco grinning down on them. She could see how satisfied he was watching his game play out.

It's like he's not even human.

Turning away, Claire looked at the lever. The full weight of this decision was on her shoulders. Her mind was surprisingly quiet. The logical part of her told her what should be done; it didn't matter what choice was made so long as she made a choice. But her emotional side was screaming for a third option. She looked to the map and saw there was some time remaining. She followed Ewan's lead to scan the map and resigned herself to spending the remaining minutes desperate for another way…no matter how slim, if there something else they could try.

Claire knew the choice she was going to make. But hitting that lever felt like admitting defeat. It felt like condemning those people to die all because Serco took an interest in her.

Nothing. They're all going to die because I got involved. I can't protect anyone. I wanted to save people, and I've doomed them instead.

Claire almost broke completely until she saw something. She followed its path on the map a few seconds longer to be sure. It was a slim chance, and she may not be reading it right, but a chance is all she wanted. Without any further thinking, she forcefully hit the lever left and walked away toward the next carriage. The others hadn't realized what happened and even Serco was left silent at the sudden move. He never expected her to make this choice with such a steely resolve.

"Arden, Lilla, get to that hospital and save those people. Ewan, I need a boost." Without waiting for a response, she moved to the next carriage. Ewan quickly followed, and Arden and Lilla were left speechless. As they shook it off though, they put their faith in Claire that she had some reason behind her.

Claire unsheathed her sword and stabbed into a panel on the roof of the carriage, then bashed it open. She gave a quick glance back to Ewan. "Follow me."

Climbing on top of the carriage, the two had to take a moment to adjust to the high wind threatening to throw them off the train. They moved up and crouched to steady themselves.

Ewan's mind raced to try to figure out what Claire was doing, but he couldn't piece it together. "There was no chance to intercept Serco's train! So where are we going?" he shouted over the wind.

"We're intercepting a different train!" she replied. "Past the next junction, there's a point where another train will pull up across the street from us. I need you to help me jump to it!"

"What other train?"

"I saw it on the map! It's running in circles right now!" she said, pausing for breath after each explanation. "It won't go to New Haven, but it should come close to Serco's train further down!"

Ewan was surprised she caught that, but something in her words made him worry. "Come close?"

Claire's expression changed for a second, but she looked him in the eye with as much confidence as she could muster. "It's the only chance we have to save everyone; I had to take it. I can knock him off his route while the rest of you go to the hospital."

There wasn't any time for debate as the train they were on reached the junction and turned left. Ewan and Claire waited to see if her prediction came true. They turned another corner which brought to a long wide open street with another train running on the opposite side a short distance ahead of them. Claire let out a breath she was holding and readied herself for the jump. It was clear to them their train was catching up to it and would soon run side by side. Claire was right in bringing Ewan as the gap between them was far too big to jump on her own.

"Ready?" She looked to him.

Trusting in her plan, Ewan charged up a platform beneath her as she prepared to jump. With their timing synchronized, the glyph pushed her across while Claire put all her strength in her legs to make it. With any fear forgotten, Claire flew across the street to the fast-moving train and came crashing down on it. Initially landing on her feet, she immediately fell back and rolled down the train. She reached out and grabbed hold to stop herself falling off. With time to catch her breath, she pulled herself up to a crouch again, just in time for Ewan to land a little more gracefully behind her.

"What are you doing!" she yelled. "You were supposed to go to the hospital!"

The minute Ewan was told this part of the plan, he knew he wasn't going along with it. "I will not let you face Serco without backup. You'll need me."

Since it was obviously too late to argue, Claire proceeded up the train for a better vantage. The two of them were speeding across the city, ready to jump trains again. Claire quickly tried to think if they could disable Serco's train from a distance when they saw it, but neither of them had enough firepower for that. The plan was put together in seconds, so she was mostly improvising from here.

The train passed street after street while Claire tried to remember each point on the map as it passed. Visualizing it, she remembered the routes and how there was only a small chance to intercept.

What if we're too late? she heard in her head and tried to push the thought away. *What if I made the wrong choice?* Again she gritted her teeth and tried to look ahead as more and more time passed.

We're not going to make it.

Chapter 19

The Greatest Plans of Psychopaths

Serco watched the drama unfold in each of the players in his exercise. He was building an idea of their personalities so far, but it was Claire that he focused on.

What decision will you make? More importantly, can you make a decision at all?

He was didn't know how to react when Claire slammed the lever one way and immediately stormed off. He was expecting her to curse his name, to despair over the horrible scenario laid before her, but this?

Does she think I was bluffing maybe? Or that the remaining mages can hold their own against me?

No. He grinned. *She's not stupid. She understands full well the choice she's made.*

His smile grew, and soon he broke out into laughter. "Yes, Claire, that's the way. Don't lament over what could have been. Instead, follow the path you choose for yourself!" It seemed they weren't listening anymore, but that didn't matter. The game was almost over, all that was left was for them to rally with this sense of loss and hunt him down for a dramatic ending. With a sense of pride in his young trainee, Serco readied himself for New Haven.

Serco sat back and waited as there was still a little time for him. "It seems there's no safe haven today," he joked to himself.

His humor was interrupted by a crash on the roof. Instinctively, he whipped his head to the monitor to see only two mages on screen.

No, it's not them. Even if they did turn right, it would take them far too long to reach me.

Nevertheless, he heard hard, heavy footsteps on the roof. Serco hurriedly moved toward the roof hatch, but before he reached it, he felt a tingle as a small charge ran through the train. He heard a crackle of electricity shooting through the front of the train, causing the console to explode into sparks.

The roof hatch flew off violently, and Serco climbed up to find an armored hitchhiker standing at the front. He wore sleek, dark armor all over his body with a yellow, glowing visor watching Serco closely.

"What are you supposed to be?" Serco asked, annoyed at the interruption.

"I'm the one who will stop your insane rampage," the armored stranger declared.

"What business is it of yours?"

"I've told you before, you're not welcome in my city."

Stunned for a moment, Serco realized what he was looking at. "Chief Ghehara. I didn't expect to see you here."

"You wanted to see the big guns, didn't you?" Ghehara replied. His voice was filtered, but it was unmistakably his.

"Too late, Chief. I lost interest in your lot," he said and extended his arms theatrically. "I found a new game to play as you can see."

"Well, it ends here."

Serco grimaced at him as he clearly wasn't impressed. "You better leave before I cook you in that armor of yours."

Unfazed by the threat, Ghehara braced himself. "Come and try."

Taking him up on his offer, Serco immediately let loose his personal flamethrower, which engulfed Ghehara. Usually, this kind of interference would amuse Serco, but he didn't have the time to waste, so there was no joy taken while his opponent disappeared into the fire. Serco halted his attack to see what remained of the chief, but as soon the flames dispersed, Ghehara retaliated by firing the built-in spikes from his gloves. These shot past Serco who narrowly managed to dodge them. He heard another crackle from the electricity charged through them as they flew past his face. He turned back to see his opponent completely unharmed and moving in close. Serco jumped back to avoid close combat. He moved quickly but carefully to not lose his footing at such a high speed and retreated to the second carriage.

"Fireproof," he grunted. *I guess that should have been obvious. Fine, then I'll blow you off the train!* He fired off his explosive shots, but the armored soldier braced himself and took them dead-on. Serco was careful not to destroy the train, but it would be more than enough to blast this nuisance far away from him. After a few large explosions, Serco was infuriated to see not only was Ghehara unharmed, but he hadn't even budged. Once again Ghehara moved up close, and this time Serco welcomed the hand to hand.

With his steel hands, he blocked the armored punches and, moving faster than his opponent, he laid into Ghehara's helmet with flames engulfing his gauntlets. From the impacts being dealt, Serco was certain this was having an effect. But it wouldn't matter as Ghehara landed some hits of his own and Serco received a shock with every hit. After taking a few hits, Serco was knocked back onto the third and final carriage.

On his side, Serco had to recover as Ghehara nearly crashed down on him. Rather than waste his energy hitting back, he continued to dodge back and circle around. Serco hit him with an explosive shot close up to give him a moment to break away. He caught his breath, and looking a bit battered, he faced Ghehara again with a smirk. "You surprised me, I'll give you that. Never thought you'd be able to keep up with me using your little toys."

"You're as smug as ever, even when you're losing."

"Heh. Yeah, if we keep going like this I might lose. But I've wasted enough time, so this is goodbye, Chief Ghehara."

Serco raised his hand to Ghehara to finish things off. As he focused, an ominous orange glow appeared on Ghehara's armor. It pulsed gently like a life of its own. But it wasn't touching the armor and instead seemed repelled by it. Serco's smile dropped, and he was left staring in disbelief.

It was Ghehara's turn to be smug. "There's a reason it's called anti-magic, Serco. I know all about your little trick, and we felt confident it wouldn't work on this armor." He moved his hand into the glow, and it was pushed away and dissolved from the touch.

"Now that we're done playing games, I'm gonna put you in the deepest cell I can find and hope I never see your arrogant face again!" He raised his hand, and another volley of spikes flew and clipped Serco in the shoulder, causing a jolt of pain. He fell back and moved back onto the middle carriage. Enraged at his failure to kill the chief Serco turned and targeted the rear carriage. Before Ghehara could move, the rail blew, and his carriage buckled and broke off from the rest of the train. It was knocked into the air from the explosive. Ghehara's feet remained secured to the train in midair until he broke off to land on the rails.

Serco stood and watched Ghehara recover and run as if he could catch up to the train. There was still a chance for his plan to get back on track although he lamented leaving the chief alive. Serco watched Ghehara for a moment longer, hoping he could feel somewhat satisfied leaving him in the dust.

****

After sitting in dread of being too late, Claire's shuttle pulled around the corner, and they caught sight of Serco on top of his train. With that feeling gone, Claire focused on the task at hand, somehow knocking Serco off the train to stop his attack. Easier said than done. If he saw her coming, he could shoot her out of the sky with ease, and they didn't have enough firepower between them to hit him off from this distance. Before she could formulate a strategy, however, she instead bore witness to an armored soldier speeding after the train.

Even after being knocked off, Ghehara refused to give up. He quickly magnetized his boots to the rail and used the current to propel himself after the train. Electricity buzzed around his legs, and even through the suit, he felt a tingle as the current in the rail became one with his armor. He easily picked up speed and was catching up to a surprised and likely furious Serco. There was a reason this technology was still experimental, and now he was pushing both it and his body to their limit. But he would stop at nothing to end this madness, as long as he has the strength to stand he would continue to chase Serco down.

As expected, a volley of explosives was being fired toward him, but he dodged or simply charged through each one. When it was clear Serco was trying to destroy the rail to stop his pursuit, he jumped to the opposite rail to keep up.

"Who is that?" Ewan mused out loud.

Claire ignored the question as they would find no answer here. "If I use the wind as a boost, can you get me over there?"

"Possibly, but I won't be able to follow. It would be crazy to jump in the middle of that."

"You wanted me to have backup," Claire started and pointed to the man riding the rails, "there's my backup. We can still finish this."

Ewan looked at Claire for what felt like the longest time, and against his better judgment, he agreed to help.

"Don't worry. Worst-case scenario, I miss the jump, and it will hurt…a lot."

Ewan wondered if that was one of the better scenarios, but despite that, he readied his platform.

****

The last thing Serco needed was more interruptions, but that's exactly what he received as Will called on the radio. "We have a problem with the train."

"I'm working on it!" Serco howled in response as he continued to shoot at Ghehara.

"Not the armored guy, I mean the train. I can't stop it. You're going to speed right past your next target."

Serco's mind raced for a way to fix this mess. He couldn't stop as long as Ghehara was in pursuit, and they were only minutes from his target. It was over. Ghehara ruined the game; now there were no consequences for Claire's choice. All that work for nothing. But right at this moment, he would trade it all for the chance to destroy the man who did this. With one more attempt, he focused from his palms to destroy the rail and shake off Ghehara.

With so many distractions, he didn't see Claire until she came spiraling through the air toward him. He barely had time to look up as her feet slammed into him, sending them both rolling across the carriage. Claire's momentum took her across to the front of the train, but she recovered and turned to face Serco with her sword drawn.

At the same time, Ghehara managed to land back on the speeding train while Serco stood between them with one hand pointed at each of them. Serco looked between the two of them, ready for any movement but they both waited and watched. His eyes narrowed at Claire. *You idiot. You really don't understand sacrifice, do you?*

With another turn, they sailed past New Haven and his plan was in ruins. Ghehara edged forward and received more fire for his effort. Glimpsing movement from the other side, he fired an explosive at Claire which she promptly ducked, and the three fighters held their position.

With no choice but to retreat, Serco saw they were nearing his first hideout. If he could make it to there, his escape was guaranteed. He cautiously lowered his arms and aimed his palms to face the ground. He would need to time this perfectly; thankfully his two opponents were holding their position. Reaching his mark, the train slowed to turn, but the second he stepped forward an attack was thrown from both sides.

An instant before a strike could land, Serco was propelled out of the way as the train exploded beneath them. The train and its three passengers were thrown off the track and flew out into the street. Flying through the air, Serco managed to fire another shot and blast through a wall in front of him.

Claire, with her sword already out, jammed it into the wall to catch herself. She instantly curled up as the burning train crashed below her. After a moment to check she was unharmed, Claire tried to make a quick survey of the destroyed train on the streets below. There were screams from the shock, but from her vantage, it looked as if no one was hurt, luckily the streets were mostly barren, or it would have been a disaster. Deciding if she should pursue, she caught a glimpse of the armored man climbing the building to where Serco smashed through. It seemed he wasn't wasting any time, so she too climbed across to back him up.

****

It was a close jump as Serco slammed through the falling debris. It wasn't completely accurate as instead of landing in his studio, he landed in the young couple's a few doors over. They were promptly huddled in the corner after a man came flying through the wall, and without saying a word, the man got up and walked out the door. Moments later he was followed by an armored soldier, who also ignored the couple hiding from the intruders.

Upon jumping through the hole, Claire immediately heard a scream and whipped around to face whatever danger was there. She only found a terrified couple who were receiving more and more strange visitors. Realizing she was brandishing a weapon at them, Claire quickly apologized and left to find Serco.

She entered a hallway in poor condition; it was an unkempt building even before they came smashing through it. Looking around for the trail to follow, she heard heavy footsteps that must have belonged to her mystery partner. Further down the hall, there was more banging and the sounds of a struggle.

It was easy to follow as there were smoldering flames leading up to a bashed-in door. Claire looked into the doorway and only caught a glimpse of Serco's furious expression before she slammed herself to the side as fire shot out the doorway and destroyed the opposite wall where she stood. More struggles from inside, Claire held back long enough to charge her sword and moved swiftly in. She ducked in low and rolled inside to avoid the next spray of fire. Before he could attack again, Claire swung the sword and let loose her kinetic impact. It hit Serco clear in his torso and forced him back. Before he could recover, he got hit by an electric shock from the side that threw him across the floor.

Claire still didn't know who the armored soldier was, but he packed more of a punch than she did. The two stood side by side as Serco struggled on the ground.

"You've lost, Serco. Give it up," Claire demanded.

Serco looked up at them defiantly. "No, it's not over. This is a pathetic ending. I won't allow it!"

But Serco looked beat, and the two facing him were in a much better condition to fight. Claire felt confident they could beat him. As they were ready for him to try something, however, they were caught off guard by something else.

A deafening sound wave hit the three of them hard. Having experienced this a few times now, Claire managed to turn her head and see the source as Sam and Hunter stood in a newly revealed doorway.

In the same instant, everyone made a move. Knowing where this would lead, Claire instantly went to attack the two, but Hunter moved faster than her and hurled her across the room. Ghehara fired his charged shot at Hunter before he could attempt to throw the chief, but it was all for naught as Serco ended any chance of a fight right there.

In the short time Ghehara and Claire faced their new opponents, Serco focused his magic once more into the ground. It sounded as if everything was exploding at once, and the floor beneath Ghehara and Claire broke away and left them to fall with half the roof from three floors above caving in on them.

"This way!" Sam called to Serco to join them.

Reluctantly, he picked himself up and followed as they were at his exit anyway.

Serco had planned this trick well in advance, so it was easy for him to topple the building in such a way that one half of the room remained fairly intact while the other collapsed on his intended victim. His half of the room even contained an access ladder which, as his usual method of travel lead underground beneath the city.

****

After being sure she wasn't getting crushed, Claire attempted to move under the rubble. As determined as she was, there was no chance of her breaking through and fighting again, so she resigned herself to slowly crawling out. After carefully maneuvering through the rubble into a more open space, she found that part of the roof was being held up by her new friend.

"Are you all right?" she managed to ask.

"I'm...not...hurt." He struggled to answer because of weight bearing down on him. She had guessed what the suit he was wearing was, and so even with the filtered voice, she recognized it as Chief Ghehara.

"Hold on. I'm going to see if I can shift the weight off of you." Claire looked at the amount he was holding and sent her magic out to feel her way through it. The same way mages could move things with their mind, she could also feel along it and get a bearing of what was above her. The rubble was slanted, and some of it was already falling off, so it only needed a little push. She found a sweet spot and moved as if she was physically pulling it to shift enough of the roof. Using the momentum, more and more of the rubble slid its way off and crashed onto the rest outside the building, allowing Ghehara to push back and release them. The physical strain had taken its toll as he took his time to walk out and into the open. Claire offered to help, but he refused and made his way over to an intact area of the room.

They were left on the second floor with a collapsed wall leading to the street and a mountain of rubble behind them. Claire checked the ground below, and it looked easy enough to leave when she was ready. Serco was clearly in the wind, and unless Ghehara's men happened upon him, it was clear he would get away once again.

Despite the high-speed train, firefight, and collapsed building, Claire was miraculously unharmed. She turned to the chief who had taken a beating throughout the entire ordeal.

"The tech armor, it's really impressive."

Ignoring the compliment, Ghehara removed his helmet and faced her. He looked exhausted, and his skin had taken on a gray hue since she last saw him. It didn't look like it was due to the fight. It looked as though he was like this since the battle started; it didn't look normal. "What were you doing here?" he asked harshly.

"I was trying to stop him," she answered, ignoring his tone.

Ghehara walked closer to her as though he was going to start a fight. "I told you to say out of this. This is my job. You'll only get in the way."

Claire was taken aback by this, but she tried not to show it. "We have a better chance of taking him together. We could—"

"No!" he ordered suddenly. "I'm telling you to stay out of our way, or I'll arrest you myself. I'm only letting you leave here now out of respect for saving my life before. But this is your last warning. You need to leave before my men arrive and find you here." Without giving her a chance to answer, he gently pushed her back, and she fell to the street. Literally landing on her ass for what felt like the third time today, Claire looked up at the chief in the broken wall as he walked away.

I can't believe him, she thought angrily. *We could work together on this; we would have a much better chance. Does he hate mages as well?*

Rather than sit and stew, she managed to brush herself off and start the long walk back to find her team.

****

His plan truly destroyed, Serco made his way through the sewers with Sam leading the way. It seemed she had three others with her, so her revolution was not truly dead yet. Not that it mattered to Serco. Their fight no longer interested him. He fumed as he considered this failed operation, and on top of that, he had someone nattering in his ear.

"They're cutting through the door. I can't get out of here. Serco, what do I do?" Will was clearly panicking, but Serco ignored him. He callously threw the earpiece to Sam, no longer caring what happened to Will.

Sam took the earpiece and listened. "William? What's going on? Where are you?"

"Boss? Oh, I'm so glad you're here. I'm still stuck in the security terminal, but they're breaking in. I don't know what to do. Everything fell apart."

"You did all this to rescue our people, didn't you?"

"It didn't work," he answered miserably. "If we don't do something, I'll get caught too."

Sam felt sympathetic to his predicament. She held up the earpiece once more to answer him. "It was a valiant effort. I appreciate all the work you've done for our cause." With that, she dropped the earpiece and crushed it under her boot. Leaving a stranded Will alone and afraid.

****

After gaining distance from the scene, Sam led them into a much wider tunnel and told everyone to rest for a moment before continuing. Serco slumped against a pillar for support and reflected on the past few hours. Claire made the choice but felt none of the consequences. It was a valiant effort she made to catch his train, but he was confident she would have failed if not for Ghehara's interference. Yes, overall she performed her role perfectly, and he hadn't given up on her yet.

Sam instructed the others to sit back and wait while she talked to Serco. The couple with them, Tanya and Marcus, did as they were told and gave them some distance. However, the other boy, Jacob, stayed close to weigh in on the conversation. Sam meant to talk to him properly as he didn't seem as good at following her orders.

They left Tanya and Marcus so they could speak to Serco and hopefully convince him to join them again. Serco supported himself against a wall and regarded them coldly. "What were you even doing there?"

"We were camped out waiting for you. It was the only hideout I knew you had," Sam answered without reacting to his mood.

"You wasted your time. I'm not interested in you anymore."

Sam simply scowled at him, but Jacob jumped in. "Hey, man. From the sounds of it, we saved you. You should show some respect!" Before Sam could silence him, Serco stood straight and stared the boy down.

"Oh, you picked the wrong day to fly off the handle." He faced his open hand toward him, and the boy froze and started sweating profusely. "All of you pay close attention. I don't care about any of you or your pointless fight!"

Sam did her best to keep her cool as getting offended would accomplish nothing. She still needed him. "Serco, that's enough. Let him go."

Serco held his grip, and Jacob started shaking as he could feel the pressure building inside. He started pleading as Serco's victims often did. "What are you doing? Stop please!"

"Serco, stop this. Let him go," Sam demanded.

Serco looked at Sam with all his anger now aimed at her and her group. "You really have no idea what you've gotten involved in. I think you need a demonstration." Serco took a breath and regained his composure but didn't release his hold on Jacob. Instead, he looked him dead in the eye. "Goodbye, whoever you are."

"Serco, that's eno—" Sam never finished her sentence as before her eyes the boy who promised to follow her lead coughed up blood and crumbled to the floor. The amount of blood that pooled was a clear sign that he was dead.

Witnessing this, Tanya screamed. Marcus backed into the wall and slid down terrified while Sam and Hunter stood in shock.

"You never even learned who you were dealing with, did you? I should dispose of you all right here." Serco pointed a hand each at Sam and Hunter, and they both felt the same pressure Jacob must have felt. Hunter looked desperately toward Sam and saw the sudden fear in her eyes.

"But..." Serco continued. "You can still be useful to me," he said reluctantly and let them go. Sam sank to her knees and Hunter ran to her side. Serco regarded them both and the two remaining mages with them.

"Now, if you can pull yourself together, we have work to do."

Chapter 20

The Calm

"It sounds like you and your group are more than capable. I would be more than happy to hire your services for this expedition," Professor Mansen told the young woman in front of him. As with everything, he held this meeting in his office in the library to get more work done. It was nearly time to leave, though, for an expedition had been planning to an ancient temple north of the city. The ruins had been surveyed many times before, but recently one of his charges had discovered a hidden door which could lead to a bigger discovery. They had learned much of the region's history through this temple, and it was possible they had only scratched the surface.

This was the second meeting between these two as he was first approached by this woman when he was still finalizing the details of the project. She seemed most eager to join them, and they required the protection against any creatures that would see their party as easy prey.

"I must say…" he continued. "I am lucky you came along. I did have someone else in mind for the job, but it seems they were busy. I much prefer to hire young adventurers like yourself. It reminds me of my early days in archaeology. Why, where else will you find such valuable experience in the field, eh?"

"I am happy for the opportunity, Professor. We're very curious to see these ruins up close," the girl told him in a quiet, friendly manner.

Pleased with her enthusiasm, he handed his guest a cup of tea. "Tell me, Professor. How much do you know about the ruins we're studying?" he asked, eager to gauge her interest.

The girl took a sip of her tea and confidently answered. "People call them the ruins of Akrath, named after the tribe we think built the temple. The temple was built to honor Mordecai, a man who held great power over the land thousands of years ago. That's about all I know from looking into it," she said and put the cup down in its saucer.

"You've done your homework. I'm glad to see you're interested in history."

"May I ask what it is you think we'll find?" She couldn't help but lean forward.

"It could be any number of things hidden away. Mordecai is one of the most prominent figures in ancient history. You can find traces of his lineage all over the continent from the western reaches to Dottinheim and even the southern Wasteland. Personally, what I hope for is to learn as much as we can about this man. As we've never found where he was buried, it's possible his corpse is hidden in the very chamber we're about to unearth!"

"I see," she replied and sat back to finish her tea. She drained it quickly and stood to leave. "So we'll meet in two days to set out?"

The professor nodded and settled back at his desk. He always ended up pacing while talking about his work.

Once she had left, he sat back and looked forward to the expedition.

Although not who I expected, she is an intelligent and polite young woman. Yes, I believe this will work well.

Leaving the library, the girl immediately pulled a hood over her face in public and avoided eye contact with anyone around. It was possible that Ghehara had seen her face when they rescued Serco, and she couldn't risk getting caught in the open.

What a stupid old man, Sam thought as she left the library behind. *He wastes his time doting in the past and ignoring the problems in the here and now.* She didn't care at all about the history of Dottinheim. But she knew he would ask so she memorized what she could about the temple. It had to be her that met with the professor though; the others couldn't keep up appearances like she could. She completely hid her frustration that he couldn't confirm what they would find in the temple. Without that information, they were acting on Serco's word alone.

It had been weeks since he wreaked havoc in the city, and people were still dealing with the aftermath. Sam hoped that her father would be struggling to deal with this after their security was hacked and they failed to protect their citizens. It would be the only silver lining for her. Sam's operation had fallen apart, and everyone but Hunter and the stragglers Tanya and Marcus had left her. It was a miracle she convinced them to stay considering what happened to Jacob. But she had no choice; if Serco couldn't give her what she wanted, he might as well kill her too. He agreed to give her everything in exchange for their help. All her hopes lay in the promises of a madman.

Sam moved quickly downtown and went back to Tanya's house. It was the only place left to hide. She returned to find the three of them waiting eagerly for her.

"Are we going ahead then?" Hunter asked while facing the window.

"Yes, we'll meet with them in two days to leave Verras."

Tanya looked anxiously to Marcus, and Sam sensed the uncertainty passing between them. "It'll be all right," she assured them. "We'll get what we need and leave. We won't have to deal with Serco after this."

Only Marcus nodded and led Tanya out for some air.

Sam joined Hunter at the window and looked over the city. "Do you think they'll stay with us?" she asked.

"After what they saw, I'm surprised they stayed at all."

Sam had to keep herself from shuddering at the mention of it. What they had witnessed shook her, and the fear of death followed soon after. But they were spared so Serco could use them to his own ends. Sam wouldn't go along with that though. She didn't care about Serco's ridiculous plan any more than he cared about their plight. But the promise to crush her father's regime was enough to come to an agreement. So she told Hunter they would go along with him for the time being. The others took some convincing, but Hunter said he'd follow her lead without hesitation.

But he seemed oddly somber. He gazed out the window with a much softer expression.

"Emil. I can tell something's weighing on you," she started. "If you have something to say, you should say it now. It might be your last chance for a while."

Hunter closed his eyes as though he was struggling to find the words.

"It's not too late for us," he said suddenly.

For a rare moment, Sam was speechless, unsure of what he meant.

"We don't have to follow Serco into this madness. We could leave Verras behind and start over somewhere else."

Sam was stunned, but she then stood back defensively. "You want to leave too? To run out on everything we've done?"

"I want this for you. I don't want you to feel like you have no choice in this. You don't have to throw your life away to stop your father."

"No! I refuse to run away after everything I've sacrificed. I will not stop until I finish what we started!" She looked at Hunter with a cold stare. "If you want to leave, then leave. It'll be one more traitor that I can put behind me." Sam turned away, no longer able to face him.

"Sam," he said quietly and moved to her side. "I won't ever betray you, and I won't ever leave you. My life is yours, and I will stay by your side no matter where it takes us. I swear to you." He gently put his hand on her shoulder.

Sam breathed a sigh of relief and turned to acknowledge him. "Get your gear ready for the trip. I want us to be prepared."

****

The weather was growing fouler as Chief Ghehara made his way to AMTech labs. It was the middle of the afternoon, but the sky was dark, and the wind picked up like a storm was approaching. The chief didn't believe in superstitions but thinking a storm is coming seemed like a bad sign. Serco had caused so much damage and slipped away again and again. He lamented to think what it would take to finally bring him in. He entered the building, but instead of going down into the labs, he took the elevator up.

He was heading up to a private conference room at Director Walker's request. It had been some time since he has met with his old friend as the director had been away making deals with other businesses in Dottinheim. He said he was acquiring the materials required for more tech armor. Eren couldn't hazard a guess at what was necessary to make a technology that repels magic. For now, he didn't need to know as this meeting was clearly to discuss his use of the prototype armor and Serco's attacks. He hoped his friend would accept that the choice he made was a necessary one.

The chief found Doctor Lambert already waiting for him. His head drooped as though he was ready to pass out in the chair but instantly turned to greet Ghehara.

"Chief Ghehara, you look well. I take it the physical symptoms have dissipated."

Ghehara touched his face as if to check again. His normal pallor had returned, and he didn't feel as tense as he had a week ago.

"Yes, it seems the side effects are gone. I take it you'll have that fixed before the next volunteers?"

Before he could answer, or more likely duck the question, a secretary approached to inform them the director was ready. The professor hurried inside, leaving Ghehara sure that the answer was no.

Director Corrin Walker stood behind his desk in his business suit as they came in. He maintained his usual calm but stern expression and waited for the doctor and his friend to line up in front of him. They had been friends since college, and both were determined to make a difference in Verras in their own way. Ghehara preferred the hands-on approach while Walker took a more political route. Despite their different methods, the two had always worked together to gain the best result. But Ghehara wasn't expecting to be let off easy. He went ahead and tested the armor with Doctor Lambert, without Walker's knowledge. And so here they both stood in front of the man. Ghehara stood firmly while Lambert was slouched over waiting to get this over with.

"You know why I called you both here?" he asked in his usual gruff manner.

The doctor grinned at the question. "You're curious as to how the armor performed."

"I'm curious as to why you went ahead with this without my authorization."

The doctor fell silent, so Ghehara stepped in. "The situation was desperate. Without the armor, we don't have the firepower needed to stop Serco."

"Hmph. It's lucky for you this turned out as well as it did. I mostly disapprove that you volunteered yourself for such an unstable procedure."

"I understood the risks, that's why I couldn't ask any of my men to do it."

"Did you understand the risks?" Walker fired back. "I don't think I understand what kind of genetic manipulation this one does." The doctor looked away from Walker's glare. The director shook his head and sat, urging them to do the same.

"At the very least you two owe me a status update. How did the prototype perform? I understand it was put under considerable strain on its first run."

The doctor jumped at the chance to talk about his creation; it was the first time he sounded invested. "Oh it was beyond my expectations. The armor itself repelled any magic fired at it with none of it reaching the user. The teslapack it is equipped with ran smoothly. Even with your little stunt of magnetizing to the rails, it easily maintained power within the suit. We gave the chief a medical check when he returned. He took some shocks when it was being charged, but thanks to the markers planted in his body, the damage was minimal."

Walker frowned at the doctor. "How minimal?"

"I was fine. Even when pushing the suit to its maximum, I only received a few small jolts," Ghehara answered.

Walker considered this for a moment, but he accepted his friend's judgment. "All right then. I will catch up on your more detailed report at a later date. What about Serco. Do you have any updates?" he directed toward the chief.

"We believe Serco has already left the city. Over a week ago, a man was found leaving through the eastern gate in the back of a carriage transporting produce. When found, he fought his way through and fled."

"You believe that was Serco?"

Ghehara sat back and remembered the full incident report. "Judging by their combat ability and the absurdity of the escape plan, I believe that was him. The mayor's been pressuring me to confirm this. He wants a press release to say we drove him out after his defeat weeks ago."

Walker sighed. "Of course he does. But if he's still in the city, then a press release like that would only antagonize him."

Ghehara agreed. It seemed like the mayor wanted to clean up this incident as quickly as possible. Of course, he would want to keep it under wraps as the leader of the rebel mages was his own daughter. William had given up his comrades after only two nights in a cell. Ghehara chose to sit on this information until meeting with Mayor Hargrove in person. He had to push for a meeting and caught him after a few days. Upon discovering this, Hargrove ordered him to keep it quiet. He couldn't afford for his family to be caught up in a scandal. Could he not see this was far more important than his political career? Despite his own opinion, Ghehara kept the name a secret but released her description to all the stations in the city. He was determined to bring them in even if it risked her name getting out.

"How long before we construct more tech armor and put it in the field?"

Ghehara snapped back to attention to listen to the doctor's reply.

"To produce new, fully operational armor and prep new subjects to use them?" He paused and did some mental calculations. "Ten days."

For once, the director nodded his approval at Lambert. "Once we have more soldiers in the field and have confirmed Serco left the city, I want us to pursue him. We'll eliminate this threat to the region and prove our capability to the people."

"I will lead the teams myself," Ghehara volunteered, eager to bring down Serco once and for all.

"Good. I'll count on you to end this. Onto the last order of business, the boy you captured. Has he given you anything?"

The chief cleared his throat and continued with the update. "He's been very cooperative. It seems he was abandoned as soon as he had done his job. He gave us the names of people involved, but beyond that, he didn't know much."

"I see. Do you know who their leader is?"

"No," he lied. "We only have an accurate description of her. If she surfaces, my people will find her."

"I see. I'll leave tracking the rebel mages to you. If we can eliminate them before the ten days all the better. But I'm more interested in how this boy crippled our network and plunged the city into chaos. It seems his magic hacked into our systems. Do we have any idea how that's possible?"

Doctor Lambert pondered for a moment. "We have no record of any magic such as this, and none of our research subjects showed anything close to this ability. With computers and technology becoming commonplace, it makes sense that magic would adapt and work along with it."

Walker gripped his hands tighter. It was worrisome that magic could be used in this way. He took a breath and acknowledged them both. "This will not be a threat to us. I founded this company specifically for incidents such as this."

Lambert smiled. "So if you have no more questions for him, I would like to study this child's ability. It could prove invaluable to my work."

Before the chief could speak up, Walker granted his permission. "You can have him if it aids in your research."

Ghehara felt a growing discontent. It never felt right leaving a kid to Doctor Lambert's care. But he had assurances none of the research subjects came to any harm. In a case like William's, they would have been locked away for their crimes anyway. They would be treated better in AMTech's research program than prison, at least that's what he told himself.

****

A few days passed, and the weather grew worse still. The rain was coming down constantly with the wind whipping it around. It was a perfect excuse to ride with their hoods up as they left Verras. After greeting the professor and his team, Sam rode in silence as they made their way out the city gates. Her group rode on horseback alongside a convoy of carriages with a dozen researchers and all the supplies for the trip. They cleared the city gates with no problems, and once they were a few hours clear of the city, she heard Hunter approaching from his post on the front right of the convoy.

"It looks like we're clear. If anyone was going to stop us, they would have done so by now."

Sam finally felt comfortable to lower her hood. "I agree. I'm surprised we made it."

"Did you think the security was going to catch us?"

Sam shook her head. "Not them. When we made it to the gates, I expected Claire to come crashing down on us."

Hunter felt annoyed. "We'll be rid of them soon. It's Serco that they want, and if they keep chasing him, they'll die."

Sam looked up and felt the rain lightly wash over her. She knew it was cruel, but the idea of Claire being gone gave her some satisfaction. She soon discarded the fantasy and told Hunter to get back in position. It would be smooth sailing from here to the temple.

Professor Mansen watched the two defenders conversing at the front. He was lucky. When Sam first approached to volunteer, he made a call to the young Ewan Solace to offer him the job first. Even though Ewan asked all about the trip, it seemed he had other business to attend. Whatever he was doing, it was a shame he would miss this opportunity.

But Ewan was not as far away as the professor would have thought. For just out of sight, a group of four mages was following the convoy.

Chapter 21

The Temple of Mordecai

Claire and her team rode slowly through the grasslands. If nothing else, the horses were enjoying the trip as they spent most of the journey at a gentle pace. Moving like this for so many hours, Claire thought at least Arden would be growing impatient, but it seemed he was perfectly content riding quietly, occasionally encouraging his horse as they moved. Since they knew their destination, it was easy enough to follow the convoy while staying out of sight. It became even easier when they reached the hills that stretched on for miles up north. Occasionally, one of them would ride ahead to keep track of the convoy as they were keeping a good distance.

After Arden went up ahead, he came back to report that they were still on the move and there was no sign of the temple yet. Although she expected Arden to crack first, Claire finally asked Ewan how much further they had to go.

Ewan tried to reach his saddlebag and fumbled his way into it. It was entertaining to let him keep trying, but soon Lilla rode alongside and pulled the map out for him.

"Arden said you weren't good on horseback," she said, handing Ewan the map.

He begrudgingly accepted. "I'm sure you're sugarcoating it, but yes, I'm not very comfortable."

After scanning it for a full minute, Ewan showed the others their rough location.

"The temples only a few hours away then."

"Do you think he's already there?" Lilla asked.

Ewan stared at the map thoughtfully. "I can't imagine he'd be anywhere else. He's waiting for the others to catch up."

Now that they were nearing their goal, Claire asked how they all felt approaching the end.

"I feel bad for using the prof as bait," Arden said as it had been on his mind all day.

"It was the best way to lure Serco out from hiding," Ewan replied without looking up. "As soon as Professor Mansen told me of his visitor, I knew they were planning something. If we stopped Sam back in Verras then Serco would be in the wind, and who knows how much havoc he'll cause next time."

Claire nodded in agreement. Even though it was his initial idea, she could see he wasn't taking it lightly, none of them were.

"We can catch them by surprise this time, like with the raid on AMTech's factory. Once we find Serco, we can work on taking out Sam's group and getting the others to safety. Then we can face Serco together."

"You make it sound so easy," Arden said dryly.

"This will be different from the last two times. This isn't his game anymore. We'll catch him unawares before he can spring whatever insane plan he has in mind. If he wants to get us involved, it would have taken a day to get here. So now we'll have the drop on him. This is our best chance to stop him."

The others fell silent as they had said their piece and could only think about the fight ahead of them.

Lilla looked at the sun starting to set. "So it'll be over soon," she said. The others turned to see she had a faint smile on her face. "This time tomorrow, we'll be done with this. We can get back to normal."

Arden snickered. "I don't even know what normal is for us."

A laugh echoed around the group.

"I don't know either, but I want to find out," Claire said, trying to be hopeful.

"There will be many more challenges ahead of us," Ewan pointed out.

Arden edged his horse to ride in front. "Ha! We'll be ready for anything after this. If someone causes trouble in Verras again, I'll beat them down."

Claire felt his confidence. They would end this tonight.

****

After a solid day of traveling, Professor Mansen's expedition was pushing through the tall grass that lined the path ahead. The sun had gone down a few hours ago, but the moonlight helped guide their way. A few thousand years ago, there would have been a road here but the countless changes in climate had taken over this area. It took months to clear out the creatures that had once inhabited the area. Although they were gone, it was better to be prepared when making the journey.

The hills had risen alongside the group as their path was relatively sunken in. There was only one way in and out, which would make securing the site easier. Sam still led the way at the front but was then joined by the professor who was riding at the front of his carriage. Sam looked at him blankly as his horses lined up with her.

He smiled back at her. "I want to be right up front when we see it."

Sam soon saw why he was eager. She could barely see a few feet in front of her, but suddenly the world opened and revealed an enormous clearing with the temple waiting for them at the end. Leading up to the temple was an array of stone columns and old structures with intricate designs carved into the stonework. It was a stunning sight, but with the dark clouds looming above, it was ominous. From the stonework around her, she saw weeds and trees growing out that were slowly crumbling away the architecture. She couldn't imagine what this place would have looked like when it was first built; it was incredible it was still standing.

They moved up, and the temple came into full view. It was built into a cliff, so it was impossible to tell how big it was inside. Sam could understand how they wouldn't know there were more chambers to be discovered.

The convoy moved in and settled below the long rows of stairs leading to the entrance. The team was ordered to set everything up while a few would go on ahead for a quick survey. The professor politely asked Sam if she'd like to accompany them, to which she accepted. She asked her own team to set up a perimeter around the convoy while she checked out the temple. This was her chance to find out what the weapon promised to her could be. If she could find it before Serco arrived, all the better.

****

They walked through the open doorway, which itself was the size of a building. Inside was a cross-section of passageways, some leading down but one in the middle continued on the same level. The professor and his ward, Jonah, led the way with flashlights to guide them. Jonah had discovered the sealed chamber inside but had yet to find a way to open it. Behind Sam, one of the researchers was lighting the mounted torches as they went. Having clearly been here before, the professor led them into the main chamber and waited for his assistants to move through and light the braziers in the room so they could see ahead.

He took this opportunity to give Sam a lesson in history. "This main chamber consists of three levels and housed many historical artifacts. Originally thought to be a place to bury Mordecai, we found evidence that he spent some time here while still alive. From ancient scrolls and the carvings on the walls here, we can see he was researching magic. Many of his followers assisted him. There are several rooms built out and smaller chambers where we believe he experimented, using people as his subjects." As he spoke, the room was slowly lighting up, and Sam was getting an idea of how large the temple was. The ceiling may well have been fifty feet above them. The level they were on was more like a series of platforms connected through various bridges that crisscrossed, leading across the immense room.

Every part of the temple was intricately designed with various carvings and symbols etched into the stonework. Sam could only guess magic was used in the construction to build such vast and detailed chambers. Once it was sufficiently lit, they continued toward the far side, and Sam prodded him for more details. "Was Mordecai a mage?"

"A very powerful one if the scrolls are to be believed. And the oldest mage we have record of. Some even think of him as the first to use magic. It would certainly explain how he made such a mark on history. One of the most important historical finds in recent times was a tome kept by Mordecai himself. It was a journal of sorts detailing his life, and although it doesn't go into specifics of his magic, it was clear he was obsessed with one thing. Immortality."

Sam frowned. She was fishing for a clue as to what Serco expected to find here, but this history lesson was telling her nothing. The only thing she learned was that Mordecai was crazier than Serco is. Maybe that's why he's interested. "So you don't even know what kind of magic he used," she said, unable to hide her irritation.

Oblivious to her tone, the professor continued. "There are many tales that we've gathered from different sites. Some talk of him regenerating lost limbs, opening portals to other worlds, or even taking people's souls and putting them in jars. These accounts are difficult to prove of course as they are a world apart from the magic we know today."

No closer to understanding this place since they started, Sam finally saw what they were here for. Jonah excitedly showed them a wall at the far side that he claimed had a hidden chamber behind it. There were lines of statues stretching across the wall, each one holding a different weapon at their side. The section they were facing was blank, with two columns on either side that stretched up to the roof. Nothing about the wall looked out of the ordinary, but the professor examined the blank space with curiosity.

Without turning away, he asked, "You told me you could manipulate sound waves. Is that correct?"

"Yes," Sam answered slowly, unsure of why he was asking.

"Can you enhance the sound from this wall for a moment?"

Seeing no harm, Sam casually waved her hand over the wall, and after a slight vibration, she stood back. "Done."

He smiled and took out a metal rod from his pack. He gently tapped the wall in a sequence. With a clear sound echoing from it, he proudly announced it was hollow.

"Thank you for your help. Now we must find a way to open it up."

"I take it we can't just break it down?" Sam asked.

Both the professor and his aide looked shocked at the suggestion. "Even if we were willing to risk damaging the temple, which we are not, the wall is very thick, and the columns on either side are load bearing. This door was specifically designed to prevent people from forcing their way in. Mordecai did seem to enjoy making puzzles out of these old structures."

Sam's expression must have given her away because the professor patted her on the shoulder. "Don't fret, my dear. I've opened many secret doors like this one. I'm confident I'll have this open soon."

Sam managed to force a smile. "Okay, Professor. I'll look around and leave you to your work."

****

Outside, Claire and Ewan lay overlooking the clearing. They kept to the hillside and moved above the gorge that led to the temple. It would be hard to spot the two up high in the dead of night. However, Claire was also straining to see the people below her. She certainly couldn't recognize any of them from here. She looked to see Ewan's eyes glowing softly as he got a close look at the people below.

"You need to teach me that sometime."

"Or we could think to bring binoculars with us," he pointed out.

"I'll make a note of it. What can you see?"

Ewan checked again to make sure before speaking. "On the right are two of Sam's people watching the entrance to the clearing. I remember them from Haven. The rest are setting up camp, but I can't see Sam, Hunter, or the professor from this angle."

Claire looked around the area. "I'm glad we circled around. There's no way we could have walked into the clearing without getting spotted. Do you see a way down where they won't see us?"

Ewan pulled himself out further and looked across the clearing. "I see a small structure nearer the temple. If no one is nearby, we should be able to drop down without notice."

"That'll work," Claire said before crawling back away from the edge. They both moved away and joined Arden and Lilla.

"We'll move further up and wait there. If they make their move, we'll be ready to head down. If nothing happens, we'll try to sneak into the temple." With the clear orders, they acknowledged the plan, and Arden and Lilla left to tie up their horses.

"Could I ask you something before we move up?" Ewan asked suddenly.

"Of course. Is something wrong?"

"I'm sorry I left it until now to ask, but it seems like my last chance."

It wasn't like Ewan to hesitate like this. She gave him her full attention and let him continue.

"When you find Serco, are you prepared to kill him?"

Claire felt suddenly tense at the serious question he had given her. It's not like it hadn't crossed her mind, but to be asked flat out felt different. Even so, she knew her answer.

"Yes. It needs to be done before he kills anyone else." She looked Ewan in the eye and didn't waver in her response. "Do you think I'm wrong?"

Ewan looked away as he gave her his assessment. "It certainly is the smarter choice. Trying to take him alive will prove extremely difficult and endanger all of us. But saying it and carrying it out are two entirely different things. If the time ever came, I'm not sure if I could do it."

Taking this in, Claire rested her hand over her sword. Although she felt sure of her decision, there was the possibility she wouldn't be able to carry it out. She wondered how her other teammates would respond to this. "I don't think Arden would do it if given the choice. It's like a code of honor for him, but if it put more people in danger, I couldn't accept that risk," she told Ewan while observing her teammates. He nodded in response.

"Lilla certainly wouldn't do it. To her a human life is precious. She hunts beasts out of necessity, but with people. She will always spare their life."

"Does it make us bad people that we would consider it?" Claire asked.

"Not to me. As long as you accept the responsibility that comes with it."

More to think about. Claire took a breath after such a heavy subject and started to move up to join the others. She turned to Ewan once more as they walked. "I'm glad we talked about this. Now I know I'm ready."

Shaping a Hero

****

Sam stayed nearby as they worked but checked out any murals she could. She easily deduced Mordecai's likeness since he was the most common theme in the murals. The ancient drawings varied from Mordecai standing above his followers being worshipped to him performing what looked like torturous acts upon them. However, another common element in many was a large statue looming behind him. Did this indicate his overwhelming presence or was it simply one of the many statues that were placed around the temple? But where the statues here were finely detailed as different humans, the one depicted in the murals was much bigger than any man, and its only feature was the markings over its body.

Sam looked away as the professor and his aides were running around, and she wondered if they had something. The professor was arranging the statues that he discovered could move their arms. He was moving them, so they all raised their various weapons up toward the wall.

"Have you found something?" Sam asked.

After moving one of the five statues nearest the wall, the professor checked it again. "I believe we're on the right track. When ready for combat like the five statues here, warriors of that time would raise their weapons to Mordecai to show their respect. It's not enough on its own. There will be some kind of lever to open the door." The professor looked around past Sam and spotted an ordinary-looking pedestal that could have easily been a placeholder for a book. He hurried over to it with Sam following closely as she was eager to get that door open quickly. If she could get in before Serco showed up, then maybe she could turn this weapon against him. Professor Mansen stood by the pedestal and tried to shift it, but it did not budge.

"Can you charge your magic into this?" he asked excitedly.

"I can try," Sam answered. She didn't have much experience charging up objects other than her bat. But she placed a hand on it and pushed her magic through. As soon as her energy entered the stone pedestal, it shifted and smoothly sank into the ground. At that moment, the blank wall rumbled and slowly lowered to reveal a hidden passage.

They all moved to it with curiosity. It was dark, but they could see it led into another massive chamber to explore.

"All right, the first job is done," the professor said, taking charge. "We'll move in carefully and light up the area as before. We will only have time for a quick sweep of the area, and then we'll bring the rest of the team in."

Before they went ahead, though, someone was already approaching from behind. Professor Mansen turned around to see a stranger casually walking toward them.

"That was well done. Took you less than an hour to get it open."

Next to the professor, Jonah looked anxious of the stranger. "What are you doing back here?"

Confused, Mansen looked at his aide. "You know this man?"

"I, uh…" he started to answer but couldn't get the words out.

The strange man looked genuinely offended. "You mean you didn't tell him I was here. I am shocked you would take the credit of the discovery for yourself. I was the one who told you about the passage after all."

Sam sighed as Serco sauntered his way up to them. It seemed he was watching them all along. As his face came into the light, Mansen recognized him too. "I know you. You're the criminal who's been causing chaos in Verras."

"Oh yes, I created quite a stir. I must thank you for getting the door open for us. Now that your job is done, I'll need you to gather your team and stay out of our way."

The professor looked to Sam, unsure if she could do anything, but she regarded him coldly. "Do as he says. We came here to take whatever's inside this chamber. Stay out of our way, and you won't get hurt."

Taken aback by this betrayal, the professor was stunned for words. Serco walked past him and had a quick peek inside the chamber. He raised his hands, and his fire emerged to spread into the room. It moved across the room with purpose, splitting in several directions and making its way down lighting the torches as it moved. Serco only lit up a small portion of the room, but it was enough to see the scale of it. The chamber they were in right now was considered to be the whole temple, but with this discovery, it would be more than twice the size. With the light not reaching the end, it seemed to stretch on forever. Serco marveled at it.

"What do you hope to find here?" the professor asked bitterly.

"A stage," Serco answered gleefully. "Here I'll find the perfect stage for my final act."

"What about the weapon you promised!" Sam shouted. She was losing patience with his theatrics.

"Why, that is the prize we'll be competing for. As soon as we lure Claire here, we can begin."

The professor shook his head dismissively. "How can you possibly know what's beyond this door. How did you find this place?"

Serco grinned. "I had a peek at Mordecai's tome. It told me exactly what was locked away in here."

The professor refused to believe this statement. "Impossible. I studied the tome myself. It mentioned no such thing."

Clearly amused, Serco walked up close to the professor. "You people need to learn to read between the lines. There were so many juicy secrets hidden in that book, but this interested me the most," he said and then backed off for a moment. "But I digress. We should really head outside to gather you all together."

****

"We have movement at the entrance," Lilla told the others as they all lay overlooking the clearing. All eyes were squinting at the temple to see who was coming out. They didn't need Ewan's eyes to tell it was Serco walking out with the others nervously following him. They didn't even need to see him as, after a quick instruction to Sam, his voice echoed out to everyone in the area.

"Everyone stop what you're doing and line up!" He fired a shot in the air to make sure they obeyed. "The guards you hired are working for me, and they're already guarding the only exit. I'm getting bored of always taking hostages so I advise you not do anything stupid or I'll start thinning out the crowd."

Thankfully, they all obeyed and grouped together. Like nervous sheep being guided by wolves, the group was led into a small stone structure to keep them out of the way. Claire was sure he wouldn't kill them outright as he needed them for whatever plan he was concocting. However, her stomach was in knots just sitting there. If he hurt them now, she would be powerless to do anything. She could only pray she was right and remain hidden.

Everything went smoothly for Serco, which is the only time Claire would consider that a good thing. He left the two she wasn't familiar with standing guard over the captives while he, along with Sam and Hunter, went back inside.

****

Tanya and Marcus took guard duty casually. They were happy to stay out of the way and it wasn't like any of the captives would try to make a run for it. They stood together in front of the large stone door that housed the survey team. Marcus noticed Tanya shaking anxiously as they waited.

"Hey, we'll be okay. The boss will get this weapon we need, and we'll be out of here soon."

She looked up at him while still trembling. "I want to be as far from that monster as we can be."

"I know. Remember what the boss told us. This will ensure future mages can practice magic freely in the city. We're doing the right thing here," he told her although he wasn't fully convinced himself. A few shaky breaths later, Tanya agreed and moved to the other side to stand guard like they were supposed to. Marcus went the other way and hoped they would be out of here soon. Marcus didn't appreciate it at the time what happened next definitely worked out in his favor. As he turned the corner, he was blindsided by a fist to the face and was instantly knocked out. Tanya turned upon hearing this, but before she could register anything, she was zapped with electricity and collapsed as well.

With a pang of guilt, Arden helped Marcus sit up. "I think that's the third time I've knocked this guy out. He must really hate me."

"I doubt he realizes what happened. You could always say it was one of us," Ewan offered.

"Focus," Claire told them in a cool tone. "Let's get these people out of here and go after Serco."

With some effort, she managed to push open the stone doors to find the survey team huddled together. They all looked at her expectantly.

"We're here to get you guys out. You need to get on your horses and ride back to the city before Serco comes back."

She saw many of them let out a breath. Professor Mansen showed up from behind the door and lowered the stone pot he held, with relief. "We appreciate the rescue. I was planning our escape as you came in."

"You were going to hit them with the pot?" she asked.

Avoiding the question, he noticed Ewan waiting behind her. "Ah, this is the team you spoke of. You have impeccable timing."

"We are happy to help, Professor. You had best hurry. Although I don't expect Serco to come back anytime soon, I wouldn't hang around."

Happily, the former captives made their way out and went off to prepare the horses for travel. Claire took the professor's arm to request something. "Can you take them with you?" she asked and pointed to their two unconscious guards. "They're not bad people, they just got involved with the wrong people." The professor eyed them for a moment, then agreed.

His gaze darted back to Claire as he realized from her request. "You're not coming with us?"

Claire shook her head. "We need to stop Serco. This is our best chance to end this."

"We could send for help back in Verras. There's no need to take on such a man alone."

"By then it will be too late. We have to do this now," she replied and backed away. Claire was leaving no room for debate, and the others followed her lead.

Ewan turned to the professor before leaving him. "We will meet again when this is over, I promise you." He bowed his head and left the professor with his peers.

After watching them leave, Professor Mansen turned to his team. "You should all make haste to the city and tell them what happened. If anyone is willing to stay here with me, I want to make sure those young mages make it out of there okay." Many of the team were shocked but could see his mind was made. Only Jonah and the professor stayed behind to await the return of Claire and her team.

Chapter 22

One Last Game

"We're taking this weapon and leaving," Sam ordered.

This statement caused Serco to stop as they reached the hidden chamber.

"I'm afraid it's not that simple," he replied, sounding patronizing.

"Why not!" Hunter demanded.

Serco smiled like a child holding back a secret. "It's not how the game is played. You want your prize, you'll need to earn it."

They were clearly getting nowhere with this, so Hunter reeled it in. But Sam had no intention of letting Serco mess them around.

"No more games. We've done everything to set this up for you, and we're not leaving without taking what we came here for!"

"Sam." Hunter took her arm and tried to stop her as they both knew what happened when she pushed Serco the last time.

Sam was beyond reason now and shook him off. "I won't let you lead us around like dolls to be disposed of!" Sam was shaking with frustration at this point. Her words echoed and died off, leaving total silence.

Serco's expression was hard to read, but when the silence reached its peak, he sighed. "You really don't understand. You've already done your part. In fact…"

In a flash, all three of them raised their weapons at each other.

"You must have known this would end badly for you." Serco smiled as his gauntlets began to glow.

Before the other two could make a move, Serco backhanded an arrow that came flying in. Lilla felt disappointed she couldn't wound him in that moment, but she couldn't wait any longer as it looked as though he was about to kill.

All three were caught off guard and instantly forgot about their pending fight. Seeing this as a signal of sorts, Claire rushed in and fired out a shockwave from her sword that pushed Sam and Hunter back; only Serco stood his ground. He looked at Claire with surprise at her arrival. "No, you're not supposed to be here. It's too early."

"We're not waiting for you to come for us again. We're ending this right here."

The rest of her team moved to back her up while Sam and Hunter jumped down to the lower level to escape. Nobody pursued as their main target was right in front of them.

Safely around the corner, Hunter stopped Sam. "We have to get out of here."

"No!" Sam yelled and threw him off. "We didn't come all this way for nothing."

"There are too many of them," he pleaded.

"We are finding that weapon. You're promised to follow me, didn't you?"

A voice screamed in his mind that it was a terrible idea, but he couldn't say no. "Always," he replied and Sam led him deeper into the temple.

****

Serco's mind was racing as Claire and her team were ready to face him. "I still have the captives," he threw out with hope. "I can blow them up from here if you don't back off."

"Did you really think we'd rush in without freeing them first?" Claire revealed and watched the color drain from his face with some satisfaction. "There's no way out this time. You'll have to fight us."

Still, his eyes were darting around for a solution.

"What's the matter, Serco? Is this not dramatic enough for you?"

She saw a flash of anger in his eyes, but he soon straightened himself. "No way out, huh? But have you considered this?" he said and pointed toward the roof. Even with her eyes trained on him, he fired a shot with his other hand and blew up the ground in front of him. This was enough to kick up dust and allow him to run back into the hidden chamber, ignoring an arrow that whizzed past him. Claire cursed and gave chase with the others.

He ran frantically ahead of them while lighting the way. The area ahead was vast and split off in every direction. Serco seemed to run with a clear purpose, however, while navigating the temple.

Ridiculous to the end, Claire thought. *He can't seriously think he can get away.*

It might prove difficult to find their way back as the chamber continued on like a labyrinth. They passed countless doorways on multiple levels. But he was an easy trail to follow as he still had to slow down to light braziers along the way. Still, he didn't give them a chance to catch up as an explosive shot came speeding toward Claire. The four of them had to stop as Claire narrowly dodged it and heard the explosion go off behind her. She turned back and could make out a light source in a doorway before moving off, and the chase began again.

Claire led the way a bit more cautiously this time, in case he left any traps behind. The doorway led into another smaller chamber, and she could hear Serco inside lighting it up. There was a tablet inscribed on the wall that led in. She paused to examine it. It showed five people standing with their weapons raised at a dark, looming figure ahead of them. Claire couldn't tell what it meant, but it was worth keeping in mind as they followed Serco inside.

They entered to find a platform laid out for them that led up a stairway and onto a throne overlooking it. Serco locked eyes with Claire before running up the stairs. They jumped onto the platform one by one, and all landed as Serco reached the throne. He turned to sit in it and crossed his legs as though he had been there the whole time.

"I'm glad you could all make it," he called to them with a sinister smile.

Claire almost groaned aloud. "Are you going to pretend the last five minutes never happened?"

Serco frowned in response but shrugged it off. "I'll admit I'm surprised you found me so quickly. But that's part of what makes you impressive, Claire."

Claire gripped her sword tighter at the mention of her name.

"You were right about my hesitation to fight you. It wasn't dramatic enough. It wasn't good enough for a hero like you. But this." He pointed out the room. "This is the perfect stage."

"So let's finish this," Arden called out. "Just like last time, we'll see who walks away."

Serco looked pleased with his suggestion and stood from the throne. "Yes, I think it's time. We'll settle it all here and see if you really are the hero."

He slowly descended the stairs toward them. They all readied themselves as they couldn't underestimate him. He may act like a clown, but he was powerful and highly skilled.

Serco continued monologuing but only had eyes on Claire. "It was fate that we face each other again. Sure I arranged the finer details, but there was no doubt the two of us would settle things. You may even succeed here, but you will learn one hard lesson." He reached the platform with them and faced them all with his hands in his pockets. "You can't save them all."

Enough of this! Claire stepped forward to get the first attack in. The moment her foot touched the ground, however, she stopped suddenly as the floor below them started to glow. The entire platform was radiating a deep crimson red. Countless symbols had lit up on the ground and shifted around each other as if they were alive. Claire instantly looked to Serco, but he hadn't moved. He stood perfectly still, grinning smugly.

None of them dared move without knowing what this was. Before they could consider a plan, the symbols scattered through the floor and over to the walls. They were multiplying, and soon the whole room was bright with an eerie red glow. They couldn't tell how far it had spread from here, but it sounded like the temple was moving in the distance.

"What is this?" Claire yelled to Serco.

But he gave no answers. "Wait for it," he said, barely containing his excitement.

At last the glowing symbols settled in place, providing light to the whole temple. Several looked very much like eyes and looked around at the people waiting in front of them.

Then behind Claire came a large rumble...followed by a crash...and another. The sound was getting closer, and it soon became apparent these were footsteps. Heavy footsteps moving toward them.

Claire refused to take her eyes off Serco, so she asked Arden, who was already facing that direction.

"It's a...statue," he said in shock.

Frustrated, Claire told Arden to cover her back so she could face it. "If he attacks, you block him. If he tries to run, Lilla, you shoot him."

Feeling confident that she wouldn't get shot in the back, she faced the danger approaching them. It was as big as the footsteps suggested. From near the chamber entrance, a massive statue walked toward them. It was also covered in the same red, glowing symbols that were scattered on the walls. But they spiraled and danced over the statue's body as it moved. It was over twenty feet tall and had no face to speak of. Just two massive arms that swung lazily as it walked.

"What is that thing?" Claire breathed.

"It's a Golem. Like the practice mannequins but far bigger," Ewan said, sounding surprisingly calm considering it was shambling toward them. Looking at him, though, she could see a hint of fear.

This thing is what he was after? Claire grew angry that again he had what he came for. She stormed toward him for answers. "What's going on?"

"The final game has started," he said with satisfaction.

"No! I'm done with your games!"

"Oh, this isn't one of mine. Our dear Mordecai left this behind for us. You better listen to the rules, or you'll be in trouble."

Claire couldn't stomach the idea of indulging him. Luckily, Arden asked in her place. "What're the rules? Are we supposed to fight that thing?"

Delighted that he asked, Serco explained simply. "That thing is the Golem of Korain. Mordecai's infamous bodyguard used to keep him from dirtying his own hands. When he approached his dying days, he decided to leave the Golem here for someone to one day unearth. It wasn't enough to simply give the Golem away, however, so he set up this little challenge. The rules are very simple. Five warriors enter the stage and the last one alive in the temple gets the Golem," he finished with glee and giggled despite horrifying everyone with this statement.

The Golem drew closer as everyone fell cold. "Even if we beat you, we're supposed to fight each other next?" Ewan asked.

"We won't kill each other to win some stupid game. You really are crazy if you think we would sink to that!" Claire cried out.

Serco burst into laughter at her response. "That's the beauty of it. You don't have to kill each other. That's why he's here. He'll hunt down anyone still alive until only one remains. The temple is sealed off, and the only way out is when everyone else is dead!" Serco's excitement was in full swing as he threw out his arms and exclaimed to the roof, "You will emerge a hero born from sacrifice! You'll never hesitate to make the hard choices after this event. After watching all your friends die so that you may live."

Pushed to her limit, Claire howled in rage and attacked. Her slash flew forward to strike Serco, but she hadn't charged the sword to full, so it was easily deflected with his armored hands.

He took a defensive stance. "Are you ready to begin?" He fired a shot, striking the Golem in the chest as it was getting close. The explosive chipped some of the rock, and it flinched back. Reacting to the attack, it charged forward toward them.

With only a couple of seconds to react, they scattered to avoid being trampled underfoot. It swung an arm at Lilla, who barely got away. It wasn't interested in who was attacking it, only who its nearest target was.

The Golem stood up in the middle of the group, and the symbols were shaking erratically. All five of its possible victims stood ready. Serco was delighted by the fighting and let loose his personal flamethrowers. Arden turned to shield himself while the others moved away. The Golem was unaffected by this, and it turned to Arden as the closest stationary target. Unable to move without getting scorched, Arden was clubbed from behind and sent sprawling across the floor.

"Arden!" Claire called out to her injured teammate.

"Keep back!" she heard Ewan shout behind her. Trusting in him, she kept her distance and watched as the Golem moved toward Serco. He jumped back and blasted it, chipping off more of its torso. Claire watched on and hoped the Golem would beat him. If it did, she would then move in.

"Leaving us to fight alone, are you?" he said, smirking at her. "Sorry but that wouldn't be any fun!" He focused energy to his palms and caused two of the beams under the floor to explode. The platform toppled and Team Arkon fell with the Golem to the floor below.

Chapter 23

How Far They Fall

Landing on the floor below, Claire instinctively tucked and rolled into her landing, which was soon followed up by the Golem smashing into the ground nearby. Seeing that her team was okay, she led them back and away from the collapsed landing to more open ground before the Golem could get close. They found themselves gathered under the throne, which gave them ample space to fight this thing. It seemed Serco did not follow and fled somewhere else. As the Golem followed their trail, Claire cursed herself for losing Serco again.

One monster at a time then, she told herself.

"Take him down!" she ordered and let loose a fully charged slash at its weakened torso. Arden followed suit with his mace, but both attacks bounced off with little effect. They both had to move as the Golem swung its arms down at them and crushed the ground.

Claire had seen Arden smash through rocks before, so why was it so weak against this thing? She now noticed the symbols dancing around its body and found her answer.

The magic must be amplifying the rock. It's not going to be easy to break.

"Keep it busy. I need to add something," Arden told her and retreated.

"Claire, bring it this way." She saw Lilla ready on a ledge with a bomb tied to her arrow. Claire eased back toward her with the Golem approaching. Claire had a plan to amplify the attack, but she needed to stay close. The moment she heard the arrow fly past, she ran in to join it. It sank straight into the Golem's exposed midsection. Claire tried to repeat the technique she did with Serco's explosive. As the bomb detonated, she directed the explosion into the Golem. As the force of the explosive reached her hands, Claire's magic repelled it and pushed the full force into the Golem. It proved effective as the attack burrowed into the Golem and fired out the other side. She hadn't mastered this, however, as her hands were left scorched.

Even with a hole in the Golem's torso, it reached around to crush Claire who was only a foot away. With only a second to react Claire attempted to get away, but there was no time. Just as she braced for the impact, a spiked ball slammed into its hand, causing it to miss by an inch and giving her the space to pull back. Arden checked the results and saw the back of the Golem's hand was cracked. The force sigil he hurriedly placed on the ball gave him the extra power he needed, not enough to destroy the Golem but a definite improvement. He was unsure until now if this would interfere with the chain sigil put in the hilt, but it seemed they complemented each other.

Ewan sneaked up on the Golem before it could mount another attack and tagged its back to continue breaking down the midsection. As the glyph formed on the stone, the red markings retreated away from the foreign presence. The Golem seemed to feel his presence though, and its arms twisted around to face behind and grabbed Ewan. Ewan struggled feebly as it was attempting to crush him. Claire moved in, but she felt a gust blow past as Lilla flew over her and landed on the Golem. She stood on its blank head and it, along with its torso, started twisting around as the symbols reacted to her presence. It struggled against her and continued twisting its body to throw her off.

Claire got close below and willed her sword to sharpen. She slashed at the body, hoping to cut it in half. Each cut made its way deeper, but she only managed a few before its leg batted her away. Unable to shake off Lilla, the Golem resorted to tossing its catch away. It reached back and threw Ewan across the room and started swinging for its new target. In the process, Claire was punched off to the side while Lilla gracefully flipped away from the swinging giant. Arden's mace once again came crashing into its body and hit much harder than before. It buried into the Golem's abdomen and timed perfectly with Ewan's glyphs detonating on its back. Both impacts punched through, and the Golem broke in half and fell to the ground.

Ewan, apparently unharmed, ran back to see what remained. They all kept their distance and watched as the Golem reached out for them but couldn't move far without its legs. After struggling on the ground, the symbols stopped all at once, and the Golem froze along with it. Its arms dropped to the ground, and it lay still, the red glow sinking into the ground.

Claire caught her breath and stared at the remains. There was a moment of relief as they had vanquished the Golem without serious injury. But it felt far too easy. She looked to Ewan who shared the confused expression. Arden's head darted between the two of them, waiting for them to say something.

"Is that it then? The big bad Golem is down?" he asked for confirmation.

Ewan's expression looked sour, and Claire agreed. "He wouldn't have left us alone if it was that easy to beat it. That thing was supposed to kill us."

As if to confirm her suspicions, the glowing symbols started gathering again. They moved to a nearby wall and danced around each other yet again. They formed the shape of the Golem, and the wall started to crack. The Golem slowly reformed itself inside the wall, and its arm broke out and reached forward.

"We have to go. Now!" Claire shouted and pushed the others to run. Not giving it a chance to fully rebuild itself, the team fled from the chamber and back into the largest room they came through. Claire and the others hurriedly moved out into the main chamber. They all stopped in their tracks once they saw what had become of it. The vast chamber was lit up with red symbols covering all the walls. They paused, and the sound of the Golem reforming stopped. It didn't appear to be following them.

"This can't be magic can it?" Arden asked while staring at the walls.

"There's nothing else it can be. It was all released when we stood on the platform," Ewan surmised.

Claire shared Arden's disbelief. The idea that this much power was buried here—it was enough to rebuild the Golem a thousand times over. Standing inside the temple, the power the four of them held was insignificant.

Claire shook her awe and looked for anyone hiding in the shadows. "We need to find Serco."

"What? No, we need to get out of here before that Golem comes back," Lilla pleaded to Claire.

"She's right. The Golem won't stop until we're all dead. We need to find an exit before anything else," Ewan told her before she could argue.

Claire wanted to argue but couldn't find the words. Begrudgingly she accepted it. Getting out alive was their priority.

Suddenly, they heard another loud crack, and the team instinctively stood back to back to find the threat. They all looked around, but there was no sign of the Golem. "Does anyone see it?" Claire asked and received no's all around. The cracking continued like when it was reforming before.

"It's close," Ewan announced nervously.

"Move!" Lilla called out, and each of them ran forward before the Golem came crashing down on their heads. It wasn't wasting time anymore and swung its arms left and right. It was closest to Claire, and she had to keep jumping back, hoping she wouldn't run out of space. She was close enough to feel the power behind each swing, leaving her no chance to counter. For a moment it seemed she was safely out of range until its arm came around again and separated from the body. Claire jumped upward with a blast of air to gain some distance, but the giant arm followed and slammed her with an uppercut.

A long red stream still connected the arm to the Golem's body, which then reared back and reconnected itself. Arden and Lilla were attacking to try to draw its attention, but Claire had already been knocked away and soon hit the ground hard.

Claire eased herself up and stretched her aching arm, but it seemed nothing was broken. She saw her team still fighting and hurried to her feet. The Golem was firmly planted between her and them. She saw Ewan watching her and tried to shout over the battle. "Just run! I'll find my way round to you!"

Her voice must have carried as Ewan nodded and led the others in a retreat while Claire ran around to try to keep up. Her pathway took her up to a higher level, but she still had a clear view of them, thanks in part to the giant glowing Golem charging after them.

****

Ewan ran ahead, trying to aim for the entrance to the chamber. He checked back to make sure no one was left behind. Lilla stayed closest to the Golem's reach, but she was the most adept at dodging it. Still, she couldn't keep this up forever, so Ewan looked for any chance to shake their pursuer. This chance came as they had to cross a bridge up ahead. With a quick check, he saw a deep pit was below them. He was far away enough to plant his glyphs at the start of the bridge and moved across beckoning his teammates to follow.

Arden and Lilla worked together seamlessly to keep the Golem busy. Lilla used blasts of air to push herself away and anytime it seemed too close Arden struck it from a distance to throw the Golem off balance. They continued their retreat onto the bridge but had to keep engaging the giant as it could easily catch up to them.

Lilla saw the length of the bridge and quickly told Arden to cross. She could hold it here and escape much easier than the two of them. Arden was hesitant to leave her behind but agreed. He promised himself he would stay within range to attack again if she needed him.

Lilla ran circles around the Golem seemingly with ease. Any other opponent would become frustrated at the constant misses, but the Golem had no such emotion and continued swinging and crushing and grabbing for her. She had her rhythm down and brushed aside any fear as she maneuvered around each attack. She would tire herself out soon though and would need to disengage before that happened.

One the other side, Ewan couldn't make any more glyphs without first detonating the ones he had. He made the choice to destroy the first set. The bridge was large enough it wouldn't fall from one side being broken, and Lilla could use this as a signal to move away. Kneeling down to concentrate, he detonated the glyphs which blasted the other side.

"What are you doing!" Arden suddenly shouted.

Ewan felt a surge of panic and looked up to see what had happened. But it wasn't him Arden was shouting at. Sam and Hunter were now on the bridge in front of them.

They must have dropped down from above, Ewan realized.

Sam turned to them with clear resentment in her eyes. "We're taking what's ours. That Golem is our prize, and we won't let you take it away."

"You don't stand a chance!" Arden yelled desperately, but Sam ignored him.

Hearing the commotion, Lilla pushed away and stumbled near Hunter.

"Out of our way," he ordered, and she was thrown off the bridge. She reached out and grabbed onto a nearby pillar. Worn out from her fight, she could only catch her breath and watch as the two stood to face the Golem themselves.

Sam smiled as it shambled toward them both. "You are the weapon we were promised, and you will come with us."

With that, Hunter pulled a pillar down to strike it, but the Golem easily shrugged it off behind him. It landed and destroyed more of the already-damaged bridge. Sam tried her sound wave next by slamming her bat on the ground, but the Golem was unfazed. With their first attacks done, the Golem suddenly sped up and charged toward them. Hunter pushed Sam out the way as the Golem's arms came smashing down into the ground. Although missing them, this impact was more than enough to break the bridge apart.

Ewan, Arden, and Lilla watched as the two of them scrambled for each other as they started to fall and the Golem still reached for them. Only Lilla could see them as they dropped into the pit. The two held on to each other and thankfully were out of reach of the Golem. But they fell out of sight, leaving Lilla to hope they weren't hurt. Despite everything they had done, she had no hatred for them. They would need to pay for what they had done but not until after they had escaped this horrid place.

****

Unbeknownst to them, Serco was watching as they fled across the bridge. He smiled at this opportunity and looked to each of them in turn.

Which one? he pondered as each of the three fought the Golem. *Which one should die first?* He carefully watched each of them in turn.

The smart, analytical one? The strong and confident one? Or the skilled and empathetic one? I could kill any of the three, and it will set Claire up on her true path. He thought carefully about this as the battle unfolded until he made his decision. He stretched out his palm and aimed toward Arden. *Physical strength alone won't get you very far, and let's face it, doing this for the thrill and the glory, you're only a few years away from becoming me. It's fitting I'll be the one to kill you before that happens.*

With a last look at his prey, he whispered his words. "Goodbye, Ar—" but his hand was suddenly struck before he could carry it out. He turned and caught Claire's sword as it came down on him. With a struggle, he threw her off, and she regrouped to face him.

"Again and again you get in my way!" he spat.

"I'll always stop you, no matter how many times I have to. I won't let you hurt my friends!" She ran in again and her sword collided with his gauntlets as they fought each other. With her sword pressed against him, he shot out his fire near her face forcing her back again.

"You idiot! How can you truly protect people when you don't know anything about loss?"

Growing more enraged, Claire snapped at him. "How dare you tell me about loss! I lost my parents to monsters like you!"

Claire charged at him again, but he immediately fired an explosive at her. With an instant reaction, it was blocked by the blunt of her blade with her free hand pressed against the back of it. As practiced, she willed the explosive away from her to deflect it. And before Serco could react, she launched another slash at him, this one clipping his shoulder and shedding blood. He readied his other hand to attack so she stood ready.

"Someone like you who kills people without remorse. I won't let you inflict that kind of pain on anyone else!"

Claire rushed in for another attack, but Serco lowered his guard and looked disappointed. He held out his palm and stopped her in her tracks. "You are far too naïve. You haven't hesitated to risk your life for others. You've made the hard choices, and you actually do understand real loss. But if you can't accept that the people around you will die, you will break when it finally happens."

Claire couldn't move her body as he rambled. She still held on to her sword but couldn't do anything to stop him. She looked him in the eyes and saw only cold indifference.

"It's a shame you didn't turn out to be the hero I wanted, but I've enjoyed our time together. I can only hope that your death will fuel others to come stop me, but it will take time to find another candidate with as much potential as you held. Goodbye, Claire."

Claire felt intense pain as the pressure increased and knew it was going to burst.

She opened her mouth and let out a final cry of anguish.

Chapter 24

You Can't Save Them All

Sam stood frozen and stared vacantly in front of her. Everything happened in a blur. They were falling, then Hunter grabbed on and pulled her in close to him.

Her guardian. Her friend.

It all seemed to slow down when she looked in his eyes, and she knew she was safe. Even falling into a pit, she knew he could stop their fall. But he never had the chance. The Golem's arm came rushing in from nowhere and crashed into them both. She was knocked away from her protector and rolled down a slope before managing to stop herself. Unharmed by the fall, she crawled her way back up, looking to regroup. She crawled her way up the steep climb, determined they wouldn't give up. They could still make it out of here with their prize. All the work, all the sacrifice they went through together couldn't be for nothing.

Back onto the ledge, the only light source was the eerie symbols that seemed to watch her. It was below this light she saw Hunter. He wasn't moving. She felt a cold sweat, but her brain was in denial at what she was looking at. He never stayed down for long; he was too strong for that. She rushed over to his side and saw his crippled body. It had impacted the wall up above and landed here.

This is where she stood, over his lifeless body. She had begged him not to go with what little life still lay in him, but it was too late. Like everyone else who followed her, he was gone. Now she was alone.

It can't be for nothing, she remembered.

Not him. He can't be for nothing. The thought rang through her head and tears ran freely down her cheek.

Somehow she found the strength to stand.

"It can't be for nothing."

The ground around her shook as her magic seeped out.

"It can't be for nothing," she whispered again, and the words echoed around her.

It was the only thing that could keep her going. She looked at Hunter one last time. "I won't let it, not after everything we did together." Again the words echoed around her, reinforcing her will. She heard an explosion echo in the distance and left to find its source.

****

Arden helped Lilla climb back to solid ground. She looked exhausted, so he supported her. It was no wonder after facing the Golem alone.

She was awesome holding that thing off by herself. She didn't even need my help.

Ewan looked over the edge of the destroyed bridge for a sign of Sam and Hunter's fate.

Should we try to climb down? They could be hurt. Everything had gone quiet, but Ewan knew it wouldn't stay that way for long and he had to make a choice.

"Any sign of them?" Arden asked. Ewan shook his head. He saw Lilla over his shoulder catching her breath. "Are you all right?" he asked. Without looking up, she gave him a thumbs-up and kept taking deep breaths.

She pushed herself too hard keeping the Golem at bay. In a way, my plan worked, but Sam and Hunter were caught in the middle of it. Ewan's train of thought was cut off as an explosion echoed in the distance.

"Claire," he said unconsciously. The others shared his realization that she was nowhere to be seen, and Serco was still out there.

"We have to find her," he said and tried to trace where the sound had come from. This place was built like a maze, and the sounds could echo from anywhere. It sounded like it came from the first chamber toward the entrance. It was the only chance they had of finding her, so they rushed away to find their leader.

****

"You are too naïve," Serco told her. Those words repeated in her mind as the pressure in her chest built up.

He's really going to do it this time, Claire realized in a panic. Her brain was desperately telling her to move, to rush him before he could do this. But her body wouldn't listen.

I can still fight this! I can't let it end here. She was reeling internally. He was still rambling, but she couldn't hear him anymore. Her vision started to blur as she tried to force her body forward. All she could see was Serco's hand with the force sigil resonating.

Seeing it like that brought back a strange rush of memories. *When magic moves through a sigil, it reacts in different ways. The sigil helps the magic move in the right direction,* Claire heard echo through her mind. It was Arden's voice. He had told her this when they were kids after Tohren visited. But why was she remembering this now?

Magic responds to the will of the user.

Ewan's voice came this time. Was this what it meant to have your life flash before your eyes?

This is a common theory I've found, and it confirms what we've seen so far. The stronger the will of the user, the stronger the magic they can wield. You are its guide, the magic responds to what you want to happen.

So what do you want to do? she heard Lilla say. *We all have different goals, and we can use magic to reach them.*

What do I want now? The pressure in her chest was ready to burst, and she heard Serco say his goodbye.

I want to live! This was her final thought before she cried out in frustration and pain, until the explosive in her detonated.

The foreign energy in her surged and shot through her body. It followed the path given to it by Claire, who commanded the magic being used on her to flow down into her right arm. Driven forward by fury, Claire took her sword in both hands to attack. The energy within her instantly moved through the sword and fired out at the man in front of her. Serco was caught completely off guard as he was ready for her to disappear. The blast released was big enough to throw him back and smash through the thin wall behind, causing him to fall away from her.

****

Claire was left shaking. Her heart was beating at an alarming rate, and all she could feel was the energy surging through her. She knocked Serco away, but this wouldn't be enough to keep him down. So without hesitation, she jumped after him.

Serco barely had time to realize what happened as he lay on the ground. He opened his eyes only to see Claire dropping toward him. Serco rolled out the way before she could finish the job. Up on his feet, he parried her sword with his gauntlets as the sword struck at him again and again. Fire streamed from his fingertips, but every time he tried to aim it at her, she slammed him with the sword again throwing his aim. Her look was fierce, and she kept up the constant attack. Striking his hands with the sword, she raised her left hand and arced a bolt of lightning, hitting him square in the ribs. With no time to breathe, the sword came in again, which he had to cross his hands and block. Holding her back, his fire came dangerously close to her face, but Claire felt none of it and kept bearing down on him with both arms.

It took all his strength to push her away and fight back with the fire from his hands. Claire continued to slam his flaming gauntlets, but he was starting to graze her. Not that she noticed. Claire felt no pain anymore and was pushed on by sheer adrenaline running through her body. When fighting before, she was careful to avoid injury but now she was relentless in her attack. With one more push, she batted a hand away with the sword and caught the other with her free hand. Serco's left hand came back around to blast her at the same time her sword moved in. She beat him to it and cut straight across his abdomen. Even in her wild rage, Claire sharpened her sword enough to cut clean through his armor and blood burst out from the wound. Leaning into the strike, Claire bashed him with her shoulder to knock him back again.

He was bleeding heavily, but Claire was showing no mercy and ran straight in. Any reason had left her, and she would surely kill him if this continued. Ending the fight the only way he knew how, Serco detonated a large explosive right between them, sending them both flying away from each other. They both took a hard hit, and their fight came to an end.

The rush of adrenaline leaving her, Claire lay on the ground. Her heartbeat rapidly slowed, and her consciousness drifted away.

****

Ewan had never questioned himself as much as he was now. He knew they had to find Claire. She could be in danger, but what if they were going the wrong way? Was it right to leave Sam and Hunter down there near the Golem? This is exactly why he never wanted to lead; he couldn't stop overthinking the decisions he made.

I wonder if Claire has these doubts. I wonder if I'll have the chance to ask her.

"There's more fighting," Lilla told them suddenly. They stopped in the corridor and listened. She was right; the familiar sounds of battle echoed down the room. Relieved that they might be on the right track, Lilla tried to hone in on the source.

"Looking for your friend?" said a voice from nowhere. It seemed to come from all around them. "You better hurry. It sounds like she's in trouble."

"Sam?" Lilla asked the voice.

It was Sam, but her voice echoed around them, and they couldn't place its source. Still moving forward, they made their way carefully into the first chamber where they first found her fighting with Serco.

"If you find her, I advise you get out of here. That Golem is mine to take."

"The Golem's not going to follow you out of here you know!" Arden told her.

"He's right. It attacks anyone who goes near it," Lilla said to back him up.

"Don't lie to me. Serco said we're supposed to compete for the weapon. So if you want to leave, hurry up and leave so I can claim it. I didn't come this far for nothing."

"We're not leaving you here. You'll get yourselves killed," Lilla pleaded with her. They stood out in the open looking for Sam or any sign of Claire. Someone was still fighting in the distance, but with the sounds echoing around, they couldn't pinpoint it.

"The Golem will only stop when everyone else is dead. That's the only way to claim it," Ewan shouted to her to try to get her to understand how pointless this was.

"So… I just have to be the last one alive. If I kill you, the Golem is mine." Her voice was quiet as if she was whispering to herself but the words came clearly to them.

This brought a chill down Ewan's spine. "No, you don't understand. You and Hunter can't both leave with the Golem. The game forces you to kill each other for it. It's not worth it." Ewan's words were met with silence. He prayed this was a sign she was seeing sense.

But his attempt only brought out laughter. It was slow at first, but it burst out into hysterical laughing all around them. Which made the scene all the more unsettling. After a disturbing minute where none of them knew how to respond, the laughing stopped. Sam barely pulled herself together to carry on her mission. "I guess I got lucky then. Emil's gone. Now there's nothing to stop me from taking my prize."

Ewan and the others were stunned by this remark. Hunter was already dead from the fall. Were they to blame?

Lilla felt the strength drain from her, and her knees almost buckled.

Was it my decisions that led to this? Ewan thought.

Only Arden stood ready for her. He knew she wouldn't give up. She was determined to do whatever she had to do to win.

Sam appeared atop a balcony some distance away from them. Arden called her out and brought the other two back to attention. She was unarmed, but the air around her was hazy as her magic was ready to strike. "I'll kill all of you!" she screamed and the sound amplified and blasted toward them.

Ewan moved quickly to the side behind a column, and Arden ran and pushed Lilla behind a half-crumbled wall for cover. The sound wave still hurt considerably, but they avoided being blasted away from the sheer force of it. Arden immediately stayed low as the wall wasn't big enough for him to stand upright.

He looked to Lilla who was still in shock. "Can you shoot her down?"

She looked back, horrified at the suggestion.

"Not lethally. Can you knock her down?" he clarified.

"I don't know."

"For Emil!" Each scream brought another shockwave.

The ground shook again, and a surge of pain rang through Arden's ears. "Come on, Lilla. I need you to focus. That's what you're best at."

Lilla took a breath and let the memory of her grandfather guide her. *He would never have lost his cool like this.* She let everything else drift away and focused only on her goal. *Focus, Lilla.* She opened her eyes, and Arden could see she was completely still and composed. Without a word, Lilla drew her arrow and waited for the next attack.

"You can't hide from me!" Part of the ceiling fell with the latest blast, and Ewan felt as though the column covering him would crumble.

As soon as the blast dissipated, Lilla rose to take her shot. But she stopped as she aimed at Sam. Lilla froze and didn't know how to react. She was supposed to block out everything around her target, but something stopped her. Ewan looked around to see what prevented her from firing and he felt fear run through him. Ewan ran out from cover and shouted, "Sam, you need to…" But he was cut off as she attacked again.

"Die!" The shockwave knocked Ewan back and drowned out anything he tried to say.

Arden tried the same thing from behind the wall. "Stop, you'll…" He had to duck again as the next blast came down.

"Just die, all of you!"

Sam was breathing heavily and wasn't sure if she could keep this up. She took a deep breath for another scream. "I won't let this—" The words choked in her throat as a large shadow loomed over her. It sneaked right up on her; she was too distracted. With all the sound amplified toward her targets, she couldn't have heard the massive footsteps coming toward her. Sam turned only in time to see its massive fist come crashing down.

With her magic still active, the last sound that amplified toward them was a snap, and they saw her body fall limply into the lower levels. The shock of Hunter's death was one thing, but they were all there to witness it this time. Sam was gone as well.

With no emotion fueling it, the Golem walked away to find its next victim as it was designed.

Ewan, Arden, and Lilla were left to absorb what they had seen. The only sound was the Golem's footsteps fading away, and a cold silence filled the chamber.

Arden gripped his weapon tighter and forced himself to say the words. "We need to find Claire."

Ewan nodded. Then with a spark going off in his brain, he realized, "The Golem goes after the nearest target. It walked away from us."

Arden and Lilla lit up as they realized what he was suggesting.

"It's going for someone else," Arden announced. With new motivation, they all hurried to follow the Golem. They could grieve properly later. For now, they had to save their friend.

****

On the hard ground, Claire started to stir. The world stopped spinning, and she tried to guess how long she was out. Was it minutes or hours? The rush of adrenaline had worn off as her body was racked with the pain she missed during the fight. She had taken a beating, and her face burned as though it was on fire. Startled, Claire opened her eyes as she realized being on fire was a real possibility.

A quick check showed she wasn't currently on fire, but she had several burns left from the fight. Gritting her teeth, Claire hauled herself up to sit and checked herself more thoroughly. Miraculously, she felt she would be strong enough to stand if need be. She found harsh burns on her left arm, part of her midsection, and judging from the pain, her cheek was also burned. She took the remains of her canteen to pour on each of them. Thankfully, the pain from them dulled, and she took time to settle.

"So you're finally awake."

The sudden voice made her jump. She looked to see Serco was sitting against a column nearby. Claire completely forgot her situation. She was so disorientated she forgot Serco could still be here. She was in no fit state to jump to her feet to defend herself, but luckily Serco looked worse. It was hard to tell with the crimson armor he wore, but she could just make out the blood stains from his injury.

"I was beginning to think I'd bleed out before you woke up. I would have hated for you to miss that," he said, somehow smiling about it.

Claire struggled to her feet and cautiously walked to where her sword lay. She watched Serco carefully while grabbing her weapon. If he was going to try something, he would have done it already, but she knew not to take her eyes off him. She faced him silently, feeling lucky he had no fight left in him. Even if she was physically able, she could feel her magic was running out. She had maybe one or two attacks left in her.

"What's with the dirty looks?" he asked. "It's over. You won."

Claire eyed him suspiciously. "You're giving up?'

Serco choked back a laugh in response. "I know when to accept a loss. You'll need to do the same sometimes."

"Why?" Claire asked. The question came out without thinking about it. She shouldn't push this, the fight was over, and she could walk away at any time, but she had to know. "You said I wasn't good enough to be the hero. So why are you letting me go?"

Serco leaned his head back and looked at her. There was no sinister smile or ill intent behind his eyes. For the first time, he looked sincere. "Maybe I judged you too quickly. You have a knack for surprising me after all. That last trick you pulled. You absorbed my attack and threw it back at me. Nobody's ever done that before. It must be fate I used it on you. I don't think I was even capable of killing you."

Fate, huh? Claire didn't like the idea of it. Maybe they were fated to fight here but what did it accomplish? She felt no satisfaction looking at the man dying in front of her. But she did have something to say before it was over.

"I think we have different ideas of what a hero is," she told him. Serco listened with interest; she was speaking his language.

"A real hero tries to save everyone. You can't write people off as a necessary sacrifice. I can't accept that. I don't care if you think there is no other way out of here. I'm going to break down the door and get everyone out."

Serco looked down and dismissed her opinion. "I guess we'll never agree. Good luck with your escape. At least you'll live to see which of us was right."

Claire looked at him closely. For once she felt no hatred toward him. Despite all his crimes, she could only see an injured man who was ready for the end.

"There is one more thing to say, Serco," she told him. "Throw off your gauntlets and surrender. Do it, and I'll drag you back to Verras in one piece." Claire stood firm and let her offer hang in the air.

"You must have hit your head pretty hard if you're crazy enough to show me mercy," Serco replied and coughed out another chuckle.

Despite the situation, Claire smiled at the comment. "It must be bad if you're calling me crazy. But I said I don't want anyone to die here. Not even you."

Serco seemed to think about it. Then, using the column for support, he slowly pushed himself to stand. "That's touching, Claire. It really gives me some faith in humanity. We balance each other out pretty well."

Claire stood defensively knowing a "but" was coming.

"But," he started and looked to the side. "I don't think he's going to let us walk away together."

Claire turned sharply to find the Golem watching them. The calm interaction between them was over, and Claire's mind raced for a way out.

This is bad. We can't run away. Can we fight it in the state we're in? I'm in better physical shape, but I'm betting Serco still has some power left.

Serco noticed her looking at him and laughed. "Are you thinking about fighting it together? What a show that would be, the hero and villain teaming up to survive."

Claire frowned at him. "You might want to take this seriously, Serco."

"These could be my final moments, Claire. I should at least face them with a smile," he said. Serco started to look like his usual self again, grinning in the face of danger.

"In any case, Claire, it's time you left."

"What do you mean?" she asked, surprised.

"I'm not going to be able to run from this, and if I'm going to go out, you can be sure I'm going out with a bang," he said with excitement. The Golem was on the move, now approaching them both.

"That's too bad. I'm not leaving you here," she said.

Serco shot her a sinister smile. "Well, you don't get a say in the matter." With that statement, the ground beneath Claire cracked and broke away. There was a split-second where she could have jumped forward and stayed, but her hesitation cost her that chance. Instead, she had one last look at him before falling down the steep slope.

Serco's gauntlets hummed with magical energy pouring into them. He shook his head. "She honestly thinks she'll find a way out of here. What a fool." He took a deep breath as the Golem drew close.

"We'll see if you can surprise me one last time." The thought of the hero that could emerge from here, his success, gave him no end of amusement. By the time the Golem loomed over him, he smiled madly at it.

"Goodbye, my murderous friend!"

Every bit of magic Serco had left was focused in front of him. The runes of the Golem were shaking erratically, and one last explosion blasted the Golem apart, taking Serco with it. The resulting blast shook the foundations of the temple. Serco would have been proud of the last bout of destruction he caused.

Chapter 25

Beyond Limitation

Claire was still feeling the pain from her last fight, and she had to maintain her balance while sliding away from Serco. Inevitably, she fell and rolled to the bottom, leaving her face down on the ground for the second time since coming here. She lay there and groaned for a while, mostly from how tired she felt of being knocked around.

"Heeeeeeeey!"

Claire barely had time to register the voice before Arden was helping her up. Back on her feet, she noticed he was holding her in place.

Oh, he's hugging me, she realized, her mind still playing catch up.

Arden let go and patted her shoulders. "Glad to see you're all right," he said with a warm smile.

Before she could respond, Lilla hugged into her as well. She held it for a moment and didn't say anything.

"You're hurt," Ewan said without the physical contact the others gave.

Claire felt her heart rise at the sight of them, giving her the energy to stand on her own. "I'm fine. I'm happy you're all are okay too. But we really need to move for the exit. I don't know how long the Golem will be busy," she told them and started to limp forward.

"Where is Serco?" Ewan asked as he followed her gentle pace.

Claire was trying to build up speed as she got used to walking again. "He's facing the Golem right now. He's buying us time to escape."

"He's helping us?" Arden exclaimed.

Claire's brain froze trying to think of the answer to that. "That's...up for debate. The point is, we don't have much time."

As if on cue, a massive explosion went off behind them. The whole temple shook; it felt like a small quake. The ceiling started to cave in nearby as several parts of the temple were collapsing. With the sudden danger, Claire found her speed again and started to run along with the others.

If I had known he had that much power left, I would have been running from the start! Claire thought, willing herself to move faster. Several platforms and pillars collapsed around them, and Claire forced her body to keep moving. It hurt all over, but the fear of being buried in the rubble was a great motivator.

The rumbling started to calm, but Claire wouldn't take the chance of stopping. As they moved across another platform, they were closing in on the entrance. The same hallway they had entered from was still lit like a beacon for them. Arden and Lilla sprinted for it while Claire struggled to keep up. Glancing over her shoulder, she noticed Ewan keeping pace behind her. Knowing he was doing this for her sake kept her moving. She could always collapse when they were outside.

As expected, it wasn't as simple as running out the front door. When they rounded the corner, they each saw it was closed. More than that, the door was covered in the red markings that vibrated silently, blocking the way out.

In front of the group, Arden used his momentum and launched his ball and chain forward. It struck the wall with a clang but fell uselessly to the floor. Claire stopped to catch herself. She waved Ewan past to inspect the door with the others.

Arden's attack only left the smallest chip on the door. Stunned for a moment, Arden reared back his chain to try again.

"There's no point," Ewan said as he put an arm up to stop him. He inspected the dent on the door. "It's too thick, and the magic placed on the door is far too strong."

Before Arden could argue, they all heard a rumble behind them. The Golem was coming. They all realized there was nowhere to run this time, as they were at a dead end.

"Lilla can break through!" Arden shouted.

Lilla stared at him. Her stomach tightened when she figured out what he was suggesting.

"Like you did back home. You can smash straight through it."

Lilla couldn't get the words out and instead looked at Ewan.

Ewan looked at her with a calm demeanor. "Give it a try," he prompted her.

Without much of a choice, Lilla took several breaths and approached the door.

It was only now that Claire remembered they weren't the only ones who were trapped in here. She took Ewan aside quickly so as to not disturb Lilla's concentration. "If the only exit is sealed, then where are Sam and Hunter? I didn't see any trace of them."

Ewan's heart sank as the image of Sam repeated in his mind. He looked her in the eye and told her plainly, "They didn't make it. We tried to save them but…" The words caught in his throat before he could finish. "The Golem." This was all he could get through, but the message was clear. He let the statement hang in the air and saw the dull shock on Claire's face.

"I see," she said quietly and lowered her gaze time the ground.

Lilla tried her best to remember what she did before, but she could only think of the failed attempts. Swallowing her fear, she faced the wall and concentrated. She cried out and thrust her hand into the wall.

But nothing happened.

Confused, Arden stood forward to see. "What happened? Why didn't it break?"

Lilla stood back and started trembling. The fear she swallowed came rushing back out. "I can't do it. I can't do it. It won't break!"

Ewan placed a hand on her and tried to calm her, but she grabbed him and started shaking him. "No, you don't understand. I haven't been able to do it since the first time. I've tried, but it won't work."

"Lilla, calm down. We can find a way out of this," he tried to say reassuringly, but the rumbling footsteps behind them broke any sense of calm he was trying to instill. Arden readied himself for a fight while Lilla continued to panic. Ewan looked to see Claire still staring at the floor as the Golem closed in.

"Claire!"

At the sound of her name, Claire felt her frustration rise. The feeling burned from her chest and spread along her arm. She directed that negativity toward the approaching Golem, and from her hand, a ball of fire shot out toward it. It exploded on impact and caused to the Golem to rear back.

The sudden attack was enough to shake them from their fear and pay attention. None of them dared to mention whose technique it resembled.

"Ewan!" Claire shouted fiercely, causing Ewan to stammer in surprise. "Help Lilla and get that door open!" she ordered then turned to Arden. "You and I will keep the Golem busy until then." Without waiting for an answer, she drew her sword and walked toward the giant awaiting her. Arden shook off the surprise and followed, ready to fight.

"No wait," Lilla called and tried to follow, but Ewan stopped her.

"No, I can't open it," she told him again.

"Don't panic. We'll do it together," he said, attempting to reassure her. "Think of your grandfather, the words of wisdom you normally follow." Lilla stared at him for a moment, and her breathing started to slow.

"There, that's good. Let me guide you this time. Focus yourself and listen to my instructions." This seemed to work as Lilla reined her emotions back in.

Confident she was settled, Ewan faced the door once again to come up with a plan. His first step was to calm Lilla as he knew she was the key to breaking through. But in truth, he didn't know how they were going to do it.

Claire is putting her faith in us, so I need to think of something, he told himself. The magic symbols were the problem; they were what was strengthening the door. He heard the fighting close behind him and tried to block it out.

When I used my glyph on the Golem, the symbols dispersed as if pushed away by my magic. I could do it here, but my glyphs aren't strong enough to break through. Lilla could try to follow up on my glyphs, but they would interfere with any magic she used.

He thought carefully of how Lilla broke through the wall. The studies he had done had given him theories, but it was his work in the field that showed how magic worked. He only had to connect the dots.

****

Claire did her best to keep dodging the Golem's attacks. She had next to no power left, and there was no chance of her getting back up if she took another hit. Arden backed her up with his own strikes to keep it off balance, but she didn't know how long he could keep this up either. With another swing, Claire jumped back out of reach. The Golem reached out for her again, and like their last encounter, its arm pulled away from the body to catch her. It was at this time Arden stood between them and blocked the arm. His feet dug into the ground, and Claire caught his back to help stand their ground. With enough space, the Golem's second arm came around. Claire pulled Arden back, causing them both to fall and avoid another crushing blow. They scrambled to their feet, and it was obvious they couldn't keep it back for long.

****

With his friends' lives on the line, Ewan felt the pressure of every second.

With the flash of an idea, he asked Lilla to join him.

"All right. I need you to think about how much magic you have left right now. You've been focusing too much on the effect you will have on the wall. You need to focus internally on your own power," he said, being sure to sound more confident than he felt. Lilla placed her arms on the wall and did as he told her.

"When you're ready, I need you to pour your magic into the door. Push the other opposing energy away and flood it with your own." This was the part he knew would work like his own glyphs. Now for the leap of faith. "Magic follows the will of the user. Once your magic is in the door, you need to tell it what you want. Force your will upon it."

Lilla nodded with her eyes still shut. Ewan held on to the door, but he was left to watch and hope Lilla could pull it off. With visible concentration on her face, she released her magic. Ewan could see the red markings move aside as her own magic pushed it away. Ewan took note of its color as he'd never seen Lilla's magic in this form. It traveled in streams as a dark green glow and moved through the door. He waited tensely for her to follow through.

Tell it what you want, he thought to her. Lilla responded as though she heard his wish.

"Break!" she screamed at the glowing door, and for a moment the markings on her face lit up as well. Obeying her order, the door blasted outward and crumbled, leaving a sizable hole for them. Lilla stood and looked with amazement at the result. Ewan patted her back harder than he intended, a habit he may have got from Arden, and quickly prompted her to jump through.

He ran back and yelled to his teammates who were being pushed back more and more. "It's open!" he shouted in triumph.

With no time to feel relief, the two ran back for the door with the Golem pursuing. Ewan made two glyphs ahead of him, and when the Golem approached, his chains shot up to slow it down. This had no effect whatsoever as the Golem easily barreled through them. With no time, Arden picked Ewan up as he ran and leaped through the opening.

Claire had no idea how close the Golem was, but she felt like it was already over her. She jumped and tucked herself to go through the opening and felt the slightest tap on her foot as she tumbled through the hole and landed roughly outside with the Golem smashing into the door on the other side. Although it had no chance to reach through the hole, the group did not take any chances and scrambled away from it.

They were immediately greeted by a cold wind, which brought the rain. Claire turned to find a storm had been raging outside, which would have been an appropriate atmosphere for the struggles they had been through. The carts and supplies still lay abandoned at the bottom of the stairs and were being ruined by the storm. Rather than flinch away from the wind and rain, Claire welcomed it. It washed over her, and she felt herself relax after what felt like an eternity of fighting.

"Oh that feels nice," she heard beside her as Arden joined and let the rain drench his face.

"We should find some cover to rest up," Ewan suggested. Claire saw Lilla hugging into him, and he awkwardly had an arm over her. She knew from Arden's embraces that he was always awkward with it, but that didn't seem to stop Lilla from trying.

They pushed through the storm and made it into the small tower where the survey team was being held. They all collapsed in a heap, and in the couple of minutes of being outside, they were completely drenched.

The group sank to the floor and lay down, all except Lilla who was still giddy from their escape. "I can't believe we made it."

"I was never worried," Arden announced confidently.

Ewan scoffed. "You looked petrified when the Golem approached."

"Oh yeah, 'cause you were Mr. Calm Under Pressure," he mocked.

"I was confident Lilla was up to the task."

"Really? Is that why you cried out Claire when it was closing in?"

Claire and Lilla couldn't help but laugh as Ewan looked completely flustered. Too tired to retort, he allowed them to have their fun.

It's funny. Claire looked at her battered teammates. *For all my talk of finding a way out and saving everyone, I barely had to do anything. Serco really was wrong to look for one hero to fix everything.*

Still, she took no pleasure in his death. Hunter and Sam were gone too. They were given every chance but wouldn't turn away from the path they both walked. Claire looked up to realize the others had fallen silent as well. It seemed the impact of the last few hours were working through their minds too.

"So—" she started, but she stopped suddenly as the ground started shaking violently.

"What's going on?" Arden asked but received no answer. Once again, Claire had to push away the fatigue and force herself to stand.

What now! she thought, angry at the disruption.

Arden pulled the door back open and was hit by the strong wind rushing in. It was hard to see between the raging wind, rain, and an earthquake. With only a moment to adjust, they saw the temple starting to move. It shook ferociously, and the entrance collapsed in on itself. A frightening crimson glow emanated from the center. But the entrance wasn't collapsing; it was starting to take shape.

"No, no, no. It can't be. We escaped. It should be over," Claire muttered to herself, watching the display outside.

The whole entrance and the surrounding columns pooled together and traced the shape of the Golem. But this was different. It was five times the size! Countless markings danced around it, furiously shaping the rock.

Not needing to watch further, the team ducked back inside the tower to hide.

"It's still coming for us," Lilla told them.

"Can we fight it?" Arden asked.

"Even at full strength, we'd have no effect against that!" Claire yelled and pointed out the door.

"Well, we can't outrun it."

"So we hide," Ewan suggested. "We keep out of sight and circle round until we escape it."

"Right. If we can get to the horses. If they're still there," Claire said doubtfully. In any case, they had to put as much distance between them and this cursed place as possible.

Their desperate planning was interrupted as the tower shook. The Golem was on the move. Each footstep causing a large rumble, it was easy to hear each step even with the storm raging above. They all waited in silence as a red light shone through the gap in the door, searching for them. Just to be safe, they backed into the other side of the room and waited. Although they did not know if the Golem could listen, they dared not make a sound until the light moved on. Claire released a breath as the thunderous footsteps moved away. After what felt like a safe amount of time, Ewan approached the doorway to see if they could sneak away.

Ewan looked suddenly tense as he continued to watch its movements.

"What's happening?" Claire asked, unsure if she wanted to know.

"It went straight to the entrance. It seems to be blocking our escape."

Claire's heart sank. "It can't be smart enough to cut us off, can it?"

"It's following commands set into it thousands of years ago. This must have been a failsafe for anyone who escaped."

Suddenly there was another thunderous crash in the distance.

"Oh that's not good," Ewan said.

"What is it now?"

"It destroyed the structure nearest the entrance. It looks to be moving along to the next. It's working its way down to us."

Claire took a few steps back. "Can we still sneak around it?"

Ewan shook his head in response. "Not with the searchlights coming from it. It's working its way down the clearing to find us."

Damnit this never ends. Claire struggled to keep herself calm. She had to find a way out for everyone.

"Okay, Lilla. I don't want to put pressure on you again, but I don't suppose you could break the Golem like you did with the door," Arden asked gently.

Lilla held her composure and answered. "I don't know if I have enough power to do it again. It's also way too big for me to take down."

"Not to mention you would need to be in direct contact," Ewan added. "It must be using the power left from the temple. Breaking it will be near impossible with the amount of magic infused into it."

Not enough power, Claire thought. *I barely have any left after fighting Serco. The small boost I got from his attack didn't last.* Suddenly an idea struck her.

"Lilla, how exactly did you destroy the door?" she asked, trying to come up with a plan.

"I sent my magic into it and then broke the rock down from inside."

Ewan knew where Claire was going with it and dismissed the idea. "I doubt the rest of us could pull that off. Lilla's specialty is earth and wind. I certainly couldn't repeat her technique."

"No, but I might have another idea," she told them. Claire didn't like asking them to risk their lives for an idea she had come up with in a hurry. Fortunately, she didn't need to ask. They instantly agreed to give it a shot and put their faith in her.

****

The Golem moved with purpose across the clearing. With every structure it smashed, beams of light shone from its body to scan the area to ensure nothing could sneak past. One of the runes reacted as something struck it, and an explosive went off at the Golem's leg. It might as well have been a firecracker for all the damage it did. The red beams of light all shot to the same direction to find the source. They all pointed toward Lilla who was out in the open after firing her last bomb. The Golem turned and leisurely walked toward its target.

Arden stood next to her in the red spotlight. He bashed his shield as a challenge to the massive killing machine, but they retreated once it was clearly heading for them. There was no escape, however, as the spotlights were highlighting them as they ran. It would catch up to them easily with each massive step toward them.

With its attention drawn away, Claire and Ewan ran out from the side to intercept it. Lilla and Arden were relying on them to strike before they were caught. This was the part of the plan Claire was least comfortable with, but without someone to draw its attention, she could never get close. Getting closer only made it look worse as it took another step right in front of her before she understood how high she would need to climb.

There was no time to waste. With the sheer size of the Golem, she had to catch it before it took another step away. At the base of its foot, Ewan tried to give her the boost she needed. With as much strength as he could pour into it, his platform threw Claire up toward the giant leg in front of her. It was the highest boost they had managed that launched her up onto a groove near its knee.

Claire held on tight while the Golem took another step forward. The minute they crashed back into the ground, she hauled herself up and was at the perfect position to strike. She was fairly certain the Golem would notice her as soon as she made contact, so she had to do this quickly. Claire placed her hands on the stone like Lilla had done with the door. The runes reacted instantly, and the miniature eyes among them faced her. Remembering the feeling of absorbing Serco's attack, she focused on the symbols swirling in front of her. They stopped all at once and seemed to be shaking in place. Feeling like she was having an effect, Claire doubled her efforts and willed the foreign magic to join her. They buzzed for a moment, then were slowly pulled down from the stone and along her arms. Claire felt a rush of pain dragging the magic into her body and absorbing it. After the pain became too much, Claire fell backward off the Golem's leg.

With the sudden intrusion, the Golem shifted its attention from the two on the ground and rotated its arm around to crush the one falling from its leg. Claire opened her eyes to see it was bending down and reaching for her. Now that she had regained some power, Claire looked back at the knee that had less magic running through it. Not knowing exactly what she was doing, she gathered her newfound power and threw it at the weak spot that she had left behind. The crimson red energy shot out as lightning and exploded into its kneecap. Still falling, Claire flipped herself to face upward again and threw another attack that blasted more of its knee away. Her attacks had the desired effect as a large chunk of the Golem's leg has been blasted off.

The Golem's arm swung around to smash the attacker, but with a yellow glow appearing around her, she was yanked out of the way and landed on top of Ewan. Her attack had failed to break the Golem's leg, and it turned around completely to deal with the new threat. Ewan got a jolt from Claire's uncontrolled power as he helped her up. Seeing the Golem towering over them, Claire tried to launch another attack, but all that came out were a few sparks. Seeing the giant coming for them, Claire let out a noise that could only be described as a whimper.

Did I burn through the power that quickly? Seeing this, Ewan grabbed her arm to run.

****

Lilla and Arden ran after the Golem as it attacked its new prey. It slammed down with both arms, and they could only hope their friends had gotten away. Lilla aimed straight for the weakened leg, hoping she could finish it off. With a quick look to Arden, she could see he had the same idea. With the Golem still holding its position, Arden held out his shield for her. She jumped on, and although not as fancy as Ewan's boost, he launched her from it with as much force as he could push through it. She summoned up a gust to fly the extra distance and landed on its leg. It was starting to move again, but she was nimble enough to climb up to the damaged knee and lay her hands on it, ready to pour all the magic she had left.

"Break!" she commanded and watched a crack push through to the other side. The Golem fell forward as it suddenly lost the support to stand and caught itself on the ground.

It was obvious to her she had no magic left to hurt it anymore. With the lower leg falling to the ground, Lilla deftly prepared to escape. She rolled onto the ground and ran back toward Arden. The Golem's arm was reaching back to crush them and soon towered overhead. They both ran as fast as they could, but the massive shadow of its arm descended upon them. It was coming too fast, and they were running too slowly. That didn't stop them from trying as the two desperately ran from the impending doom bearing down.

Arden saw something approaching from their side and had to look twice to confirm he hadn't lost his mind in the fray. Two horses ran into the danger toward them with only one rider between them.

"Grab on!" he yelled as he led both horses toward them. With ease, Arden ran and hauled himself up on the horse and pulled Lilla's arm to swing her up. With both of them mounted, they sprinted away as the Golem missed them by a hair.

"Oh, that was a close call!" Professor Mansen shouted. They continued at full speed to gain some distance.

"What are you doing here?" Arden called over to him.

"Why, this reminds me of my adventuring days. I couldn't let you youngsters have all the fun. Hahaha!" he said after narrowly avoiding being crushed by a giant, magical Golem.

****

Claire and Ewan had recovered from the last attack and again ran to engage while it was distracted. They had avoided the arms, but the force of the smash threw them back. With its attention drawn elsewhere, Claire ran around to its other arm. With the Golem pressed to the ground, Claire took the chance to steal more of its power. She took it at a much faster rate this time, and before the Golem could react, Ewan boosted her up and on its hand.

She tried to run along the arm before it could react but didn't make it far as it raised upward to throw her off. Being lifted into the air, Claire focused magic beneath her, and she tried to imitate Ewan's technique with some success. Instead of a smooth platform boosting her jump, she blasted herself away and flew across and onto the Golem's back.

With some relief, she witnessed Arden and Lilla riding on horseback and so continued up toward the head. The runes were moving frantically and shining light toward her, but it was too late. She made it to the base of its neck and plunged her sword in beneath her feet. Claire gripped her sword tightly, and after all the struggle she had been through, her will was absolute. She had one command for her newfound power and willed it to obey her. She shouted her frustration at it and flooded all the power she had into the sword, which in turn forced itself into the Golem. Repeating Lilla's technique, she commanded the Golem to break. The energy flooded to the head and ran through the shoulders, which were followed by a large crack burrowing its way through the arms. The Golem was helpless as both arms were blasted off and fell to the ground. Claire leaned back and let out one last battle cry as the rain drenched her.

The professor and the young people he saved circled around to the front to find Ewan, but before they could attempt another attack, they all bore witness to the Golem's destruction. It collapsed in front of them, and they stood in awe at the sight of Claire kneeling on top.

Arden cried out along with her in victory and continued cheering while Claire slowly stood and jumped down toward them, the occasional red sparks still emitting from her body. Claire landed in front of them and smiled to herself even though she felt dizzy from all the effort.

It's finally over. Claire felt her body finally relax after all the hardship. She could have laughed, but instead, her body suddenly seized and collapsed.

"Claire!"

She could hear faint voices as they checked on her.

"All that energy running through her must have wreaked havoc on her body."

"Can you help her?"

"Yes, I know some first aid from my travels. Get to the caravan, I have some supplies there. We need to get her back to Verras now!"

Yes. Let's go home together. That sounds nice. This was the last thought Claire remembered having before losing consciousness yet again.

Epilogue

For several days, Claire was left to recover in a hospital bed in Verras. She knew trying to absorb a foreign power was risky, but she couldn't have predicted the damage it would cause to her body. Her muscles were torn, and it would be a while before she could move around much. The doctors promised her a full recovery, so she could endure the discomfort for now.

With Claire on bedrest, her team had time to take in what happened. The deaths of Sam and Hunter were especially hard to accept. They had only begun their journey and already had to learn some hard lessons. As much as Claire rejected Serco, the lessons he tried to force upon her rung true. They couldn't save everyone.

With Serco gone, the city seemed calm, and the time seemed to pass quickly as Claire received visits from her friends. Arden was as battle hardy as ever. He congratulated her on beating Serco alone and destroying the Golem with her newfound ability. Lilla kept bringing gifts to try to make her feel more comfortable. Jamie, Wren, and the professor stopped by to show support, and give their thanks. But when Ewan visited, he was clearly bothered by something. After everything that happened, he felt it was uncomfortably quiet. He tried to understand her new ability as a way to distract himself. But there was a worry in the back of his mind that he could not shake.

Despite their involvement in stopping Serco, they were never questioned about the events at the temple. The professor and his team reported everything that happened, but no one came to hear the mages' side of the story. It was as if nothing had changed, but the silence on the subject made him nervous. Any time he brought it up in front of

Claire, he received a punch from Lilla to remind him not to add more worry. Not that Claire minded. Even in her weakened state, she wanted to be kept up to date.

Despite continually being warned from his teammate, Ewan insisted on talking about it.

"It's possible the mayor will blame us for his daughter's death. It was strange of him not to come question us."

Claire felt the burden of that blame, even though they gave Sam every chance to stop.

"Blames us?" she heard Arden shout. "Where exactly was he when she was recruiting mages to fight the government?"

"Whatever his motives, it might prove difficult for us to keep working with the tech soldiers growing in number. To make matters worse, I hear they're becoming a part of Dottinheim's military."

"Maybe we should leave then. We've done enough here, and they don't appreciate our help, so let's pack up and go."

"It's worth considering."

Claire sat back to think about it. She saw Lilla hit each of them for pushing their decision on her while she was still recovering. One more problem, but her main concern was what to tell Isaac. She had been messaging him to avoid suspicion, but it wasn't something she could hide forever.

After several more days of avoiding her brother, Claire regarded herself in the mirror. She still looked rough and was yet to be discharged from the hospital. Lilla was sitting with her today. At least she didn't have to feel alone with her team checking up on her.

Looking back at the reflection, her eyes were naturally drawn to the burn scar on her right cheek. She prodded at it but couldn't feel anything. It seemed it wouldn't heal any further.

"Does the scar bother you?" Lilla asked her.

"No. The scar is fine, but it reminds me of him," she told Lilla, sounding more sad than angry.

"Did you feel sorry for him? In the end, I mean," Lilla asked. Claire had been quiet on the subject, and this was the first time she had even briefly mentioned Serco. Lilla knew from experience it wasn't good to bottle something like that up.

Claire expression morphed into what Lilla could only translate as pity. "It was such a waste. He endangered so many lives and ended so many more for his stupid crusade. In the end, he threw away his own life as well."

"He tried to save you though. Or at least that's what you thought he was doing."

"Yeah. He wanted to make the perfect hero. He wasn't even convinced it was me, but he was willing to take a shot." She moved away from the sink and paced into the living area. "He was so caught up in his romantic idea of a hero..." Claire paused again, not sure if she should keep going, but Lilla prompted her to go on.

"The thing is, we got through the temple because we worked together. Even Professor Mansen rushed in to save our lives. Without any magic to protect him, he was more heroic than we were."

"It sounds like you've learned some hard lessons," an all too familiar voice spoke from the doorway.

Claire's heart sank as Isaac was standing only a few feet away. Immediately, she was hit with a pang of guilt. Normally, seeing her brother had the opposite effect. He wasn't looking at her the same way either; there was a clear look of disappointment written on his face.

He turned to Lilla who wasn't sure how to react. "Could you give us a minute?"

Lilla looked desperate to say something, maybe ease the tension or defend Claire, but no words came. She reluctantly nodded and left quietly.

"How...did you find me?" Claire asked averting her gaze.

"Well AMTech is doing what they can to cover up what happened to Serco, but the news of a young woman rushed to hospital after the incident did reach my ears."

"I'm sorry."

"Sorry for what? Breaking your word?"

Claire felt a numb pain run through her, but she did her best not to show it. "I'm sorry I couldn't stay away, but Serco would have killed countless others if I didn't interfere."

"Really? From what I hear, he redoubled his efforts after he met you."

Claire looked away again. She couldn't deny what he was saying. It was impossible to say what would have happened if she never got involved.

"Do you know why I told you to stay away from Serco?"

"To protect me," Claire muttered miserably.

"It wasn't just about you," he said harshly. "It was about Arden, Lilla, Ewan, and anyone who would get caught up in the crossfire. You weren't ready," Isaac continued before she could get a word in. "You nearly got yourself killed."

"I made a mistake. I know that. Things spiraled out of control, and I kept trying to fix it. I didn't know what else to do."

Isaac placed a hand on her shoulder to look her in the eye. "You should have told me. Putting out dumpster fires is part of my job. The other part of my job is deciding if people are ready for something like this."

Sensing her physical discomfort, Isaac guided her toward a chair, so she wasn't forcing herself to stand anymore. She let out a shaky breath and tried to absorb what he was saying. Thinking back, Claire didn't feel sure of anything she did or if she was cut out as a leader.

"So what am I supposed to do now?" she asked him.

Isaac raised his hands and shrugged. "Hey, you chose this path yourself, right? I know you won't give up. So there's only one thing I can tell you. Pick yourself up, learn from your mistakes, and don't lie to me again.

The look on his face was stern, but he was the same caring brother that she had always known. It was strange how much she felt like a kid again being lectured by him. Looking out the window, Claire could see all the people who called Verras their home. "It's been really hard…but you're right."

Managing a slow smile, she looked back to Isaac. Although her body was beaten, her eyes looked as determined as when she first set out.

"I'll do better, to earn the trust you and my friends have given me. After all, we still have work to do."

Printed in Great Britain
by Amazon